TEDDY'S WAR

DONALD WILLERTON

ROUGH
EDGES
PRESS

TEDDY'S WAR

TEDDY'S WAR

To my father and mother, in honor of their sacrifices during World War II

Chapter 1

My father died at four o'clock in the morning on the last Thursday of April, 1986, from complications brought on by pancreatic cancer. His diagnosis had come several months before, catching us by surprise. We rushed to be supportive, thinking he had time for a successful round of treatments, but the cancer was relentless, taking a strong, healthy man and reducing him to a frail, fragile shadow. I had never witnessed that level of intense suffering by anyone, and it kept me shaken as he dwindled away. When his suffering was over, I felt as much relief as grief.

My father was a well-known, highly esteemed businessman who was the head of a family-owned corporation with offices in several locations in the US. He was kind, smart, and a brilliant manager, and his memorial brought more than a thousand employees and acquaintances to the largest church in downtown Boston, where my sister and I grew up. His cremation took place the following week, after which the family held a private ceremony to place his urn into the family crypt in Minneapolis.

The days following his memorial brought friends, politicians, and city dignitaries to the house to offer their condolences. It was too much of a burden for my mother to welcome the constant stream of well-wishers by herself, so Nancy and I stayed to help. My wife took the kids home so I could stay as long as I was needed, while Nancy sent her kids to stay with her in-laws.

My mother is a handsome, strong, down-to-earth woman, and had reacted to my dad's sickness with an avalanche of love, care, and constant attention. Even as the disease made him miserable, depressed, and physically compromised, she marshaled forces to provide unceasing comfort and compassion. Only in her alone time did she weep at being left without the husband she had loved for forty years.

A week after my dad's death and three days after the memorial in Minnesota, we all returned to the house in Boston, and my mother finally admitted to being exhausted. The next morning, having given the housekeeping and kitchen staff a paid four-day weekend, she quietly posted a *Do Not Disturb* sign on the front gate and promised not to open it again until she was rested.

It felt good for my sister and me to be at her side in a house recently swamped with memories, and we promised to keep ourselves busy and fed without her assistance. That left us puttering around the estate while my mother slowly settled into her new role of widow. She was by nature a gregarious, motivated, and work-proud woman, and having nothing to do produced a nervous energy that kept her drifting around the house, which was the opposite of resting. We were attentive to her, but tried hard not to become nuisances.

I was gazing through the doorway of the library, missing my dad and pondering what to do with all of the books crammed into the shelves, when my sister came down the back stairway carrying something in her hands.

"What's that?" I asked.

"It's a treasure chest! I found it in the attic."

Nancy was holding what looked like a child-sized trunk with a humped top. It couldn't have been more than eighteen inches long and a foot high and deep. As an antique store addict and a coveter of trunks in particular, I'd never seen one so small and yet so traditionally shaped. The attic had been our favorite and most visited play area in the house, and if the small trunk had been there years ago, we hyper-curious kids would have found it, which meant my mother had only recently put it there.

I followed my sister into the dining room. She spread kitchen towels across the table, placed the miniature trunk on top, and set about examining its small padlock. We had many old keys in a drawer in the garage—surely one of them would work.

My mother drifted into the room, gasped, and reached around Nancy to place her hand over the lock.

"I need to think about this," she said. "I have some things to tell you about your father, but I had intended to wait a bit. Right now, I'm not sure I'm up to it. There are memories inside this trunk that need to be treated carefully."

She might as well have fired a starting pistol, as there was now no stopping my sister. Nancy had been looking for a diversion to help Mom burn off some of her restlessness and an unexplored trunk seemed like a good one.

"Memories? Dad's old memories? Yours? Memories of what?

"What do you mean by *carefully*? How come we've never seen this trunk before? It hasn't always been in the attic— did you put it up there?

"Where did it come from? Do you have the key? What's inside?"

My mother held up both hands to stifle the onslaught of questions, saying nothing but obviously feeling conflicted by what might escape if the trunk were opened. She slid out a chair and patiently sat down. "I put the trunk in the attic only a few days before Dad died. It's been inside the big safe in the file room. I thought the people from the downtown office might need to get into the safe as well as the files, and I didn't want them to mess with it, so I moved it upstairs."

The file room was a room off my dad's office at the back of the house, full of filing cabinets surrounded by shelves of carefully cataloged company reports from years past. In the corner was a massive six-foot-high railway safe, an antique monstrosity first used by my grandfather. I had never seen it open. I didn't even know if it could be opened. I thought my dad kept it only as a relic of his father's time as the head of the family business.

My mother sat with her head down, musing as she slowly rocked back and forth. Then she sat upright and tugged at a chain around her neck. I'd never known her to wear a neck chain before, so this was also a new addition. She undid the clasp on the back, and as she took it off, a small key and a diamond-coated, heart-shaped locket slipped to the bottom of the chain.

"Okay," she said, "but keep your hands to yourselves. I'll take out what I want to show you when I'm ready. If you'll be patient with me, I'll tell you everything about your father's journey."

Journey? Journey to where?

My mother slid the trunk and the towels in front of her, put the key in the lock, twisted it open, and then refastened the chain, locket, and key around her neck. She slid the lock from the trunk's clasp and tipped the lid back.

I stood to look inside. I don't know if I had expected stacks of money, jewels, Spanish gold or guns, but it held only envelopes and bundles of papers in neat piles spread across the bottom. I also saw a single VHS videotape with *Margie* written on the label. Overall, the lack of a more tangible treasure was disappointing.

4

My mother spoke with a wistful voice. "I've had this trunk since Dad and I were first married. A sorority sister gave it to me as a wedding present. It has always been mine alone, and your father was respectful enough to never look inside. I hadn't thought about it in years until a month ago."

"What happened a month ago?" my sister asked.

Mom folded her hands on the edge of the trunk and let her eyes wander around the room. Her smile and bright eyes were always the highlight of my childhood, but the strain of the recent months had brought worry lines and sadness to her face. She took a deep breath and settled against the back of the chair. "The two of you were in the loop when we first heard Dad's diagnosis, but you weren't here during the following months of surgery and chemo and the constant urgency to find ways of getting Dad back to health. It wasn't to be. Pancreatic cancer is one of the worst ones, and we finally accepted that we could fight all we wanted, but he wasn't going to get better.

"Your dad sat me down one evening and told me of his decision to forego any more treatments and to accept his death. He hoped he might feel better without the treatments and wanted to make the most of the time he had left. He loved his life, and I loved being his companion. He wasn't afraid to die, but he really didn't want to stop living.

"He asked if he could take a day or two to be alone up at the cabin, and I told him to take all the time he needed, provided he'd have someone drive him up and back.

"He agreed and was gone for three days. What I didn't know was that he asked Jim Powers to drive him. You remember Jim? He's been the company historian and video-grapher for years. Dad asked him to bring his videotaping equipment to the cabin and help him make a video. There were things about World War II he needed to tell me, he said, that he could not tell me in person.

"I already knew most of what he had done during the

war. When he came back from Europe, he told me lots of details about his time there, but he always refused to talk about his last six months. Whatever he had done, it was something he could not talk about.

"I guess he'd been thinking about it and finally decided he needed to explain what happened. After he came back from the cabin, he told me about making the video. I told him we could have talked about it and accomplished the same thing, but he had decided against doing it that way. He had a lot to say, it would take a lot of time, and knew he couldn't handle talking for long periods of time because of his pain. He didn't want to shorten the story or to leave any parts out, so he decided, instead, to videotape his story in pieces, resting when he needed to, and then have Jim put the pieces together into one session.

"Most of it had to do with his brother, Jake."

I interrupted. "Uncle Jake was Dad's brother who died in the war, right? He was a pilot in the Navy."

"He was in the Navy, first," Mom said, "but he died while in the Army Air Force in Europe. Uncle Jake had gone through a Navy training program to become a pilot, beginning around 1938 or '39, I think. After Pearl Harbor, he flew dive bombers off an aircraft carrier, became a pilot instructor, and then switched over to the Army Air Force in 1943 to train pilots flying bombers over Europe. We had always been told he died when his plane was shot down in 1945."

"Not while in the Navy? I don't remember Europe being mentioned. You think he didn't die from being shot down? You think you weren't told the truth on purpose?" I asked.

My mother closed the lid of the trunk and gave me a stern look.

"It's been hard for me to even sit down lately, and I'm a little low on energy. Telling you this story is going to be hard enough, so you're going to have to be patient. I know it's your nature to ask a lot of questions, but if you'll listen first, most of your questions will be answered. If they aren't, you can ask later."

Whoops. I held my hands up in apologetic surrender. "Sorry. I'll stop." The look on Nancy's face reinforced the decision.

My mother nodded with a small smile and tipped the lid back open. "Dad made the videotape in January. A month ago, he sat with me and we watched it together. It was incredible. The story he told was a chain of one remarkable event after another. I've never heard anything like it, and couldn't even imagine him doing the things he did.

"After seeing the tape, I wondered what else I might remember about the war, so I got the trunk out because it has the letters Dad wrote me during the war. While he was sleeping one afternoon, I read through everything I had saved. When we talked that evening, I told him that you two not only needed to see the videotape, but needed to hear the full story of the war years. He wasn't sure. He had prepared the tape only for me and sometimes talked to the camera as if he was talking to me. He hadn't planned on sharing it with anyone else.

"I still thought you should hear everything, including what happened before the war and after. He finally agreed, but made me promise I would tell you all of it, with nothing off limits and nothing glossed over, whether I wanted it known or not. He could no longer be hurt or embarrassed by anything, and wanted to make up for all the years he had avoided telling the truth. The videotape itself only concerns his last six months in Europe, but he said I should tell the whole story, starting with him and Jake in high school.

"I promised I would be as honest as I could, so prepare yourselves." She took a deep breath. "Okay, I'm ready to do this, but I need to start at the end so you'll know why he couldn't tell me in the first place."

Chapter 2

She lifted a large manila envelope from inside the trunk, opened it, and pulled out a single sheet of paper. She passed it to Nancy, who looked at it and handed it to me.

"This is your dad's military discharge paper," she said.

Some background would be helpful. My grandfather, Olaf Elias Gunnarson, was the head of an immigrant family from Norway and worked as a lumberjack in northern Minnesota in the late 1800s. After chopping his own trees for a while, he hired others to do the chopping for him, eventually making a successful business out of providing trees to sawmills. Over the next few years, he began buying sawmills to make his own lumber, and then bought railroads to distribute his lumber. He became one of the richest men in the state.

I should appreciate him more because I'm living off his spoils through a trust fund, but Olaf Senior was all about building wealth, and power was the tool he used to get it, even if he had to bludgeon people along the way. He was becoming a corporate robber baron when he dropped dead of heart failure in 1951, aged 71.

He died the year I was born.

I'm sure he was disappointed to die so soon. He'd gotten a taste of empire-building during the war, and had then leveraged his wartime railroad business into nationwide prominence. His ambition reflected his size, as he was a big man. Photographs show him to be a little smaller than Paul Bunyan. Seriously, he was like six-seven or six-eight, built like a tank, and had hands the size of pie plates—a true Norwegian lumberjack who would have made a good Viking.

As he was becoming one of the richest men in Minnesota, Olaf somehow managed to find time enough with my grandmother to sire three sons.

The first son was Olaf Junior, the eldest by something like twelve or thirteen years. He had graduated from Harvard almost a decade before the war started and was working for Olaf Senior. My grandmother could never tolerate her son or her husband being called *Olaf*, so the family just called them *Junior* and *Senior*. She thought it sounded more American.

After Pearl Harbor, Senior maneuvered Junior into a position with the newly created War Production Board, helping to convert existing industries into factories for manufacturing the goods needed for waging war—arms, ammunition, planes, vehicles, tanks, ships, and so on.

The second son, Jacob, who wouldn't respond to any name other than Jake, opted to enroll in an Aviation Cadet Training program in college, staying long enough to give himself the two years of education required for becoming a Navy pilot. As soon as he could, he was flying planes in the Pacific. His going to Europe must have been something I missed as I was growing up.

The third son, my dad, Theodore—called Teddy after the San Juan Roosevelt himself—was two and a half years younger than Jake. He graduated from high school in 1941, attended the University of Minnesota for a year, and then was called up in the draft. Fearing he'd end up in the infantry or, worse, that Senior would convince the Draft Board he was needed at home to work in the war side of the family business, he signed up for the Army Signal Corps radar operator school in late 1942.

Years later, when my grandfather died, the management of the family wealth went to Olaf Junior. Junior was a study of his own, but he enjoyed being a stocks and bonds investment manager more than playing tycoon. He created a trust fund to keep the family members at the level of near-rich and left any part of the business involving people to Teddy.

When Junior succumbed to an immense girth and hard arteries in the mid-1960s, my dad sold most of the investments, used the money to pump up the trust, consolidated the businesses into one company, and then brought the company into the new age of employee stock-sharing, retirement programs, and healthcare benefits.

He was smart enough to keep us wealthy but never had the killer instinct of his Gunnarson ancestors. He grew the company by diversifying and adding new partners, keeping executive salaries relatively low so the company was well-juiced, nimble, and employee-focused, which earned him immense respect and loyalty from his employees.

Mom and Dad encouraged Nancy and me to not rely on the trust fund and to develop our own careers. Nancy became a respected Boston lawyer and then married a surgeon, while I became a high school history teacher.

Okay, back to the trunk.

I'd never seen my dad's military discharge paper and gave it a quick perusal after Nancy read it. Everything seemed fine. He joined up, went to war, won some standard medals and ribbons, was cited for being in several campaigns, and came home whole and undamaged.

My mother then slid another paper from the envelope and passed it to my sister.

"This is his real discharge paper," she said.

Nancy's eyes bugged out as she read it and passed it over to me. I gave her a questioning look and then looked carefully at what she had handed me.

It was an enlarged photograph of a regular-sized paper. The paper in the photo didn't have the same military appearance as the previous one, but appeared to be more a legal document describing a Third Army Review Board that had met on the 27th of April, 1945. It had a couple of paragraphs of information followed by three signatures at the bottom. A summary sentence stood out in the middle of the page:

> *Technician 5th Class Theodore Gunnarson, ASN 38230913, Company A, 555th SAW Battalion, Army Signal Corps, is found guilty of 1) desertion, 2) theft of government property, 3) disobedience of direct orders, 4) unauthorized travel behind enemy lines, and 5) impersonating an officer.*
>
> *In conjunction with a reduction in rank to Private, he warrants dismissal from the United States Army with a DISHONORABLE DISCHARGE, effective on his current separation date.*

My dad had been given a dishonorable discharge from the Army, which didn't make any sense at all. "This can't be right," I muttered. "He got an honorable discharge like everybody else."

My mother laid the envelope next to the trunk. "Actually, he didn't. Your father was accused of a number of crimes against the Allies, including desertion and treason, found guilty of most of them, and was court-martialed while in Germany. He remained in the Army until the war was over in Europe, after which he returned to the States and was dishonorably discharged when his enlistment ended."

My jaw dropped. "Treason? Desertion? Dad? You're kidding!"

She gave a small smile and shook her head. "You remember your dad ever telling you about the war?"

Well, no, actually. Neither my sister or I had been told much of anything, as far as I knew. I asked Dad a couple of times when I was in junior high, but he never gave details of his day-to-day duties or locations during the war, saying only that he'd played around with radar sets in the Army. I've asked friends whose fathers or mothers had been involved in the war effort in Europe or the Pacific and they cited the same lack of conversation. None of their parents told them war stories of any consequence.

For my own part, when World War II was taught in high school—too quickly and with too little explanation—I did some outside reading, and the more I read, the more fascinated I became. That led to an undergraduate degree in history, and then a master's in American history with a specialty in military history. I had enough certificates and good-enough grades to go into a PhD program, but decided I had spent enough time getting educated and chose high school as the place where students would be most likely to be excited by the material.

"Not much that I can remember," I answered her question. "He was a radar operator and served in Europe. I remember seeing a few photos of England and Paris in his desk drawer, and maybe one of him in front of a windmill in Holland."

"Well," my mother continued, "his receiving a dishonorable discharge was one reason he never told you about the war. He told me what he could when he came back, but the major event in his last six months was classified as TOP SECRET—it wasn't declassified till decades later—so when he couldn't talk about what was most important to his military career, he chose not to talk about any of it.

"The videotape fills in what happened in those six months. If Dad could have told the whole story, he would have been seen as the hero he always wanted to be."

The hero he always wanted to be? What are you talking about? My curiosity went off the scale, and I almost swallowed my tongue keeping quiet.

"The first one looks real enough. How did he end up with two?" Nancy asked.

My mom nodded. "The honorable discharge is a fake. Remember Junior working for the War Production Board? He came into direct contact with the highest levels of the military, and he made a lot of important friends. Throughout the war, he used his contacts to keep up with your dad and Jake, watching them move around during the different campaigns.

"After the war ended, Junior found out what had happened to your dad. He was afraid that if anyone knew he'd been given a dishonorable discharge, it would affect the Gunnarson businesses. He immediately used his political clout and military friends to get the Review Board's report declared TOP SECRET, which meant it would be taken out of the usual records and locked up. Junior then had a regular honorable discharge paper drawn up and placed in your dad's personnel file.

"No one besides a general, your dad, Junior, and a file clerk knew of the switch. The real one was returned to the Army since it was now part of a classified report, but Dad took a photograph of it in case he ever needed it—remember that copy machines hadn't been invented. Meanwhile, Junior sent him a copy of the fake one."

"What in the world did he do?" I asked.

My mother leaned back in her chair, her hands in her lap.

"The video and I are going to tell you what happened. Please understand," she said, looking at us with an earnest expression, "Dad felt bad about not talking to you about the war. Since the report used by the Review Board became classified and no one ever told him it wasn't, he assumed he couldn't talk about it."

"Because he was ashamed?" Nancy asked.

"No, no—it wasn't shame. He was perhaps embarrassed, or perhaps he felt guilty or even juvenile for having been so naive, but never ashamed. He did many good things in the war, in lots of important places, but the war wasn't as simple for your dad as it was for other soldiers. He reacted differently from most men, and some of his conflicts came from his life before the war. That's why, if you're going to see the whole picture, we have to start with the school in Tucson and a young girl named Lilly."

"Tucson? The Tucson in Arizona? Dad went to school in Arizona? Who's Lilly?" I asked, forgetting my promise.

"He and Jake both attended a special school on a ranch in Arizona," she said. "It was in the late '30s, and that's where they met Lilly, a young girl at a tuberculosis asylum near Tucson."

"Ranch? As in *cattle* ranch? What are you talking about?" It was becoming obvious I'd been left in the dark about a lot of things I should have been privy to. I was the history guy, you know—I was supposed to know things.

My mother slid the two papers back into the envelope, held it while she took several twine-tied bundles of letters from the trunk, set them next to it, replaced the envelope, closed the lid, and stood up.

"Well," she said, "how about some cookies? You two need a snack?"

That was her signal we were now going to talk about serious things. My mother, bless her heart, could only talk seriously when her hands were covered in flour. All my life, when something needed to be discussed that involved hearts or minds, or when I had girl problems, or had big decisions or complaints of one sort or another, or when Nancy had just broken up with a boyfriend or he with her, or things were going badly at law school, my mother used working in the kitchen as an excuse to keep her hands busy while searching for the proper words of wisdom to help us out.

In her mind, the smells of baking cookies and cupcakes were directly connected to the heart. The taste of sugar, lovingly prepared, allowed people to be less afraid to speak of personal problems, and less resistant to good advice, and any discussion taking place in the kitchen was likely to go smoother and be more truthful than anywhere else. My dad would sit in on the conversations, but his major role was being a self-avowed taste tester and would snitch samples of the goodies while they were still warm. He rarely said anything he didn't feel strongly about, but liked being together with the rest of us when important things were discussed.

We all moved to the kitchen. Nancy and I sat in the chairs around the counter as my seemingly re-energized mother went about gathering the bowls, the mixer, the flour and sugar, the bags of chocolate chips—my favorite—and other ingredients.

"In the 1920s and '30s," she began, "it was popular for wealthy families to send their sons to ranch schools. They were typically cattle ranches, dude ranches, wilderness outfits, or other outdoor-oriented businesses that had been transformed into secondary education boarding schools by adding academic curricula to their regular work. Modern thinking believed the outdoor environment was healthy for boys, and being involved in physical work as well as regular curriculums helped build character and leadership skills."

She began creaming butter and sugar together and then stood for a moment, thinking.

"Mountain Crest Ranch School," she finally said. "It was an all-boys school in a mountain valley north of

Tucson, with a maximum of thirty or forty students. Each student had their own horse, which they had to care for, slept outside on sleeping porches year around, and performed calisthenics every morning. They worked in vegetable gardens and orchards collecting their own food, learned to work with ranch animals, and also learned outdoor skills like backpacking, camping, fixing trail meals, hunting, and fishing.

"The educational part of the ranch included a spectrum of classes taught daily by top-notch instructors who were mostly graduates of universities on the East Coast. The curriculum was tailored to prepare the kids for college, so it included history courses, classical and modern literature, Latin, a full range of math and science, and so forth. Graduates from the ranch schools were routinely accepted into Yale and Harvard and other elite universities."

Mom had gotten the mix to the proper state, blended in the dry ingredients and the chocolate chips, and began scooping tablespoon-sized mounds onto cookie sheets. Before she slid them into the oven, she stopped, washed her hands, and retrieved yet another large envelope from a cupboard next to the sink. She pulled out several pages of handwritten notes.

"After deciding you should hear what happened at the ranch, we realized that what I knew would take about two minutes to tell, and it didn't sit well with him. He wanted everything to be heard so you could understand the personalities involved and how it affected what happened later on. It was too late to make another video, so he decided to write a story describing everything.

"He spent the next two days, when he was feeling okay, writing out what it was like at the ranch, who was who, and what happened with Jake and Lilly. He wrote it in third person like a novel, obviously enjoying seeing himself back at the ranch. It was clear he loved the ranch and treasured every moment he was there. It was a true shame he and Jake had to leave.

"See—I'm already getting ahead of myself. He described the buildings, the grounds, the mountains, the lakes, and especially his horse. Giving up the ranch was one thing, but he truly missed his horse when he didn't go back. He put in every agonizing detail into his story he could remember, and I heard him laughing over some of the parts. He had almost finished it when he ran out of energy and had to quit."

After sliding the baking sheet in the oven, she organized the sheets, straightened the edges, and began reading my dad's journey.

Chapter 3

"Did you just kiss your horse? Good Lord, have you no decency?"

Teddy Gunnarson drew his brush through the mane of Sugar, a beauty of a tall Morgan, while his brother, Jake, clowned around with his horse, a muscular, full-blooded quarter horse named Maybelline.

Jake laughed and then planted another kiss on Maybelline's significantly large nose. "Ah, there's nothing like a good horse! I missed you so much, darlin'."

"Well, I missed Sugar, too, but I don't kiss him. It's only been a couple of months, you know."

Jake and Teddy had arrived at the Tucson train station the day before, were met by Manny Ortega with the ranch truck, and then spent an hour loading sacks of oats at the feed store to bring back to the barn. It was after sunset when they carried their suitcases into their dorm rooms. Early morning brought their first chance to get to the stables, both wearing khaki shorts, big bandannas, tall socks, high-top work boots, and Stetson hats, the typical apparel of ranch school students during the summer. It was too hot to don the standard long-sleeve work shirts, and exposure to the sun

18

was viewed as healthful, so shirtless was the choice for the day. Jake loved going without his shirt, regretting only the lack of girls at the ranch to admire him, while Teddy was perfectly happy with having no girls around to observe the bulges of flab hanging over his belt.

"Well, you'll have to take my word for it, but it's a lot easier to kiss May than Big Lips."

That sent Teddy into rolls of laughter. Dorothy "Big Lips" Rayburn was one of Jake's periodic targets for romance back in Minneapolis. She was known for resisting all advances from the local herd of boys who routinely vied for being her center of attention, raising her to celebrity status as a girl whose eventual conquest would become legendary.

"At least May's got less hair on her snout than Cindy Branigan has in her mustache," Teddy finally squeaked out.

It was now Jake who was snorting through his nose. Cindy Branigan was a daughter of one of the ladies in their mother's social circle. Her celebrity status had long been established, but on the opposite end of the spectrum as Big Lips, confirmed by a string of boys claiming to have learned various extracurricular activities at her hand. Touching lips to the wispy hair on her face had been elevated to a rite of passage by those who had accomplished it firsthand.

It was the end of August, and the Gunnarson boys had returned to the ranch a full week before the start of the regular fall semester, while most other students would be arriving over the next few days. Accustomed to riding the train together, Teddy returned with him though he was only starting his second year, and the extra week left him unassigned. Intending to work on his fly-fishing skills in the high mountain streams, he was looking forward to being alone.

Senior boys like Jake were traditionally invited to take part in the Mountain Crest Ranch Rodeo, a one-day affair held at the ranch's athletic field and an important part of every senior's year. The horse wranglers, cattle herders, seasonal gardeners, maintenance people, and a few of the school's teachers joined in contests of barrel racing, calf roping, horse racing, and bronc riding. Students, parents, friends, and local dignitaries from Tucson were invited to watch the events, share in the festivities, and tour the school's facilities. The pictures and movies taken by a photographer would be used in brochures and presentations advertising the school to prospective students.

"You'll be taking geometry and American history this semester?" Jake asked. "I'm finally done with Latin, thank God, and now have to suffer through physics and calculus, plus biology. You ought to be glad you inherited the smarts of the family. I'd been happy to skip the book learning, especially Latin. Why learn a language that's dead, dead, dead? And who the hell cares about the equation of parabolas, anyway?"

Jake would be eighteen in October, beginning his fifth year at the school, and was scheduled to graduate in the spring. Teddy was fifteen, with just one school year finished. Except for a week-long horse-packing trip into the nearby mountains in June, the two brothers had spent their summer at home in Minneapolis, working part-time at one of the Gunnarson sawmills.

"I'll be starting Latin," Teddy replied, "which I am not enthused about, but I'm looking forward to geometry and history. And I'm moving up a platoon, so I get to learn survival skills and map reading, which I think will be fantastic."

"You'll love it. I did. I loved every bit of it. There's not another place like this on Earth."

Having risen early, the boys were working in the barn while the rays of the sun still reached far inside the big open doors, spilling light into the horse stalls. Outside, the surrounding campus still glistened with early morning dew.

The ranch sat on gently sloping land between two roughly parallel mountain ridges that ran from a tall mountain peak in the north down to the flat landscape of Tucson, the ridges eventually disappearing as they plunged beneath the ground in true volcano-country fashion. The valley between the ridges was narrow close to the city, but broadened enough halfway up to establish the ranch in the 1880s.

Though the valley was originally a scattering of large pastures and orchards alongside a year-round stream, a small dam was built in 1896, creating a lake and a small pond, and spawning the centralization of buildings, corrals, barns, and hay sheds. The pastures and orchards up the valley were preserved, and fields of hay and a number of vegetable gardens were put in to support the growing ranch operations. Electricity reached the valley in 1911, the buildings were upgraded, and a dude ranch was developed to entice the not-so-far-away California wealthy into spending their summers experiencing the Western life. However, the heat of southern Arizona made the early years rough going financially, and the ranch became a prime candidate for cashing in on the national movement of developing ranch-based schools for America's wealthy youth.

Captain Joseph McCall was the ranch manager. Tall and rugged, the former Arizona forest ranger was a seasoned veteran of living in the outdoors. After a decade of leading other rangers, he joined the ranch fifteen years before, and helped orchestrate the conversion of the ranch first into a dude ranch, and then into a successful school.

Known for being a man steeped in the tradition of the frontier pathfinders and pioneers who had helped explore, settle, and develop the southwestern United States, McCall taught his students to be independent, smart, skilled, and educated. He was strict and authoritarian, but was admired by every student. He told an endless stream of stories about men like Kit Carson, John Fremont, and Charlie Good-night, who had explored and opened the early American West, believing they were good role models for developing character. The boys soaked up every tale like water in the desert.

Jake let Teddy lead the way as the horses plodded along a trail into the mountains above the ranch. The kitchen cooks had made them sandwiches, so they'd make it up to the small lake below the peak for lunch and have some time to fish before the clouds gathered. A little sprinkle would be okay, but they wanted to be headed home if a mountain shower moved in. They had packed ponchos in their saddle-bags, just in case.

"What do you have to do for the rodeo? It's on Saturday, so you only have the rest of the week to get things ready. I'll be around if you need any help."

"I'm making the trophies and ribbons in the crafts shop tomorrow," Jake answered, "then working on the posters for each event. Setup for everything begins on Thursday. On Saturday, I'm entered in a couple of the roping events and the last horse race, but the Captain recruited me to escort a special visitor after lunch. I'm supposed to take them for a ride around the ranch.

"He didn't say who it was, but last year Jimmy Edwards had to babysit some politico's little kid who whined all the time. The kid wasn't big enough to ride alone, so he had to sit behind Jimmy's saddle. It was torture for all concerned. I kind of expect the same thing, and am not looking forward to it. I only hope it's not some fat lady. Ol' May, here, she doesn't take to carrying people whose rumps are broader than her own."

That brought a guffaw from Teddy.

"Speaking of which, I noticed you let your stirrups out. Are you growing again?"

Teddy laughed. "Afraid so. I've grown a half-inch since June, making it three inches in the last year. According to

Mom, I haven't even hit my growth spurt. If I can get rid of my gut, I'll be in pretty good shape by Christmas."

"Well, you're taking after Senior, for sure, so don't be surprised if you wake up one morning with your feet hanging off the end of the bed. I'm pretty much guaranteed to be the shrimp of the family. I make up for it by being adorably handsome, but it's tough being in a family of giants. Good thing the captain chose you a tall Morgan horse. He must have been able to tell you were going to be big."

TEDDY PULLED on his reins to get Sugar to stop. "Did he figure that out when I had to take off my shirt and drop my pants in his office the first day I was here?"

Jake grinned. "The ol' personal physical exam in the captain's office? Everybody gets to do it. I guess he's looking for bumps or pimples or irregularities in your bone structure, though I expect he's also checking out your weenie as a forecaster of growth."

"Well, I hope he doesn't do it again. It was damned embarrassing, standing there all shriveled up. I'll do my own forecasting."

Jake laughed. "Maybe we can get Cindy Branigan to help you out with that."

Teddy grinned, gave Sugar a nudge, and started up the trail again. An hour later, they topped a hill that led to a steep switchback down to the lake.

Chapter 4

"Jake," Captain McCall said, "this is Miss Lilly Hollister. Miss Hollister has been a patient for a year or so at the tuberculosis sanatorium down the road, and she has never ridden a horse. I'd like for you to take her for a ride around the ranch and show her our facilities. I think Pinky would be a good mare for her to ride, so if you'd rope her out and saddle her up, you can escort Miss Hollister around for an hour or so while her nurse, Mrs. Duncan, and I watch the rodeo."

"Nice to meet you," Jake said as he regarded the fine-looking young lady in front of him. She certainly was not fat.

"Hi," she replied with a nod.

"Don't let the surgical mask fool you," Captain McCall continued. "Under that mask is a delightful smile, but we must respect her need to be cautious around us. You also need to go slowly, as she needs to remain relaxed and as calm as possible."

Miss Hollister was, in fact, shapely, perfectly groomed, damned pretty, and he had overlooked the mask. He was guessing she was fifteen or sixteen, and she was definitely a looker. She had combed her blonde hair so that it fell uniformly below her shoulders and wore a stylish headband that held it back from her face, highlighting a pair of clear blue eyes that were the loveliest he had ever seen.

"Uh, well, yeah, of course! My privilege!" he stammered. "Let's walk over and get Pinky ready to go."

As Pinky was being caught and saddled, Jake took his time explaining the various breeds of horses, pointing out how Pinky differed from his own horse, May, and from his brother's horse, Sugar.

Jake helped Lilly into the saddle, explained the use of the reins, and then supposedly gave the young lady control of the beast, though Pinky was well-known for being a follower and would dutifully stick with May while ignoring the person in the saddle.

May and Pinky plodded contentedly around the ranch property as Jake pointed out the features.

"This is the dormitory. It houses all the students and a few teachers, and it also has classrooms. Those are sleeping porches around the outside. We sleep outdoors all year around, though we lower tarps during snowstorms, windstorms, or other violent weather. We also meet outside at six-thirty every morning to do fifteen minutes of calisthenics."

"I sleep on a screened porch," Lilly said, anxious to get a word in. The sanatorium had a number of cottages with sleeping porches, arranged in a loose rectangle on the valley floor between two ridges—the same valley where, a mile above, the ranch had been built. She had been there a year, being calm, eating healthy food, and impatiently waiting for her lungs to heal. After being diagnosed with tuberculosis, she had come to the sanatorium when she was fifteen and considered it a major catastrophe when her sixteenth birthday came and went without her ever having been kissed. She had wept at the occasion, and a dark curtain of loneliness had fallen over her.

"This is called the hotel," Jake said, pointing at a different two-story log building with a row of large windows on its first floor. "It has the ranch kitchen and the dining area, more classrooms, and a central meeting area downstairs. The top floor has bedroom suites for visiting teachers and dignitaries. We eat three meals a day with most of the vegetables and fruits coming from our own gardens and the orchard, and we all learn how to butcher the cows we raise in a herd north of here, so we also have meat. The cooks are really good, and all the servers come up from the valley.

"This row of buildings includes the nurse's station, the crafts shop, and three houses for the ranch manager and the headmasters. This is a pond that's fed by a stream over there. We swim in it during the summer."

Jake rambled on and finally pulled up next to one of the large gardens.

Having looked for an opportunity, Lilly pulled a handkerchief from her pocket, lowered her mask to expose her whole face, and pretended to mildly wipe her lips. Then, making sure Jake was watching, she smiled at him as sweetly as she could and thanked him for taking her around.

That did it for Jake.

Lilly had perfect white teeth set against a perfect set of lips. With her endearing eyes and glistening hair, her face took on an appearance far beyond what Jake had ever experienced. It was as if an angel had descended upon Pinky's back. Jake was smitten into silence, and from then on, Lilly did most of the talking.

Fitting her mask back around her mouth and nose, Lilly, in as much of a lady-like manner as possible, gushed about her family, a description of her house in Pittsburgh, her school, her friends, her life at the sanatorium, her lessons, Mrs. Avery, her home teacher, Mrs. Duncan, her nurse, her pets back home, a description of the countryside compared with that of Arizona, what she had found in Tucson while on a field trip, and even the color of flowers outside her cottage.

She finally ran out of all the words she'd been saving since Mrs. Duncan told her of the day's arrangements, which would include meeting a real horse that would likely have a real boy on top. She knew a kiss would be impossible because of her condition, but even being close to a handsome boy was definitely a major step forward.

The dark curtain of loneliness began to lift.

Jake, meanwhile, kept May and Pinky headed toward the orchard and then the pastures, where he helped Lilly down from the horse so she could rub the head of a cow. Jake maintained their leisurely pace past the rodeo grounds, not even slightly remembering that he and May were entered in the final horse race. Then it was back to the stream, to the lake, past the maintenance sheds, around the corrals, and finally, the stables.

After dismounting, Lilly closely followed as Jake led the horses to their stalls, showed her the tack room where he put away Pinky's saddle, and then turned Pinky into the corral behind.

It was a surprisingly long afternoon. It wasn't until Captain McCall hunted them down that they returned to Mrs. Duncan and the rodeo festivities. McCall was peeved that after telling Jake to take one hour showing Miss Hollister around, he had taken three.

Chapter 5

"Are you crazy or are you just stupid?" Teddy asked when Jake told him his idea.

"I'm neither," Jake replied. "This is a great idea. Lilly has never experienced the high country, right? We know that the high country is awe-inspiring and inspirational, right? We know from our own experience that it brings us closer to God and his creation, right? And I'm pretty sure it's a healthy thing to do, too.

"Imagine if Lilly could sit quietly beside the lake and breathe deeply, focusing all her appreciation into a soul-immersing experience. Don't you think she'd be better for it?"

"And 'just stupid' wins the prize! McCall is going to crap his pants. He doesn't like us to even be around ordinary girls, so sneaking away with a tuberculosis patient is going to give him fits. You've only known her since August, you've seen her on a few weekends, and even then, you've only been able to talk to her through the screen of her porch. Besides, don't you know that tuberculosis is a real disease? It's not likely that somebody can just *sit quietly* their way out of it. I don't know much about it, but—"

"See, that's where you're correct—you don't know much about it. I do. I can tell you right now she'll be happier and healthier just seeing the mountains and the lakes than she's ever been lying around and *being calm* every day for over a year. She needs to drink in the wonders of nature. She needs to touch the granite spires she sees out her window. She needs lifting up!"

Jake had decided the best thing for Lilly was to take May over to the sanatorium early one Saturday, sneak Lilly out of her cottage, put her behind his saddle, and the two of them would ride up to the lake for a short visit. They'd be back right after lunch, and no one would be the wiser.

Jake circled the first Saturday in November on his calendar. Captain McCall was on a recruiting trip in New York and would be gone that weekend, so he'd never know a thing. Lilly's nurse always took Saturdays off, so she'd be out of the picture.

Onward and upward! Jake told himself.

When the first Saturday finally dawned, Lilly began an early morning sidewalk stroll outside her cottage. The patients were allowed to walk anywhere within the compound and were encouraged to sun themselves frequently. As she had taken walks before, no one was suspicious as she strolled by, her face mask firmly in place. Mrs. Duncan had the day off and was shopping in Tucson, leaving a nurse from a different cottage to look after Lilly.

Lilly left a note for her substitute nurse saying she would be spending the morning visiting friends and would take her breakfast and lunch with them. She'd be back sometime in the afternoon. Carrying a required sweater should she get chilled, Lilly walked slowly and calmly up the sidewalks, past the gardens, and up behind a maintenance shed, where Jake was waiting. She nervously took his hand, slid her foot into his stirrup, and clumsily swung her leg over May's rump. She settled herself behind his saddle on a blanket Jake provided as a cushion. He had their lunches in a small pack tied onto the saddle horn.

"Are you ready?" Jake asked.

"Are you sure we should be doing this?"

"I'll take care of you," Jake said as he touched his heel to May's flank. "We'll make it to the lake, you will be properly awe-inspired, and we'll have sandwiches for lunch. We'll be back in time for your afternoon nap. It will be a glorious day."

He turned his head and looked into her eyes. "You're going to see everything I've been telling you about. You will be truly amazed."

At least Lilly was already accomplishing one goal: During their talks in the months since the rodeo, with Jake sitting outside her screened porch while she stayed inside, she had yet to significantly touch him, but was now hugging him tight around his waist, snuggling up against his muscular back, and burying her covered nose in the smells of his shirt.

Jake turned May toward the road and set her into an easy walk. He could barely restrain his pride at having pulled off such an adventure. It was the beginning of a whole new level of friendship with this wonderful girl, and he was sure he would soon be her Mountain Man hero.

"MY BACK IS HURTING."

Jake had never ridden behind a saddle, so it being uncomfortable surprised him. The hurting, though, could also be from the trail. It was more rough and uneven than he'd remembered, and May's gait was not as smooth as usual. He had been on this trail a couple of years before, and had chosen this way because it left the road a good distance before reaching the ranch, zig-zagging up and eventually passing above the ranch, making them less likely to be seen by anyone out for a ride. But the trail was rougher, steeper, and narrower than he'd remembered, especially on the switchbacks.

May's reaction to the mountain trail was normal—swaying, rocking, pounding, placing her hooves down hard on the inclines to put power on her back legs where she needed it, making small jumps as she negotiated sharp turns. This caused Jake to rock back and forth and up and down in his saddle and to shift the pressure from each of his feet against the stirrups. For an experienced rider, the situation was normal, and he hardly noticed the motions.

Lilly, on the other hand, felt every hard jolt as the forces rippled up her spine. Her legs ached from hanging without support, and the swaying back and forth was making her queasy. The blanket provided some cushion, but not enough to make a difference. She tried to rock and sway with the movements, but it was totally different from riding Pinky around the ranch.

Stretching to relieve the pain in her back and on her thighs, she couldn't help but hold on tighter to Jake. Feeling Lilly's increased movements against him as she squirmed, it gradually dawned on Jake that Lilly's problems were due to her lack of stirrups. She had no way to use her legs to cushion her body against May's movements.

He took his feet out of the stirrups and told her to place her feet in each one, but her feet did not reach—she was too far back from the saddle's center and was several inches shorter than her golden knight. Jake finally let the attempt go and hoped it wouldn't be too much farther—she would just have to bear up.

The trail leveled out as it turned northward to follow the ridge. Lilly felt the decrease in steepness, but May continued to sway and rock and pound, and there was no relief for the pain in her tailbone. It wasn't long before Lilly was constantly squirming with small grunts and an occasional gasp as she tried to stretch out the aches in her back, along her sides, and in her neck. The pain finally reached her rib cage, and she found herself laboring to consciously inhale and exhale to keep her chest relaxed.

A few minutes later, she began to cough.

Jake pulled May to a stop in a small meadow. He did not know where they were exactly, but he had been watching the distant peaks. The peaks did not seem much closer, yet they had been moving for two hours since leaving the road.

He lowered Lilly to the ground and dismounted. "How are you doing?"

Lilly did not want to complain. She did not want to tell him how uncomfortable riding behind him was, and she did not want to seem weak. A year of mostly lying prone had taken away the comfortable fit between her bones, joints, and muscles, making her stiff, awkward and unbalanced when her legs were spread so far apart. She knew there was little hope of compensating for the constant motions of riding a horse.

More importantly, apart from the aches that squirming no longer alleviated, she already felt tired—she had lost her energy. That was a major indicator Mrs. Duncan always looked for and had preached to her about. "Back to bed with you," she'd say, and Lilly would inevitably feel better after a few minutes of lying down.

Her bed was now a long way off.

"I'm doing okay," Lilly finally responded with a forced smile, forgetting she still wore her mask. "I need to walk around and work out some of the aches. I'm turning out to not be much of a horsewoman."

"You're doing fine," Jake said, hoping to encourage her. He was surprised she seemed so out of shape because she looked fit and healthy. Her breathing sounded fine except for an occasional cough, so he guessed the muscle aches were from the swish and sway of May's back end, which he couldn't do anything about.

"We're almost there," he said, not really knowing but hoping again to encourage her. He wished he'd selected another trail, but maybe they were closer than he imagined. They had to be close, right? The trip to the lake from the ranch took less than two hours, and this part of the trail had to be higher up than where he usually started. It should be taking less time.

Onward and upward! he told himself.

He put Lilly in the saddle and adjusted the straps so her insteps were secure in the stirrups. He now sat behind the saddle and reached around her to handle the reins, which gave Lilly a spark of enjoyment. It was already past mid-morning, and they had to be close to the lake. He gave a harder heel to May and she increased her speed.

Lilly had pulled on her sweater while they were stopped but still missed the warmth of Jake's back. He had been a good windbreak, too. The surrounding forest and its shade made the air cooler than in the valley, and she now wished she had brought a heavier jacket. The blanket would have been welcomed around her, but she didn't dare ask. She assumed it was required for anyone riding on the back part of the saddle.

She did agree with Jake that the lack of stirrups had been one of the problems, and the riding became more tolerable. Her rib cage was still hurting, but being able to press her legs down to raise her a little off the saddle was a godsend, allowing her legs to cushion May's movements and straighten her body more upright. She could relax and focus on keeping her breathing regular. Everything should now be fine.

May's faster gait, however, brought a different motion, bouncing Lilly up in the saddle and slapping her bottom against the leather as she came down—bouncing up, slapping down—once more, twice more, an infinite number of times more. She tried standing up all the time, but her legs couldn't handle the constant strain.

Her cough had gone away as she relaxed over the short rest break, but her chest cavity was now absorbing a lot of the shock from the increased bouncing in the saddle. She soon felt her bronchial tubes flexing behind her breastbone. That was a bad sign.

Her coughing began again, and she had a faint taste of blood in her mouth.

Jake noticed when Lilly began to cough, but was focused on something else. The early morning had been perfectly clear, but clouds had now gathered above the west slope of the mountain range. Clouds forming in the afternoon was normal in the summer and to be expected—they would typically build up around noon, rain for an hour or two, and then disappear before suppertime.

Clouds in the fall, however, did not readily go away. The cooler air and reduced sunlight meant they were more likely to increase, and occasionally, release rain, hail, or snow. Or all three.

They needed to go faster. Jake added more pressure to May's flank, and she responded by stepping faster, almost to a trot, making the ride even more uncomfortable and causing Lilly even more pain.

In a few minutes, Lilly motioned to Jake to stop so she could manage her coughing. He had become disillusioned with riding behind the saddle, so he readily slid off and helped her down.

Embarrassed, Lilly stepped down the trail to cough as discreetly as she could, but once the cough started, she could not hold back. Her cough ratcheted up to a full-blown hacking episode, and she collapsed to her knees as she held both hands over her mask. The problem was not only the force of the air coming from her lungs, but she also struggled to breathe in. How high up in elevation were they? A couple thousand feet higher than her cottage? She had been lectured about the benefits of the dry air at the high altitudes of the Southwest, but she'd never been so high.

When Jake came up behind her to see if there was anything he could do, he saw that her mask was hanging loose from her mouth, dripping gobs of blood onto the ground.

Jake made his first good decision of the day and called it quits. They would head back. After Lilly had calmed herself and quieted her coughing, Jake draped the blanket around her shoulders and helped her back to May. Trying to be careful and considerate, he hoisted her onto the saddle. Using one of the stirrups to boost himself up behind her, Jake turned May around and nudged her back down the trail.

Coming up the trail, Jake had tried to judge how far they were from the lake. Now, he was looking in the opposite direction. He could see a few rooftops of the sanatorium cottages in the far distance and was happy to find a familiar sight: the flagpole of the ranch below him.

It wasn't that far away.

The sun was now covered by clouds, and the air was increasingly chilly as Jake leaned against Lilly, holding the reins, listening as her cough came and went. He kept placing her hands on the edges of the blanket, urging her to pull at them to keep it swaddled around her. He was already working hard at holding her, trying to cushion her against May's movement, trying to keep from sliding around, while also trying to hold the reins.

Urging his horse down the trail, he realized another problem. Coming up the trail, May had used her strength and the movement of her body to adjust her gate as she moved uphill. Going downhill, especially with Jake urging her to hurry, May was now landing on her front hooves, changing the rhythmic bounces into sharp, thudding jolts.

Lilly's head began bobbing up and down, her mouth now huffing as each jolt sent a shock wave through her. She worked hard to keep her eyes on the trail, anticipating each jolt from May's steps, thinking that if she knew one was coming, she could lean forward and lift herself off the saddle, letting her legs take most of the shock.

After a few attempts, she no longer had the strength to keep her legs straight. The jolts kept pounding through her body, causing her shoulders to hammer down on her chest cavity. The repetitive pains in her chest were beginning to collect, and spasms started twisting inside her chest. She had also begun to shiver. The blanket was good, but she was chilled wherever the breeze found an opening. She tried to hold the edges, but her hands were feeling cold and weak, and weren't responding like they should.

As Jake was mentally listing all of the mistakes he had made, he had to quickly grab Lilly as her head suddenly dipped and she fell forward against May's neck. Pulling her back up, Jake moved the reins to one hand, wrapped his other arm around her, and pulled her back into his chest.

This close embrace would have been one more achievement for Lilly to tell her friends back home, but she hardly noticed. She was trying—really trying—not to cough, not to spit up, not to appear weak, and not to embarrass herself any more than she already had.

She hadn't noticed when she fell forward, nor had she felt her face brush against May's mane.

Chapter 6

Jake didn't remember the trail being so narrow and steep when they had been coming up. Regardless, he needed to get Lilly back as soon as he could. She needed her nurse, she needed her doctor, and she needed them right now.

Holding Lilly upright was wearing him out, and to make things worse, she had begun flopping sideways, like she had no strength left, forcing him to lean even farther back, pulling her more strongly against him. It had begun to sprinkle, and then increased to a light rain. He pulled the blanket up over her head, giving her cover. He himself had no cover, but could do nothing about it.

Jake spotted what he was sure was another worn path to his left, going down the slope and almost directly pointing toward the ranch. But as he had looked, he noticed smoke coming from the firepit at the ranch. If there were any way he could cut through the forest, he could reach the ranch far sooner than stuttering back down the hillside with the zigzags.

Knowing he shouldn't be doing what he was doing, Jake extended the reins to the left, and May, hesitating, stepped onto what to her seemed a trail even rougher than the one she was on.

The drops of water hitting Jake's back increased, while Lilly kept on coughing, spraying blood across her mask. May had stepped her way down a couple of hundred yards, sliding in two places because of the increased incline. The forest around them was overgrown with brambles and thickets and had a much different appearance from what Jake had seen above. After a dozen more yards he found a full-sized pine tree fallen across the trail.

They could not continue going down, and because of the thickets, they could not go around.

Damn it! Jake said under his breath, but he had no time to hesitate. He turned May around and kicked her in the flanks. It was harder going up, but they had no choice. He had made another mistake.

He felt May's jumping and bucking and slipping and jolting as she made headway, and he felt every shockwave as it moved through Lilly's body. Her face mask was matted and soaked with more blood than it could hold, and he felt the blood spraying across his forearm when she coughed. Looking her in the face, he saw the blanket around her head was soaked in blood as well.

Jake kept kicking May's flanks, regretting the rough treatment, but knowing he had to force her to keep going. If the situation wasn't bad enough, he was behind the saddle and had nothing to keep himself from sliding over May's rump except grabbing onto the saddle horn, leaving only his elbows to cradle Lilly. It was awkward and ferociously painful.

Finally reaching the original trail, Jake had to give May a rest. She was heaving with each breath, her large chest going in and out, her head bobbing up and down as she snorted, straining to suck more oxygen into her lungs.

Jake slid off of May, but Lilly refused to get down,

shaking her head. She was afraid that if she got down from May, she'd never get back up. Her energy was gone. She tried to say something but could get out only the beginning of a word before she resumed hacking into her mask.

She suddenly yanked the mask away, smearing blood across her cheek. There was no embarrassment anymore, only fear and urgency and panic and disgust. Blood had also run down her neck and onto her white blouse, the same pretty white blouse she had worn to the rodeo, the blouse that had made her look so attractive.

Jake couldn't help it, and they were hard to distinguish from the raindrops, but his eyes were filling up with tears. What had he done?

May suddenly jerked her head around and gave a loud snort. Another rider was coming on the trail in front of them.

"Jake! Jake!"

A man jumped from his horse and ran toward them. It was Manny Ortega. The ranch had discovered Jake's foolish plans, and when he and Lilly had not returned, had sent out the ranch hands to find him.

Manny slid Lilly from the saddle and laid her on the ground. He held her as she coughed and then vomited blood onto the ground.

"Help me get her wrapped up., then you follow me."

Jake, cold, stunned, and terrified, did not fully comprehend what was happening. Finally understanding Manny's command, he clumsily helped Manny use a clean wool blanket to wrap Lilly tightly into a mummy form. As the blanket was finally tucked around her head and neck, they both got her standing, and Manny draped a poncho around her.

The cowboy climbed into his saddle. Taking the reins and draping them loosely around the saddle horn, he lifted as Jake pushed, and Lilly was soon cradled in Manny's arms.

Using soft whistles and movements of his knees, Manny's horse turned and was soon trotting up the trail from where he had come.

Ignoring the sodden mess of the blanket on the ground, Jake slung himself into the saddle, using his hand to scour the rain from his hair and eyes. Pulling tight on the reins, he kicked May into a leaping start and was soon close behind Manny, focused on the seemingly lifeless body ahead of him.

Chapter 7

"You mean she died? Lilly died? My God!"

My mother had read up until my dad had had to quit and then recited the rest of Jake's story from memory. She gathered the pages and slid them back into the envelope. Her expression was one of profound sadness.

"She developed pneumonia, which was typically fatal for tuberculosis sufferers, and died two days later. Jake was devastated, of course." She took a deep breath and continued. "He knew he was responsible for Lilly's death and could not be consoled. When Captain McCall found out what happened, he immediately dismissed Jake from the school, stating that he was disobedient, irresponsible, and displayed a clear lack of character. Jake took a couple of hours to pack his bags, shine his saddle and bridle, give his precious horse one more combing, and then was gone on the next train home.

"Your dad was devastated, as well," Mom said, "as much from Jake's dismissal as from Lilly's death. Everything had happened so fast it left him stranded, emotionally and physically. He finished the semester and rode the train home alone for Christmas. Once past the holidays, he decided not go back. He worshipped Jake, and when McCall refused to listen to Jake's explanations or to recognize the string of events working against him, your dad no longer felt the same about the school.

"His belongings were sent home and he finished his school year in a regular junior high in Minneapolis. The next fall, he enrolled in the same high school I attended."

We were silent as my mother wiped the cooling racks clean, stored them away, and wiped down the counter. Her telling of Dad's journey, so far, had taken six dozen cookies. She motioned us to the dining room, where we sat in chairs clustered around the table opposite the trunk.

"Were there any charges? What did Lilly's family do?"

"I don't know if Dad knew anything about Lilly's family or their reaction or whether they'd made any contact with Jake. Society back then wasn't as predisposed to pointing fingers and meting out punishment like it is now. Dad didn't even know if Jake attended Lilly's funeral."

"What did Senior do? Or Lady Gunnarson?" I asked. "Did they feel like Jake needed to be punished?"

"Don't be too hard on them," Mom said. "They knew Jake to be different from the family mold, and even if they felt he was responsible, they couldn't miss the intense guilt Jake was suffering. They tried to comfort him but finally accepted moving on to be the best thing."

"What did Jake do when he couldn't go back to the ranch?" Nancy asked.

My mother took another deep breath, let it out, and crossed her arms on the table. "His dismissal meant not receiving his high school diploma. I'm sure he had no desire to hang around home, so with Senior's influence, he was accepted into an aviation cadet program at the University of Minnesota in Duluth. He spent the spring semester on campus and the summer at Navy training camps, and then became a regular student. He never went back to Minneapolis, as far as I know."

"Got to admire him for going to college," I said. "How was he emotionally?"

"He didn't recover for about a year, according to Dad. He had been a smart, vibrant, risk-taking, passionate, driven sort of kid, especially when it came to athletics and outdoor adventures. The ranch had given him a small group of people to be around and the freedom to wander the countryside, and he loved learning all the outdoor skills. After he was kicked out, Jake struggled to fit into a college environment where students attended only classes. Dad went up to Duluth a couple of times to visit and found that Jake had resigned himself to living without happiness and shied away from any relationships. There was nothing he could do, so Dad left him alone.

"Jake's salvation came when he discovered flying. It took more than a year of training to become a pilot, but before he left for the Pacific, his boyish exuberance and extraverted personality had come back. He transferred his infatuation with Lilly into loving hunks of metal with big engines and wings. Flying renewed his sense of purpose, I think, and his focus, for sure.

"After Pearl Harbor, Jake's training was accelerated. The Navy dropped the requirement for two years of college, and it wasn't long before he was on the other side of the world. Other than a letter every now and then, Dad thought he'd never see him again."

"Did he ever see him again?" I asked.

My mom used her hands to give me a *don't get ahead of me* sign, and I withdrew the question.

"Speaking of letters," Nancy said, "is that what you took out of the trunk?"

My mother reached over to the bundles and scooted them in front of her. She carefully removed the various pieces of twine and sorted the papers into piles, each pile being a stack of letters with different sizes of stationary, different colors, and different styles, lined and unlined. Where there was an envelope, it was stapled to the accompanying letter. She shuffled things quickly and when she was finished, she took two letters from the big pile, added them to the last pile, and separated it from the others.

"These are the letters Dad wrote while he was away," she said as she touched the piles in front of her. "He left in November of '42, and I didn't see him for three years."

"Did he keep the letters you sent to him?" Nancy asked.

"He did, but he burned them all later."

"What? Why in the world did he burn them?" she asked.

My mom looked at her hands. "You'll understand when you hear the story."

"Now," I said, "you and he didn't get married until after the war, right? You were *betrothed* before he left?"

Mom smiled. "Yes. We were *betrothed*. We met in high school, became sweethearts, graduated, and then started college together. We wanted to get married, but we knew he'd be drafted and would have to leave. That's a rotten way to start a marriage, especially if I ended up a widow. It was in vogue at the time for distressed young girls to swear fidelity to their boyfriends who were going off to war, so Dad and I became officially engaged in August of 1942. He enlisted in October and left the last of November."

I reached over and pulled her left-most pile in front of me. "You've obviously sorted them for some reason, and I assume it's okay if we read them. Should I start here?"

"Yes, that would be fine." She held her hands over the piles as she talked about them. "Your pile has the first letters, written during boot camp in Miami and his radar training in Tampa Bay. They were written on the family stationery he had taken with him. The next two piles are from when he was stationed in England. For those, he used the Army stationery. This pile is when he was in Normandy, then Belgium, Holland, and then Belgium again, at Bastogne."

"He was at Bastogne? When?" I asked, surprised.

"He was there when the Battle of the Bulge started but left before the Germans surrounded the town."

"Oh, my God! I wish I had known. I would have loved to talk to someone who was actually there."

"I wish he had told you, too, but I'm not sure what his perspective would have been. At that point, things had begun falling apart for Dad, I think. He was becoming disillusioned with what was going on around him, and was getting depressed and a little hostile.

"Well, I'm getting too far ahead," she said. "The letters from when he was training in Florida are about 95 percent practical information—pretty dry. You can skim through them, if you want. After those, read the England letters, then the others. He didn't write as frequently once he was on the continent. I'm not sure why, but maybe because he was seeing a lot of things he didn't want to tell me about. He was never one to gripe about things, but the war wasn't as tidy as he needed it to be.

"After that...well, Dad may have been exhausted because of the constant fighting and moving around and everything. Whatever it was, the more he saw and experienced, the more he was dragged into the more horrible parts of the war. Let me know when you get through Bastogne because I have a couple of letters you should read before you go on."

"And the stack you moved to the side?" I asked.

My mother pursed her lips. "Read your dad's letters, then we'll get to those."

She reached over, picked up the stack on the side, and slid them into the big pocket of her apron. That was a pretty cautious move for a bunch of letters, and I tried to read the addresses before she got them into her pocket but failed.

"Okay, well, it will take you a while, so I'm going to make a cake."

Things were moving right along. It was now cake time.

Chapter 8

After scanning through a couple, I agreed with my mother: My dad's letters from his first months in the military were as dry as a bone, although he had a good sense of humor about the situation. I scanned most of them:

> February 20, 1943
> Dearest Margaret,
> There are many men here, training in different areas like radio communications, radio repair, and even torpedo detection. We don't have infantry or artillery people, since most of our training involves some kind of electrical work.
> At boot camp, we were all individuals, commonly referred to as maggots. Here, I'm trained as a member of a 32-man squadron—a First Lieutenant, a Second Lieutenant, a few sergeants, and several Technicians, Fourth Class and Fifth Class. I am a Technician Fifth Class. I don't know many names,

and it's surprisingly hard to tell who's been to college and who hasn't. Of course, we're all young.

Each of us currently has specific duties for what we're doing, but I assume we will be cross-trained on all the components and duties.

Enlisted men live in dormitories, with common showers and bathrooms, and two-person bunks. I have to sleep on my side if I don't want my feet to stick out from under the blankets. Officers have separate quarters. Everything looks like Florida pine construction: loose-grained but probably more rot-resistant.

I hope everything is fine at home.

Yours truly,

Teddy

April 26, 1943

Dearest Margaret,

We've finished the formal training curriculum and are practicing real war situations. As a graduation exercise for the whole camp, a make-believe war was planned out over a many-square-mile area south of the training compound involving our school and an infantry school in the next county. The officers lumped the schools together and divided us into an army of good guys and an army of bad guys, with judges for every battle. Good guys wore white armbands, bad guys black, and judges blue. If a judge points at you, it means you've been hit, and you're supposed to lie down and play dead. When the battle is over, all the dead people move off the field and sit in roped-off areas.

It was like a giant game of Capture the Flag. Just offense and defense. There must have been a strategy on each side, but of course, the officers don't tell us anything about it—we just do what they tell us. Once it started, the commanders really did try to win. My unit set up once, then moved, then moved again. It took all day. They had some planes flying around, but not one of them acted like they had been shot down, so we weren't even sure if they were ours or theirs.

It was fun, but I'm pretty sure real war is not this way. Or maybe it should be: we could go to Europe and yell at all the Germans that they'd been hit and should lie down and play dead. Seems reasonable to me.

That does it for us. The next time we go to war, it will be the real thing.

We now go to England. They haven't told us any details and probably won't. We'll get up one morning, and they'll tell us to get our stuff and get on a train. I've heard we even have to ride the train with the window shades pulled down.

I hope to write you before we leave for England.

Yours truly,

Teddy

"DAD WAS NOT EXACTLY the romantic type, was he?" I said to Mom as she kept walking in and out of the kitchen, checking on our progress. "I mean, he hasn't seen you in five or six months, and all he can say is *Yours truly*? You'd think he would have slipped in an *I love you* or *I miss you* at some point."

My mother smiled and shook her head. "No, not a romantic. He was naturally shy to begin with, and his Gunnarson upbringing had instilled a strict protocol about keeping correspondence formal and unemotional. At least he took after his mother more than Senior, and he was considerably better than Junior, who had the emotions of a brick. Still, he was reserved in the way he wrote letters.

"At least in the beginning. He got better in England, where things were more interesting, and then grew a lot more personal once he was on the continent and saw combat. He wasn't born to be a fighter, and he did a lot of thinking once he saw the war up close.

"Some of it he told me, some of it he didn't."

I scanned through the pre-England letters and then started on the England pile. The new ones did take on a different tone. I wondered if he wasn't needing my mom to talk to. Someplace along the line, I expected him to sound lonely.

> July 20, 1943
> Dearest Margaret,
> You would love the countryside. I've never seen such lush pastures and fields. Of course, it would be a lot prettier if we hadn't turned the whole southern part of England into an armed camp.
> Places here have funny names: Fording Bridge, Milbourne Ferry, Ranscombe Downs, Newbury-Greenham Common, Sturminster Marshal, Strat-

ford-On-Avon, Stow-On-The-Wold. That's just what
I've seen on signposts. They all sound poetic. Maybe
Shakespeare named everything.

They have large estates over here, surrounded by
crooked roads with scattered villages and towns. The
architecture is dominated by stone. I haven't seen
any good lumber trees.

Our training includes presentations at movie
theaters and town auditoriums, but we mostly put up
our equipment and stay in the pastures around
airfields. They move us around a lot, I guess because
it happens in war, and they want us to be able to
knock everything down and put it all back up as
quickly as possible. We're also required to dig foxholes
every place we go. If I don't get anything else out of
war, I'll know how to set up tents and dig holes.

The people in my unit are interesting but are
pretty common, on the whole. Especially the south-
erners. I don't want to call them uncouth, but they
are certainly lax and uneducated, and their accents
are hilarious. I have to slow down my ears to listen to
them. Some of the guys love to decorate their
foxholes, if you can believe it. It's not something that
I apply myself to.

Yours,

Teddy

"Did he always use V-mail?" I asked.

"Oh, he always did whatever the Army told him to do,"
my mom replied.

"What's V-mail?" Nancy asked.

Ah, this is what history majors live for: "Sending mail back and forth between the troops and their families was a high priority for the military. They valued the morale boost that a letter from home brought to somebody sitting in a foxhole in the middle of nowhere.

"But sending and receiving mail in a mobile army in the middle of a war creates a lot of problems, the first being that there's no telling where any particular soldier will be at any particular time. What country will they mail the letter from? How will they get the right stamps? Where will they be when they receive mail? What addresses should people back home use?

"The military came up with V-mail, short for 'Victory mail,' a standard sheet-sized form that provided only one side to be written on, with the address written above the body of the letter. Once written by someone in the States or some GI in Europe, the letter was sent to a special Army organization that photographed the one-sided letter with a frame-by-frame movie camera—one letter per frame—and then sent the film to the corresponding organization across the ocean.

"Each frame of the film was projected on special paper, printed and folded, stuck into an envelope with the address showing, and was delivered to the recipient. No postage was necessary. In the US, the regular mail service took care of the delivery, and overseas, the military did it. The address of the GI was linked to his military unit and would stay with him for the whole war. Between when they started V-mail in 1942 and the end of the war, more than 556 million pieces were delivered to servicemen overseas, and those servicemen sent some 510 million pieces in return. It was a pretty clever solution."

"Well," my sister said, "part of one sheet of paper certainly doesn't allow you to say much."

"No," my mother said, "but your dad was smart. He'd

take several V-mail sheets and write all he wanted to, and then numbered each one so I knew in what order to read them. When I received several pages that made up one letter, I stapled them together.

"However they did it, I got letters from your dad relatively quickly, sometimes even within a couple of days of his mailing them."

> December 15, 1943
> Dear Margie,
> We're on watch 24 hours a day and switch off people so we don't get hypnotized looking at tiny blips on tiny screens. It's easy to fall asleep, too, especially when not much is going on.
>
> This last week, the battalion said we'd be in the same place for a couple of weeks and gave out five-day passes to rotate through the unit, since we wouldn't be having much Christmas. I decided to take a bus to London.
>
> Roger Bernard went with me, as did Skinny Walker (funny name). They've been in my unit since Florida.
>
> Roger's a diesel mechanic back home in Great Falls, Montana, and can fix anything. Skinny is from Waxahachee, Texas, and looks like his name. His family has a farm where he and his brothers work for their dad. They are both nice guys, but obviously don't have much money.
>
> I expected London to look like hell because of all the bombing that took place during the Blitz. They haven't done any new building, so there are lots of empty spaces, but everything has been cleaned neat

as a pin. I was told they start cleaning up bricks the day after a bombing and pile them in their parks until they could be hauled off or reused.

The people of London are interesting. The island is as close to the continent as twenty-one miles and even Berlin is within a few hundred miles. I thought everybody would be nervous and fearful but I don't see it. In the pubs, people act the way you'd expect—drinking, singing, laughing, playing instruments, dancing (they're a lot more energetic in their dancing than we are). Alcohol is not rationed as much as other things, so I expected to see drunks all over the place, like Saturday nights at home. I didn't see one. They do have curfews, and all the lights have to be turned off or the windows blacked out with heavy curtains.

I haven't talked to anyone who thinks Britain is going to lose the war. They are a strong and resolute people and refuse to consider they aren't up to the task. They tell me it wasn't much different during the Blitz, even though a fourth of all Londoners slept every night in shelters underground. They had already sent 80 percent of their children to stay with families in the countryside. America is here now, so bombers aren't expected anymore.

Roger, Skinny, and I went to see Big Ben, Parliament, Westminster Abbey, and other big sights, but missed the Tower of London. Many of the usual attractions aren't open, but the local markets are going full steam. The rationing is significant, since it's been going on for years for sugar, oil, meat, etc.

America could learn a lot from the English farmers about how they responded in getting vegetables and fruit into the city. The three of us bought small sacks of fruit, but we thought the Londoners needed it more than we did, so we gave them away.

It's time for me to go to work.

Yours truly,

Teddy

April 21, 1944

Dear Margie,

Nobody knows where or when the invasion will occur, but once started, the bigwigs want to be able to flood Europe with all the men and supplies needed to go as fast as possible.

That means England is filling up with men, women, hospitals, vehicles, planes, airfields, training sites, and a whole lot of storage depots. It must be an incredible challenge to manage all of this stuff. They're even building prisoner-of-war camps.

Here are a few more of the men in my platoon. (I already told you about Roger and Skinny.) Bryan Matlock is 19 and is from Ft. Stockton, Texas, where he works at an automotive parts store. Jimmy Standfield, who is called "Chicago" for some reason, is from Chicago. He's 21 and owns a pizza restaurant with his brother and parents.

Harry Sizemore is from some little town in Washington state, is 21, and works for the highway department.

Our First Lieutenant is Jonathan Buffy, a high school math teacher from Des Moines, Iowa, and he's one of our oldest—29. Our Second Lieutenant is a regular Army soldier out of Ft. Bragg, North Carolina. His normal job is working at a repair depot and is 26.

There are two brothers from Louisiana, Lorenzo and Lackady LaClerque (I don't think I spelled it right). I don't know how old they are or who's older than whom. They're both alligator hunters, and they are quite a pair. They're always telling stories about bayou gators, rumrunners, voodoo dolls, and ghosts. They keep us entertained and seem like really nice people, even if they do believe in voodoo dolls.

There are others, but these are the ones I know best. We've been together since Tampa, so I guess we'll be together when we get to the war.

Thinking about you and sorry it'll be a while before I get back.

Teddy

July 4, 1944
Margie,
You haven't heard from me as much because of D-Day. I'm now sitting on the bluffs in Normandy, France, looking over a beach full of the Allied army. The invasion plans put everybody under tight controls for the last few months—our locations disguised,

moving people around only at night, using evasive maneuvers, even launching a ghost army with all the sights and sounds but wasn't a real army—just a bunch of blow-up dummy tanks and trucks and airplanes. I hear it worked great. They even put General Patton in charge to make it look real.

We took down our equipment and tents the last of June and drove in long vehicle convoys that stretched for miles in every direction. I'm afraid we clogged every road and made the locals mad. We were moving to a port on the coast. You can't believe all the equipment: tanks, Jeeps, 1-ton, 2-ton, 5-ton, 20-ton trucks, artillery pulled behind tractor-trailer rigs, cranes, bulldozers, road graders, rocket launchers, and our radar trucks. (I can use the word radar now, as long as we don't say where it is or how many there are.) It was quite a gathering of military machines, thousands of every kind of vehicle I've ever heard of. Once we got past the assembly point, we joined a line of heavy vehicles being guided into the belly of a huge cargo ship with big clamshell doors on the front. Everybody stayed with their vehicles until the doors closed, and then we ran onto the deck to watch.

We were next to a troop ship. I bet a thousand men marched on, all carrying rifles, machine guns, or bazookas, plus all of their living gear—pup tents, canteens, clothes, steel helmets, jackets, ration boxes, knives, shovels, etc. Made me happy to be in a unit with trucks.

Our ship was towed out of the harbor, but once

out at sea, we circled around for a day and then moved south across the Channel. Let me tell you—I'd never make a sailor! The ship was rocking and rolling and pitching back and forth. It was cold, too. I was seasick and threw up over the railing a couple of times. How do people do this for months at a time?

The Channel was clogged with ships, one after another from horizon to horizon. It almost made a solid corridor of ships from England to Normandy. Lots of barrage balloons were up in the air.

Our ship had to wait until the sailing lanes were clear and the tide was right. When the tide is out, the ocean is three hundred yards from the shore. When the tide is in, the ocean's right up next to the bluffs. What they do is sail the ships up close to shore when the tide is in, and then let them settle onto the sand as the tide goes out, leaving the ship stranded. They then open the big doors on the front, let down the ramps, and move all the vehicles out. They have to empty the ships before the tide comes back in.

The troop transports aren't that picky. They unload farther out because the troops can wade some of the distance to get to the beachhead.

Once our ship settled, we drove our equipment out of the ship and onto the beach, then got in line with other vehicles to wait for directions to go into the bluffs above the beach. We drove on a road that probably didn't exist a month before and went to an airfield that probably didn't exist the week before. I can't believe the sheer size of the operation involved in invading another country.

When our ship was empty, they loaded a long line of captured German soldiers. They're headed for prisoner-of-war camps in England.

My unit is now stationed in the bluffs, not far inland from the beach landing zone known as Omaha. We're set up at the second airfield to be built here. They build airfields as fast as they can so the fighter planes can be as close to the front as possible.

We have officially joined the battle for Europe. We landed yesterday, twenty-six days after the initial invasion.

When we got to our setup point, we jumped out of the vehicles, got our equipment in place, put up our camouflage, and set up our tents. We were moving like madmen, happy to finally be part of the fight, and scared to death by the sounds around us—planes landing and taking off, tanks roaring by, forklifts and bulldozers grinding around the airfield, and most of all, the sound of artillery going off. Boom, boom, boom, noise that never quits.

We aren't like we were—slow, even-tempered, complacent—but are now excited, scared, diligent, obedient, and pulling for each other. We're in the war! We're for real!

Have to go.

Yours truly,

Teddy

Chapter 9

July 9, 1944

Dear Margie,

They didn't tell us how noisy it would be. It's hard to think straight, if you can think at all. We see every kind of plane flying around us, but it's the cargo planes that are constantly landing and taking off. We've also got fighters based at the airfield, and they buzz around us like flies. Enemy fighters sometimes fly over, as well as hundreds of our B-17s.

The Navy destroyers are still lobbing shells twenty miles inland, and the tanks clanking by are just mind-numbing.

To all that, add our artillery guns. We have the regular single-shot artillery pieces close to the front, anti-aircraft guns with multiple barrels (think of a bunch of rifles all put close to each other) that fire an unbelievable number of rounds a minute, and last but not least, the rockets used for softening up the country for an infantry attack.

I never take out my earplugs.

Thinking of you,

Teddy

July 10, 1944

Dear Margaret,

This place stinks. Something else they didn't tell us in England. First, we get the breezes off the Channel, so we smell the sea. That wouldn't be so bad, but the beach, up and down for miles, is a 24-hour-a-day landing point for thousands of ships bringing vehicles, cargo, and people. It's guarded by several hundred ships of the Navy, Merchant Marine and Coast Guard, patrolled by constant flights of aircraft, while the beach itself is covered with thousands of soldiers, trucks, tents, material depots, foxholes, repair tents, hospitals, command posts, and latrines, all with their disgusting smells.

Second, the airfield next to us is used 24 hours a day, bringing in a continuous stream of planes ferrying food, medicine, ammo, water, gasoline, and a thousand other things, and then loading up the wounded to go back. The planes are always being refueled, and the smell of gasoline sticks to everything.

Third, the whole countryside smells like exhaust because of the trucks, Jeeps, and tanks moving around, and the artillery shooting up the countryside, filling the air with smoke. Bombers are dropping bombs not much more than ten miles away, close enough to make the ground shake. That keeps dust in the air.

And lastly, the vegetation would smell pretty good if we weren't tromping on it all the time. Most of the tents are set up in fields where the dirt was already churned up by the tanks.

With it raining so much, we smell like mud mixed with cow manure. There are trees, but they're pretty thick, and we can't move between them. I don't know what kind they are, but they certainly aren't what we have in the sawmills back home.

That's just the general smell. Then there's the pungent stuff. There are latrines set up wherever there are large groups of men. The normal method is for the GI to take a shovel and find some place in the woods, or dig a hole and put a box with a toilet seat over it, but there are too many men in some places, so they set up trench systems. They dig a long, narrow trench and use stakes to position a slanted 2x8 board a couple of feet above it, then drape a tent over the whole thing. Men drop their pants, back up so that their thighs are against the board and their fannies are hanging out in space, and then do their business. One time, when there were a lot of men, the board collapsed and several men fell into the trench. I won't tell you how that turned out. I've learned to hold my breath and do my business as quickly as I can. At least I hang out farther over the trench than most; it's funny to watch the short guys.

It rains two days out of every three, making the smells sodden with water. Everything is tainted by mold, and nothing—I mean nothing—ever dries out.

Anyway, I'm surrounded by stink, and there's no getting away from it. I'd give anything to shove my nose up against a good Minnesota pine.

Teddy

"I bet he hated every moment he was there," Nancy said. "He was always so particular about being clean and good smelling. Remember all the bottles of Old Spice we gave him every Christmas?"

"Maybe," my mom said. "He certainly had been raised that way. I think he settled down after a while, started blending in, and was soon having the time of his life."

"You're kidding."

"Not a bit. Dad had a strong streak of curiosity, and now he was seeing things he had never seen before, on a scale that must have been jaw-dropping. He was also around all sorts of people he had never been around before.

"Think about it. He'd grown up in a rich, industrial, aggressive family in a monstrous house, with good clothes, and a well-established political system. Watching Senior wear a three-piece suit every day and smoking dollar cigars probably made him think the whole world looked that way. Even when he was at the ranch school, all the students came from wealthy families. Servants cleaned his room and washed his clothes, and every student was treated as if he were going to be a future leader of the country.

"The influence of Senior was deeply engrained in him. Senior treated his lumber and railroad businesses like a war with him as the commanding general. Everything was about

63

strategy, about assembling the forces needed for battle plans, about finding the advantage in every situation, and charging ahead when everything was ready. Senior expected to win every battle, so he did not shy away from running roughshod over anyone who got in his way. He expected his sons to follow him. Junior fit in fine, but Jake was obviously not inclined, and Dad was not naturally aggressive. He didn't like confrontation or manipulation, so Senior was disappointed in him most of the time. When he was in high school, Senior made him work for him during the summers, hoping he'd catch on.

"Then suddenly, Dad's in the Army and he's not around Senior anymore. He's surrounded by people from all over the United States, from all walks of life—rich, poor, and poorer—mostly his own age but some older, from different cultures and geography and all living together in a foreign country. I can see him mentally organizing everything into social systems, listening to how people talked, how they interacted with each other, who got lonely, who got angry, who was scared to death, who wasn't fazed by anything, who laughed and entertained, and who stood in the corner watching everybody else. He was a good watcher of people. I bet that even how the military operated was interesting to him. The fact he reports on going to the bathroom means he can't believe what he's seeing. At the same time, he's fascinated that it's the official way of doing things.

"Now, I'm not saying he didn't find himself out of his comfort zone. From some of his letters, he was pretty uppity to begin with and wasn't sure he wanted to be friendly to people who seemed so common. That's one of the words he used. After his curiosity kicked in, however, he was entertained by it. The longer he was there, the more he didn't mind people who were different. He even grew to like the common people and began to identify with them."

"I notice he didn't mention body odors," I said. "The

Army had portable shower units for the troops when they got a break from the fighting, but soldiers who were in combat rarely bathed and rarely changed clothes for days on end. I remember one report of a guy who landed on D-Day and didn't get off the front line until thirty-seven days later. He had worn out his clothes and was pretty stinko by that time."

"I want to thank you for being so explicit," Nancy said, wrinkling her nose. "Read some more."

"Okay, but I'm switching to a new stack."

"This is where things began to change," my mom said. "He got a new job."

Chapter 10

July 21, 1944

Dear Sweetheart,

Back in England, our trading off with long shifts
worked okay. Here, knowing where planes are is far
more critical, so we always have to be in top form to
get it done right. That means we get tired faster and
rotate more often.

If we're not part of the operating crew, we're
repairing equipment, setting up tents and camouflage
netting, taking down tents and camouflage netting,
repairing tents and camouflage netting, and digging
foxholes. It seems like we're always moving, eating,
sleeping, or helping out somebody else. There's always
work to do. I've gotten used to being busy unless I'm
asleep.

At least we have reasonably good food. We have
two cooks assigned to our squadron. That's pretty
common because the Army has a goal of providing a

hot meal to every soldier at least once a day. It certainly works for us, but you have to remember there are more than a million soldiers over here, so it's impressive when it happens. Our cooks don't always do the cooking. Several things are prepared at a central kitchen and then loaded into insulated cans to be distributed to the local units.

There's even a central bakery that bakes a huge number of loaves of bread a day.

Of course, the people on the front who are in combat get boxes of rations that include cans of meat substitute, rice or beans, fruit, cookies, and typically chocolate. Each box also includes a can opener, a few cigarettes, and a small packet of toilet paper. Nobody really likes eating rations, but it's better than going hungry.

We're tied to an aircraft control squadron. They take the locations of the planes we see in the sky and put it together with what other radar units see. You may have seen pictures of a place where everybody is moving around a large table that has a super-sized map spread across it.

Men or women with headphones use long sticks to move little statues around the map to show where the planes are located. That information is used to keep up with who's friendly and who's not and where they are, what are bombers as opposed to cargo planes as opposed to fighters, where our artillery shouldn't fire into the air because our bombers are flying over, or where our anti-aircraft batteries should fire into the air because it's the enemy.

Our aircraft control room looks just like that. It's very interesting, and I go over to watch when I'm not operating and when I'm done with my other duties.

Since there are so few German airplanes where we are, we've switched over to mainly looking for artillery. We use the radar to measure the trajectory of shells coming over, then reverse the process to find the location of the enemy guns, which we give to our artillery so they can blow them up.

We can also track moving vehicles.

Remember I told you I sat in on some radio repair school classes while in England? Repairing radios is a lot easier than repairing radars. Well, listen to this. I was at the control room three days ago. Nothing particular was happening, so I was standing outside talking to some ordnance people, the guys who hook up bombs to the undersides of the dive bombers that refuel at our field.

This Jeep drives up and a Captain Hornfeld gets out. He's turning the air blue about his radio being jammed, and he can't get it to work, and he can't talk to his men, so he's looking for somebody to get him a new one. I volunteered to fix his radio instead.

I'm looking at it and it's obvious to me that his antenna has been knocked out of whack, so I fix it, we try it out, it works, and I tell him that I'm over at my unit if he needs help again. The Captain thanks me and goes on his way.

Well, he's back the next day with a bunch of radios, big and small, dumps them at the airfield, and requests my help. More radar units like mine have arrived from England. My unit is training the new guys in the reality of combat, so my lieutenant tells me to help him out. I also don't mind a break from the radar business—it's important, but the intensity wears me out.

There are repair shops down on the beach and around each division who take anything that's out of commission and repair or replace it, including radios. They are way more talented than me and have scads of parts, so I loaded up what Captain Hornfeld brought, took them to the shop people, and spent the day working my way through the pile. Sometimes I can repair them, but sometimes they have to be replaced.

At the end of the day, I've returned with every-thing, just in time for Captain Hornfeld to show up. He's impressed and finds out that I'm from Minneapolis, while he's from St. Paul. He recognizes my last name and now he figures I'm hot stuff, so that's it—he requests I be assigned to his unit as his personal radio repairman. If I can't fix them, I go get new ones, ASAP.

I got a new job.
Life is funny, isn't it?
Teddy

July 23, 1944
Dearest Margaret,

I should have stayed with my unit.

Captain Hornfeld is a maniac who thinks he's bulletproof. The reason his radios keep breaking is that he's constantly zooming all over the countryside, road or no road, through minefields, snipers, enemy fire, ditches, forests, and barnyards, checking on his men and directing the fighting along the front line. He keeps hitting ruts and ditches that kick his radios out of the Jeep and into the dirt, and he's run over a few. He's an infantry commander, and he pretty much stays on one radio or the other all the time. And when he says he needs his radios to get his work done, he's not kidding.

I'm now one of the soldiers riding in the Jeep with him. Besides a bag of tools and spare parts, I have to carry my rifle because the infantry are those poor souls on the front line, the ones firing real bullets, launching grenades, jumping into foxholes, and dodging whatever is coming at them. And getting killed. I've been near the combat zone twice and in the camps of the squadron leaders, as well as being back at headquarters solving radio problems.

Sometimes, I'm with the Captain when he's on a hill, watching a battle take place in front of him. It's interesting how combat takes place, and he's pretty smart about the tactics involved.

The fighting has not gone well. These damned hedgerows are incredibly hard to get through. A hedgerow begins as a bunch of piled rocks a farmer has stacked up to separate his different fields and pastures. Over the years, trees and bushes grow out of the top while the roots grow down through the rocks and into the dirt, making the hedgerow almost impenetrable except where there's a gate or a road through it.

There must literally be a million hedgerows all over the countryside. There are no regular fences like we think of them, and by the way, there's not a right angle or straight line in France. I swear every road curves around a tree, a rock, or somebody's house. They curve, jut, swing wide, cut across fields, and are as rough as any backcountry road in America. My teeth are loose at the end of every day.

Anyway, hedgerows are where tanks get into trouble. Whenever a tank tries to go through a hedgerow, instead of punching right through it, the treads crawl up the mess, sometimes way up into the air. I've watched them. That exposes the underbelly of the tank where it has thin armor.

The Germans wait until they see the belly of the tank and then fire an explosive through the thin steel and blow up everybody inside. The tank crews have been routinely dying miserable deaths. I saw one crew where everyone scrambling out of the tank was on fire.

Hornfeld and I were watching some hedgerow fighting when a new tank showed up. This tank had big iron teeth welded on the front, and when it ran into a hedgerow, the teeth cut into the base and kept the tank from rearing up.

Lo and behold, it pushed right through. Hallelujah! Some guy finally figured out to use old metal from the beach obstacles to make big teeth, and that's the solution for defeating the hedgerows.

I hope he got a medal for that.

The Germans also dig trenches behind the hedgerows and connect them into long channels around the fields so they can attack and then run away without having to show themselves. The trees and bushes are thick enough that they've even hidden big artillery pieces next to the hedgerows and can kill a lot of people without our ever seeing where they are.

Fortunately, that's where our artillery comes in. Infantry (the soldiers) works hand-in-hand with the armored divisions (the tanks) and the artillery (the big guns). The foot soldiers call in any locations where they suspect enemy artillery is hidden or where machine nests are hidden, or where mortars are hidden, and the artillery lobs some shells into the midst of the German defenders.

That's sometimes the situation, sometimes not. No matter what, it's the infantry that's fighting for every foot forward. The bodies keep piling up, and the replacements keep being sent in.

I, myself, will stay with the Captain in his Jeep. At least the driver knows to dodge any bullets coming our way.

Thinking about you,
Teddy

"So," Nancy said, "how is it that a guy spends a year training in radar and then some arbitrary officer reassigns him to repair radios?"

I was making up the answer, but she wouldn't know the difference. "I'm betting that Captain Hornfeld wasn't playing by the rules. If he were a successful commander, his superiors would have let him do anything he wanted if somebody didn't complain about it. It was war. What mattered most was to win."

My mother just smiled.

> July 23, 1944
> Dear Margie,
> I was in the Jeep with Captain Hornfeld as he was watching the countryside when a soldier ran up to us.
> The man was filthy—mud covered him from his boots to his helmet, his uniform was torn, his helmet had a dent in it, he had a dark beard, and I could smell him as he talked with the Captain. Nobody in my unit would ever get away with this.
> His eyes were bloodshot, with big dark circles under them, and he had a way of looking that made me think he was hollow.
> He was a squadron leader, a sergeant. He spoke carefully to Captain Hornfeld, pointed at the Captain's map a couple of times, got orders, and trotted back down the road.
> "There goes a hell of a soldier," Hornfeld said after he left. "He's twenty-eight, has two kids and a beautiful wife, was in Africa, Sicily, and Italy, and

came ashore with my unit the second day of the invasion. Been wounded twice but keeps coming back. He's a lawyer in Phoenix with his own firm.

"Nicest guy you'll ever meet, but put a gun in his hand and tell him to kill the enemy and there's no stopping him. He knows how to separate himself from the horrors of killing people, like a professional. That's what's going to win this war. We all have to become professional killers."

"I hope you're not counting on everybody becoming professional killers," I said. "I'm not the type."

He gave me a grim look, then said, "You haven't been here long enough. When you finally discover the German soldier behind those hedgerows over there is looking to take away every freedom you and your family have ever enjoyed, you'll warm up to the idea that you need to kill him and the guy next to him."

Maybe killing isn't as complicated as I'd imagined.

Teddy

Chapter 11

July 24, 1944

Dearest Margie,

I'm still a Jeep jockey with Captain Hornfeld. There are two stories I want to tell you.

The Captain dropped me at an artillery battery supporting his company. Their radio had quit and he couldn't talk to them. He doesn't tell them where to shoot, but he always likes to know what they're doing.

So, he drops me off at the battery to see if I can fix the radio.

This battery is made up of four separate artillery units, each with an eleven-man crew, each firing a BIG gun called a "Long Tom." Each of the guns sits in a flat pit three feet deep under a camouflage net, and the four are placed around a rough square about the size of a city block.

Each piece fires a 155mm shell that weighs 108 pounds. When they load the gun, they run the shell into the chamber, followed by three little sacks of powder charges. When everything is in, the cannoneer closes the breach and pulls a cord that sets off the charge.

Each 108-pound shell goes about seven miles, and if the shell has explosives in it, it makes a hell of a hole. Each of the four guns is connected by telephone wire to a central executive post, where an officer receives commands from a command center a half mile away, which is connected to the division command center that is located miles away.

Anyway, you see how it works. Somebody at the division level decides where each artillery unit is to deliver that 108-pound shell, gives them the coordinates, the gun crews make all the adjustments, load up, and pull the cord.

There's a forward observer someplace out there who will tell them if they hit the target.

When all four guns are firing at the same time, they cover a lot of territory.

So, I'm looking at the radio to see what I can do. This particular crew is part of the Arkansas National Guard, and half of the gunners (there have already been replacements) are from towns in Arkansas.

But here's the kicker. I was talking with them when one guy showed up from the crew next door. He grins at me and says, "Hey, Mr. Gunnarson! Que pasa?"

It took me a minute to recognize him. It was Carlos Ortega. He was one of the servers in the dining room at the ranch school.

"Carlos! What the hell? What are you doing over here?"

He laughed and we kidded around for a few more minutes. I remember him because he's Manny Ortega's son. Manny's the ranch hand who found Jake and Lilly. I thought Carlos was about twelve when he was bringing me my supper, so he couldn't be but eighteen or nineteen now.

"How's Mr. Jake? My dad said he'd joined the Navy."

I laughed. "He was a Navy pilot on an aircraft carrier. But now Jake's someplace up above us. Jumped ship in the Pacific and is flying B-17s over Germany. Haven't heard from him in a while."

"A Navy flyboy in Europe! Must have gotten tired of rice and sake."

We were telling everybody stories about the ranch when the Captain drove up. I had already fixed their radio with a new earpiece, so I hopped in the Jeep and was gone again.

It was good to see Carlos. He's all grown up.

The second story is about me making another trip to the ordnance guys on the beach at the repair shops. I got there in time to watch them bring in a tank that had been shot by a German bazooka. It had a three-inch hole in the side and a tread that had fallen off.

You should see the truck and crane they send out to get a tank and bring it back to the beach—they're huge! It's an enormous operation to bring a disabled tank in, but they do it all the time, sometimes under fire. Bill Holiday is a sergeant from Stockton, California, and runs the operation. He was a bulldozer mechanic in a Caterpillar plant when he joined, so he's used to working with big machines. He's thirty-eight, married with kids, so he didn't need to join up, but he did.

He says they'll clean the hole up and weld several one-inch thick pieces of steel over it, fix the tread, and it will be ready to send back the next day. It would take a couple of weeks to get a new tank delivered from England, so that means these repairmen are saving lives.

Believe it or not, the repair shops are mobile. Once the Army gets off the beach lands of Normandy, the shops will follow. They even have lathes and machining tools installed in the backs of trucks so they can park and have repair capabilities in a few minutes. They repair everything the soldiers need—rifles, pistols, machine guns, artillery pieces, tanks, trucks, Jeeps, radios—and rehabilitate the equipment left behind when men are killed.

I'm impressed with these people and it was good to see Carlos.

I'm thinking about you more and more and miss you terribly.

Teddy

July 26, 1944

Margie,

Hornfeld's dead. His driver, too. They were crossing a field when they hit a mine. I was back at camp fixing things. I guess I just missed having a short career.

I also heard Carlos Ortega was killed when a German fighter strafed the battery. Caught him in the open. Damn. I wish he could have sat with us back at the mess hall at the ranch. I know he couldn't have, but I wish I would have asked.

A new captain was assigned in Hornfeld's place, and he couldn't understand why Hornfeld had a radio repairman who was actually a radar operator. I was sent back to my radar unit, so I'm back to watching blips on the screen and sleeping in a big tent instead of a two-man pup tent, which is a better deal.

I already miss Hornfeld. It was a dangerous job, but I saw a lot. I think I gave him somebody to talk to.

Fighting battles is a lonely business.

Teddy

August 17, 1944
Margie,

Something big has been happening. We've moved the radar south and east and have been assigned to a different artillery battery.

General Bradley was the commander of the Normandy invasion, and after enough equipment, men, and materials had been accumulated within ten or twenty miles of the Normandy beaches, he decided we needed to be getting on down the road. He thought one big push would get the Army out of hedgerow country and into central France, pointed toward Paris.

He called in a thousand B-17s, plus hundreds of fighters and dive bombers to soften up the country-side (two hours of saturation bombing) and then the Army went for it.

The infantry divisions led the charge over a front that was about a hundred miles wide. The artillery divisions were close behind, and when our battery moved, we went with them.

The big push worked and we're out of the densest area of hedgerows. It was the heaviest fighting we've ever experienced, and we were moving almost every day. That part of France in the south and east is more open, so everybody is talking about turning the speed up and chasing after the German army.

Speed sounds good to me because I'll get back to you sooner, but there aren't many roads that can handle a lot of traffic, so congestion has been a big thing and is keeping anybody from getting a head of steam. There are convoys ahead of us that haven't moved for half a day. It makes you understand just how big an army has to be to wage war and how important clear roads are. Thankfully, we're out of the low country that was flooded by the Germans, so there's more mobility with tanks and half-tracks going across fields.

We passed an area that had a lot of temporary crosses. I recognized them from similar areas near the beachhead. There are special units, called Graves Registration Units, that gather up the dead bodies and bury them. They don't embalm anybody or use coffins—they just wrap them up in mattress covers, gather all the information and personal possessions, then bury the bodies as soon as they can, leaving a wooden cross stuck in the ground.

The burial sites I saw are temporary cemeteries. The Quartermaster Corps, under which the GRUs operate, have already negotiated with the locals and bought land for permanent cemeteries. When time permits, they'll dig up the bodies in the temporary locations and rebury them in permanent sites.

There are a lot of people dying. Hundreds a day, I think. I bet it's hard on the GRU men, working in all the blood and guts. I can't even imagine the horror of taking bodies out of a burned-out tank.

I've also heard another Allied force has invaded the south of France, but I don't know any details. Write me what happened or maybe send me a newspaper article.

Teddy

"Did you hear that?" I said. "He finally said something halfway romantic—called you *sweetheart*, *miss you terribly*, *get back to you sooner*. Maybe he's picking up the talk from everybody else. Soldiers in battle are famous for pining about the girls they left behind.

"Anyway, he mentions the Graves Registration Units. In planning the invasion, there were Graves Registration Units assigned to each division. It was their responsibility to follow the fighting and get the dead bodies out of sight and buried before they started decomposing and before more troops passed by. Some GRU people even parachuted in with the troops on D-Day to get a head start on the bodies that would be piling up.

"At the end of the war, there were 359 American military cemeteries around the world for soldiers who died in World War II, seventeen of which were in Europe and North Africa, plus a big one in the Philippines. Those who died on ships at sea had their bodies wrapped up and dropped into the ocean and never even made it to a cemetery."

August 20, 1944

Margie,

From what I've heard, some of the biggest battles of the war so far took place last week, and it looks like the Army is finally out of Normandy. Patton's Third Army has been moving quickly to chase the Germans out of the south, and Bradley's chasing the Germans out of the west. They expect to be side by side soon and move north to Paris.

Meanwhile, we're moving, too. I wonder what Paris looks like. I hope they let us go into the city. I bet they'll be happy to see us.

I saw more cemeteries, bigger ones, with a lot more crosses.

There are thousands of German prisoners of war

everywhere I look. They're lined up for miles, all marching down the roads, hands on their heads, being moved to the coast. They're even using the Queen Mary to ship them back to England, where they're put into POW camps. I've heard they're being sent to POW camps in America.

The French Resistance destroyed a lot of the railroads and bridges so the Germans can't move their armies around like they need to, which means they can't get to us as fast as we can get to them. We just keep shoving them backward.

Thinking of you,

Teddy

"THEY BROUGHT POWs to the United States?" Nancy asked.

"Oh, yeah," I responded. "On D-Day, the Allies had captured hundreds of prisoners by late afternoon, many of whom weren't Germans, but conscripts from places like Poland and Italy. They were inclined to surrender rather than fight. There was no room on the beachhead to keep them, so once a cargo ship was empty, they marched them aboard and took them back to England. From there, they were taken to POW camps in Africa, Australia, Italy, and yes, the good ol' U.S. of A. By the end of the war, America had more than seven hundred POW camps with about half a million prisoners."

My mother was shocked. "You've got to be kidding. Where?"

"In every state in the Union, except for Nevada, Vermont, and North Dakota. Most of them were in the southern states because of the milder weather, but they were placed in abandoned military camps—all those training camps that had been built at the beginning of the war to train soldiers, for example—as well as old prisons and jails and even converted football and baseball stadiums. They were all over the place."

"What did the prisoners do?" Nancy asked. "Sit around and play cards?"

"Well, remember the government had drafted a large part of the American workforce into the military, so prisoners were used to take their place, especially on farms and ranches and businesses that involved outdoor labor. Prisoners built houses, churches, and community buildings, they harvested crops, plowed fields, and repaired equipment. Worked in factories, too. Many of those from Italy had been craftsmen—stone masons, fresco painters, sculptors, tile workers, brick layers—and were put to work in organizations that looked like the WPA and the CCC. There's one church in Texas that's famous for the interior decorations done by Italian POWs from a nearby camp.

"We did well by them. Most of the POWs were treated better than how they'd been living. Life under the Nazis or the Italian Nationalists was terrible. Many POWs, once sent home after the war, moved back to America."

August 30, 1944
Dear Sweetheart,
Paris was really something, but we didn't stay very long. Eisenhower wanted to bypass it because it didn't seem like much of a target—there were more French police than German soldiers. Plus, the citizens had staged their own rebellion and overrun the Army. However, we had to make DeGaulle look good, so every-

body showed up so we could march down the streets and look victorious.

That tower is impressive. Beats anything we have.

My unit didn't have much time there. Since The Stars and Stripes publishes maps of where everything is happening, I guess I can tell you that we've left Paris and are now headed toward Belgium. That puts us next door to Germany, so I expect the fighting is going to ramp back up.

The bombers stationed in England are still bombing cities and industrial centers, but there's not much opposition from the Luftwaffe. Using the P-51 Mustang with added fuel tanks as an escort for the heavy bombers has made a major difference in protecting the bombers, as well as shooting down German planes. There's not much left of the Luftwaffe. That leaves us supporting the ground troops more, which is okay with me, but one day, the radar business may be out of business.

It's a gorgeous country.

Teddy

Chapter 12

There were more letters, but I stopped when the dates showed a break in the action. As I had finished each one, I passed it to Nancy. She was more interested in conversation than reading, so had glanced through them, lost interest, and was already in the kitchen talking to Mom.

I followed.

"Did you write him much?" my sister asked.

"Oh, yes. I wrote him back every time I got a letter, and wrote him once a week when I didn't."

"What did you say?"

"There was quite a bit going on, so I mostly kept up a running commentary about who was doing what, what events we had attended, and how I was fitting in. The Gunnarson family, as you know, was a prominent family in Minneapolis and was expected to be a public presence at every major gathering. Being engaged to your father, I was treated as part of the family, which meant that most of my time was dictated by the Gunnarson schedule. It kept me hopping.

"If you remember the pictures of the old Gunnarson mansion, it had four wings and thirty-seven rooms. I was living with my parents when Dad left, but it wasn't long before I was given a bedroom and a dressing room of my own and was staying where I could always be within reach of Lady Gunnarson. She was a major figure in the Democratic Party, and I was expected to be her shadow. I went with her to rallies and war bond parties and showed up at collection points for aluminum and rubber and other rationed materials. We both worked one day a week for the Red Cross. On the social circuit, we also hosted ladies' teas and held coming out parties for various daughters, cousins, or friends of the ladies."

Nancy smiled. "Were you a debutante?"

Mom laughed. "Since I was already engaged, I was considered taken, so I wasn't being shown off at the socials. I was, however, expected to wear something a little nicer than the war uniform Eleanor Roosevelt made popular."

"Were you rich?"

Mom hesitated. "No, I wasn't rich, really, but since I was going to be an heir to the Gunnarson fortune, I was assumed to be rich. Your grandmother certainly expected me to look as rich as the daughters of her society friends, so she bought me a new dress every week, let me drive one of the Packards they kept in the garage, and never hesitated to think I should be wearing whatever was the latest craze among young and stylish women. Back then, a selection of dresses, shoes, and hats would be delivered to the mansion every week, and I would try them on in the privacy of my own room, under the eye of Lady Gunnarson, of course. I wish I'd kept some of those hats—I looked simply adorable.

"That level of rich was different from what I was used to, and it was more than a little intoxicating. I was a young and impressionable girl, so I fell right in with Lady Gunnarson's wishes and enjoyed being aloof from all the peasants around me."

"But your father *was* connected to railroads, right?" I asked.

"Yes, but my father *worked* for the railroad, which was totally different from the Gunnarsons. Let's review things.

"Senior's family came over as Norwegian immigrants into the Great Lakes area around Duluth. Having a lumber background, the family, with Senior in the forefront, bought the lumber rights to acres of forests in the northern part of Minnesota. He cut down trees, chained them into huge barges on Lake Superior, and floated them to lumber mills along the southern coast of the Great Lakes.

"It was a tougher business in the winter when the lakes iced up, so he bought into a railroad that ran from northern Minnesota down to St. Paul. What he couldn't do by water, he did by rail. Once it proved profitable, the family business became a progression of leasing more lumber rights, cutting more trees, and investing in more railroads to carry them.

"Senior then started his own lumber mills because he could sell lumber faster than whole trees. It worked until the Depression hit and people weren't building houses anymore while the steel industry was ramping up and all public buildings were suddenly steel and concrete. Senior fired everybody at the mills and shuttered them beginning in 1933, waiting for the business to come back.

"He had enough money in railroads to hold him steady, and when 1939 and '40 brought the lend-lease programs with Britain, he was in a perfect position to make up the lost income. The military was already ramping up, and after Pearl Harbor, the mobilization of America meant building hundreds of new camps to train soldiers, which required lumber for barracks. They all needed rifles, which meant wood for rifle stocks. Then there were cots, big hoops on the back of trucks for covers, wooden pallets for shipping goods, lots of wood for making train cars, and the always-needed railroad ties.

"Senior reopened his lumber mills, then bought more. He owned a lot of railroad track by then, plus the locomotives and cars, all of which were desperately needed for moving lumber around the country. He tripled the family's wealth within a year or two and tripled it again by the end of the war.

"Meanwhile, my dad started out by *working* for the railroad. He was a locomotive engineer, got himself into directing train traffic, was the supervisor for loading trains, and then selling space on trains. Eventually, he became an adviser to railroad investors and owners. He bought into a railroad himself, but he was never more than small potatoes compared to the big players like Senior. On the other hand, he was as well positioned as anyone to make money during the war.

"We were pretty well off by the time I was a teenager, which was in the late 30s. There was enough family money to make me into a budding socialite, but instead of the outrageously expensive finishing schools that most moneyed girls went to, I convinced my parents to send me somewhere I could get a real education. Learning to speak French and knowing which fork to use at dinner was not in the least bit interesting to me. Instead, I went to public schools in the upper-class neighborhoods and planned on graduating from college.

"When I was fifteen, I started high school at Woodrow Wilson High School in Minneapolis. That's where I met your dad. He was tall, handsome, and really smart, so we started dating and continued until we were both freshmen in college. Then the war interrupted things."

"You said you didn't see him again for three years," Nancy said.

"Three years and ten days."

"You kept count of the days?" Nancy asked as she laughed.

"Not me. It was Dad. He's the one who kept count of the days."

"And you said he wasn't romantic," Nancy said to me.

"I said he wasn't romantic," I replied. "I didn't say he wasn't clerkish."

MOM HAD STARTED a second cake when Nancy and I returned to reading Dad's letters. Once it had cooled, she began stirring up the icing as we took another break. Transferring the layers to a glass cake stand, she began spreading buttercream frosting between them as she built the cake upward.

"What are the letters in your pocket?" Nancy asked after we finished, never one to be patient.

My mom stopped with her flat knife, considered the question for a moment, and replied, "You're finished with Dad's letters?"

"Are there more?" I asked.

"Only two in this stack. The rest are letters to me from Jake."

I did a quick calculation. "Wait a minute," I said, a little confused.

"You met Dad in high school when you were fifteen or so. Jake was already in the Pacific when Dad graduated high school, so you must have met him during high school, but you said he never came back to Minneapolis after he had moved to Duluth. Did you meet him before he left for the Pacific? Or was he writing letters to a future sister-in-law whom he had never met?"

"No," she said slowly. "I did not meet Jake before he left. I met him later. It was afterwards when we started writing each other."

"You met him later? In the middle of a war, sailors don't

get furloughs. He wouldn't have been back in Minnesota for years."

"I'm sure that's true, but remember the battle of Midway? Jake had his time in Duluth cut short because of Pearl Harbor and was assigned immediately to an aircraft carrier after his training. He had only been there a few months and was flying a dive bomber when Midway happened. Hotshot that he was, he went all out and actually sank a Japanese ship, more or less by himself. Well, needing a boost in morale, the Navy gave him a lot of publicity, pinned medals on his chest, and put him in charge of the training program, where he taught pilots for most of a year.

"He made it through a few more of the major battles but was the type who liked to move on. My guess is that the military brass in Europe were screaming for experienced pilots, so Jake negotiated a training assignment with the new Eighth Air Force being developed in England."

"Jake was definitely a good pilot," my mom continued, "and I don't have a problem thinking he might have been one of the best pilots in the Navy. When he went around his Navy commanders and proposed to the Army that he could help train pilots for the different bombers being churned out by American factories, the powers that be jumped at the chance. It wasn't long before Jake was on his way to Europe.

"He did some bomber training in Los Angeles for a few months and then signed up to fly a new version of the B-17 to the East Coast before he was sent to England. His training wing commander gave him a week so he could stop in Minneapolis and visit his family. If you count his college years, he hadn't been home in almost four years."

Mom finished putting swirls in the icing, gave it a final approving look, and covered the cake with the glass top.

We walked back to the dining room, where she finally sat down.

"That's how I met Jake," she continued. "This was in

August of 1943. I knew all about him because your dad had told me endless stories of the two of them growing up.

"So, one Saturday morning, a crowd of family and friends gathered at the airport, cheering as the biggest plane I'd ever seen dropped down out of the clouds. Jake circled that B-17 around the control tower like he owned the place and then lined it up and gently set it down on the runway. He taxied up close to us, swung the tail around, and shut down the engines. People started clapping and cheering like he was a visiting king."

"What did you think of him when you first saw him?" Nancy asked.

Mom's eyebrows shot up, and she suddenly had a wicked smile.

"Oh, he was a sight to behold! He looked just like Clark Gable in *Gone With the Wind*. You know, Senior looked like a bull with whiskers, Lady Gunnarson was the size of a cow—"

"Mother!" Nancy exclaimed.

"Well, she was. She stuffed all she could into a corset, but she was as stout as any animal that grazed for a living. Then there was Junior, who looked like the Pillsbury Dough-boy, and your father was only a couple of inches shorter than Senior, so he blended in with the rest of the family. When we got engaged, your dad was six-five, weighed two hundred and fifty pounds, and still hadn't stopped growing. He barely made it under the maximum height for the draft.

"Anyway, Jake was never much more than six foot or so, but he made up for it by being broad-shouldered, well-proportioned, and athletic. When Jake came down through the hatch in the bottom of that plane, he caught the eye of every woman in the crowd, young and old. He was trim, muscular, well-tanned, with wavy black hair, and a thin little mustache. He had this sheepskin flight jacket on that gave him a rugged look, and I can't make you understand how bright his smile was. He even wore his pilot's cap at a rakish angle, just like Rhett Butler. Every female on the tarmac fell in love with him. He was every inch a man. He exuded manliness."

Nancy grinned. "What happened to the already-spoken-for future daughter-in-law who was supposed to be meeting her brother-in-law?"

"Went out the window," she said. "But give me a break. The war was on, there were hardly any males around who weren't either boys or old men, and it was just natural that someone like Jake would capture the heart of every young woman who met him."

"Did he take your heart away?" I asked, grinning.

I saw a wave of pain move over my mother's face. She stopped smiling, looked thoughtful, and then sad. "That wasn't all he took."

She removed the letters from her apron, put the top two back in her apron, and laid the rest on the table. "These are from Jake, and I guess you might as well look at them now. There aren't many. He wasn't much of a letter writer, he never used V-mail, and he never put a date on anything. He always snuck his letters into the official correspondence bags being flown back to the States. Maybe you ought to read them out loud.

"Don't cinnamon rolls sound good for breakfast? I think we need cinnamon rolls," she said as she stood and walked back into the kitchen.

Chapter 13

Hey, Good-lookin'!

"WAIT A MINUTE," Nancy said, looking straight at me. "You're not going to interrupt these letters with more of your factoids, are you?"

"What? I thought you liked hearing my information."

"I don't mind, but you can go on for hours. Surely you won't have as much to say about what Jake was doing. I need to get home before Christmas."

"Oh, the air war in Europe has lots of tales. But how about if I leave everything to the end and only talk about whatever he says. Is that okay?"

"All right, but I get to be ringmaster if you get carried away, so watch yourself."

HEY, GOOD-LOOKIN'!

Sorry I've been out of touch, but that's the Army Air Force for ya! I've been flying all over England trying to whip my Greenies into shape. When I joined up as a bare-chested youth after high school, I wanted to fly airplanes, but I swear, most of my Greenies joined up to avoid being drafted as ground-pounders. They think pilots get a lot of sack time in a soft bed and a personal chef for meals. I don't think they considered they might get shot at.

Boy, did their first encounter with the Jerries over the English Channel wake them up! We were training for formation flying in our B-17s when we were caught off guard by a squadron of Messerschmitts Bk-109s. We were practicing, so we didn't have a fighter escort with us —just our gunner—and he hadn't loaded any ammunition before we left. It was supposed to only be a training flight!

It was quite a circus. The Messerschmitts were probably patrolling the coast of Belgium and hadn't really intended to shoot at anybody. Well, they got off enough rounds to make several of the boys lose their breakfast. Of course, I herded everybody back to the airfield and the Messerschmitts didn't follow, but I saw a lot of white faces at our debriefing.

I bet the guns will be loaded next time.

How are you, sweetie? Is Mom still trying to train you up to be a proper Gunnarson? She still believes in corsets, you know, but don't let her talk you into one. Of course, she needs them, ha ha ha. Anyway, my family will be better off with your quality of woman, so don't let the darkness of the family mansion get you down. Tell you what, I'll teach you to fly when I get back. It's marvelous, looking down at all the ants below.

It's freedom, kid!

Jake.

HEY, Babe!

You would love Britain! It's as pretty a country as any I've been in. It's like flying over golf courses all the time—green grass, lakes and ponds, deep green forests, little streams running between fields. And the manor houses are fabulous! Unbelievable! Makes me wish I had a bigger cut of the Gunnarson fortune. I'd buy me a castle, kidnap you, and we could be king and queen of our own little kingdom.

Keep up the good work with the Red Cross and everybody. Don't let Mom get too far out of hand with all the political stuff. You gotta feel sorry for her. She's never been allowed in the business meetings where they talk about family money, and the old tightwad keeps his thumb on every dollar, so she only gets whatever he doles out. She gave up her independence a long time ago, but don't be surprised if she gets her wind up and suddenly does extraordinary things—sometimes she realizes how much she's missed.

Tell Junior he must be doing a good job. We've got supplies stacked up all over the airfield and more bombs and ammunition than we know what to do with. Maybe the bigwigs are planning something.

Don't let the bedbugs bite.

Jake.

PEG,

It's serious time. We're flying regular missions into Europe, though I can't tell you where. I can't see much, being as far up as we fly, but we must be pulverizing every brick used to hold up a wall. Lots of fires. I wouldn't want to be a Kraut.

You asked me once if I ever thought about all the people being killed. I told you I didn't, but it's not quite true. I walked through Coventry once—that's an ancient British town with absolutely wonderful stonework, but the Luftwaffe bombers pulverized it—and the Jerries were merciless. There was hardly a wall left standing. That helps with the guilt a lot, but I still wish they'd surrender so we wouldn't have to keep the destruction up. There's a lot of architecture down there dissolving into the dirt and probably a lot of good people. I guess it's quid pro quo.

There's one German town with a massive cathedral. I mean, really big, built in the 1200s or so. As majestic a display of architecture as any in Germany, as I hear it. The bigwigs sent down the news that we were to avoid bombing it. Oh, sure, it's noble and all well and good, but it means we have to fly really low so our bombs are sure to miss it. Well, you know what that does—flying through the flak is like swim-

ming through pond scum. We've lost a lot of planes and good people by having to protect our enemy's property!

Am I scared? Damned right! You'd have to fly without a brain not to be. Sometimes I put an extra parachute under my butt just to feel that much farther from all those guns that are shooting at us.

But don't worry about me—I'm really good at dodging things!

Jake.

PEG,

One more day, one more bombing run. I don't think there will be a square inch of Germany we haven't bombed the hell out of.

I was thinking about us. We had a special week, didn't we? Damned war! It makes everything crazy, and it makes things all stretched out, like rope that keeps getting pulled tighter and tighter. The strands wear out and start popping loose and pretty soon, the whole rope tears apart. I think emotions are the same way—the war has stretched us all too thin, and we do things we don't mean to do.

But sometimes magic happens because of it.

That week is in my heart and will never go further.

Trust me.

Jake.

"OKAY, WAIT A MINUTE," Nancy suddenly said as Mom was rolling out a long tube of butter, sugar, and cinnamon. "Maybe he's just flirting, but does this man have no respect for his brother? Mom, I don't know what the two of you did, but he's making you out to be a partner in some romantic escapade. This idea of everything going crazy and magic happening sounds like a two-bit high school hustler to me."

Mom was surprisingly calm. "You need to give him a break. That letter was written maybe a year after he'd seen me in Minnesota, so he's been flying in combat for a number of months. He was lonely, for sure, but I imagine the intensity of the war was high, and at the same time, the danger was awfully repetitive. If he's not respecting me or Dad, it's probably because he's scared."

"I can believe the stress, strain, and battle fatigue," Nancy said, "but he should still keep his verbal paws off the woman who's engaged to his brother."

PEG,

I sprained my arm. I was landing a 17, and one of the wheels popped, which swung everything to hell and back, and my arm got yanked in the wrong direction. That was a couple of weeks ago, but I must have done something more significant than we thought. It still appears to be weak, and I have a hard time even raising it above my head. If that's the case, I may be washed up as a bomber jockey.

Well, to hell with it! I'm going to ask to be reassigned to fighter planes supporting the ground troops. You only need one strong arm to fly those babies.

I want to go help the infantry. There's not much to the Luftwaffe anymore—we shot most of those buggers out of the sky, no kidding. But there's a lot of strafing needed down below, shoving our bombs into bunkers and trains and tanks. I'd love to fly a tank-buster and take some of those Jerry commanders out by the seat of their pants.

So maybe Holland or Belgium. I'll make somebody an offer. We're not losing bomber pilots like we were in the beginning, so I'm not needed as much. I'd like to get back to smaller planes, anyway. I'm tired of flying long missions.

I'd be happy for some down time!

Still smelling your perfume, Babe!

Jake.

"OKAY, CAN I SAY SOMETHING?" I asked.

"Sure. I had my squeal, so go ahead," my sister said.

"I'll keep it short, but I want to emphasize the kind of

guy Jake must have been. He makes everything sound humorous, but being in a bomber crew might have been the worst job in the war. The bombers were based in England, and some of the targets they were bombing were deep inside Germany. The Allies had no fighters that could fly as protective escorts for the distances the bombers needed to reach their targets. For most of the war, fighters would escort the bombers only about halfway to the targets and then had to go back home. When they left, the bombers were on their own, at which time the Luftwaffe would just pick them apart.

"I used to have the numbers of lost planes memorized, but in general, any flight of bombers flying in northern Europe and especially over Germany would routinely lose ten, twenty, maybe even thirty percent of the planes. In April and May of 1944, the Eighth Air Force lost 671 heavy bombers on various missions, mostly from being shot down by anti-aircraft guns. A room full of men at a particular airfield who had had breakfast together one day might be missing twenty or more guys by the next day. It happened day after day. Eventually, forty thousand airmen lost their lives.

"No wonder he wanted to move to fighters."

PEG,

I pulled it off. I had my thirty missions in, so they reassigned me to a theater airfield. I got my own P-47 Thunderbolt, a hell of a plane to fly! I'm no longer a trainer, either, so I'll be spending my time cutting the balls off the German army.

How have you been? Holding up okay, passing out donuts and coffee? Lots of front-line movement here and lots of surrendering going on. You can't count on the old paperhanger giving up, though—the idiot just won't quit even though his country is falling apart around him. I'd like to save one last bullet for him and fire it up his ass!

So, I've been thinking about after the war. Obviously, I'm not taking over the family business. Nobody thinks that's a good idea. Don't want it anyway——I'm just not the kind of man who'd be good at riding a desk for the rest of his life. I'm thinking that maybe I'll go to Alaska and be a bush pilot. I don't feel good unless I've got wings under me, and I hear that there's a lot of country up there.

You, of course, will be a highly successful, beautiful, and enchanting wealthy heiress with a mess of kids and a wonderful husband. I still want to teach you to fly.

Keeping the troops safe,

Jake.

Chapter 14

Jake certainly wasn't Dad. As I read each of Jake's letters, I paid attention to the personal quips; he obviously wasn't shy or apologetic. What did Mom mean about Jake taking more than just her heart? Was she talking virginity here—or less, or maybe more? Did he steal a kiss? A lock of hair, a pair of panties? Did he feel her up while in one of the hangars? It was 1943, so anything in the 'fooling around' category could have been a basis for a regretful memory. His quips indicated a pretty significant intimacy, though. I assumed the week he was talking about was when he stopped at home on the way to the East Coast, but I had no idea about the magic he was referring to.

Nancy walked into the kitchen once we'd finished Jake's letters, while I sat alone for a while.

I was sure that any level of messing around between a good-looking guy and a beautiful young woman had to be noticed by someone else in the house. Lady Gunnarson never missed a thing—she was still pretty sharp when she came to visit us in Boston when I was a kid. The mansion may have been a big house, but there had to be a lot of echoes down the hallways, and I bet she was tuned in to hear every one of them. One guilty laugh could be imagined into a whole love affair.

"Mom, did you fall in love with Jake?"

Nancy's question brought me back to my chair in the kitchen. I could sit alone later.

My mother stopped slicing the dough for the cinnamon rolls and now seemed frozen in mid-movement. I couldn't tell if she was reacting in surprise to Nancy's question, or had suddenly become aware of the question and was trying to remember Jake's presence from so long ago, or, as an expression of fear crossed her face, I wondered if she had suddenly become afraid of her answer.

Maybe all of these memories were bringing my dad's death to the forefront, and she was tired of talking about the war. Maybe it was time to quit for the day.

But the dark cloud passed, and my mother slowly resumed working with her hands.

"No. I did not fall in love with Jake," she said distinctly. "You know I'm not a believer in the *love-at-first-sight* nonsense, but I also remember lecturing you both that just because you weren't in love with someone didn't mean you couldn't be captured by them."

"And the inverse," Nancy said with a smile. "Being captured didn't automatically mean you were in love."

My mom laughed. "It's nice to know that you listened. Anyway, I was infatuated with Jake from the moment I met him, like everybody else. But in my case, he represented all that I was not experiencing with the Gunnarson family. I was only twenty, hadn't nary a boyfriend before your father, was swept up in the typical girly things of the time period, and acting like I was wildly rich had inflated my ego to the size of the Hindenburg. I acted much bolder than I really was, and I was feeling more privileged than I should have been.

"But when I went to bed every evening, I couldn't help but be sad. I was so young and self-centered. It had been a year since I had seen your father, a year since I'd been kissed or had even held hands with a man. I certainly didn't feel like the independent grown-up woman I was supposed to be. I hadn't married your father yet, but I'd been enrolled in his lifestyle—his parents, the mansion, their wealth—and I certainly was already dominated by his mother.

"I felt stifled, but I also felt cheated. Getting engaged had seemed like a great idea at the time, but after your dad left, there wasn't anything with the least bit of passion in it. What could I do? Showing disappointment and frustration with the travails of love wasn't what an influential woman did in those days. Even Eleanor Roosevelt went into the bathroom and turned on the faucets so no one would hear her cry.

"When Jake dropped out of the belly of that bomber, a light turned on in my darkness, and I was surprisingly unable to resist. He was older, more mature, alarmingly handsome, and a genuine war hero who had traveled the world and had a personality that could disarm even the staunchest of the morally righteous women in Lady Gunnarson's circle of friends.

"After Jake checked in with the tower, the family held a big party for him. Of course, he didn't tell anybody he was coming until the day before, so it was all ad-lib, which ticked off his mother to no end. Lady Gunnarson was a planner and an organizer and would have put out written invitations to half the city, which is probably why Jake didn't tell her. At the party Lady Gunnarson had managed to pull together, he was a perfect gentleman in a great-looking uniform decked out with medals and ribbons, surrounded by a crowd of adoring girls who had appeared out of nowhere.

"I was a perfectly respectable lady, recognizing the accomplishments of a real live hero and basking in his reflected light.

We went to church on Sunday, followed by a big lunch down-town at some restaurant. He got me to go to the YMCA swim-ming pool on Monday. Oh, my goodness—what he looked like in a swimming suit! Maybe all Navy officers looked that way, but how somebody like that came out of an ancestry that produced Senior, I'll never know. We went to the USO that night, and he was the smoothest dance partner I'd ever had."

She shoved the pan of cinnamon buns into the oven hard enough they hit the back wall. "I need to say this, however. I wasn't exactly detached from his attraction. I was a perfectly respectable young lady at the party, but when we went to the swimming pool, I wore what I thought was my most revealing suit. By 1940 standards, it didn't show much, but I was not a dainty woman. I had an impressive bust, and I knew how to show it off. Likewise, when we went to the USO that night, I wore a sheer, tight-fitting dress and wasn't afraid for him to hold me close.

"Was I flirting? Absolutely. Was I enjoying myself? Abso-lutely. Was I inappropriate? Probably. Did I think I was doing anything wrong? Absolutely not. It was wartime, and USO dances were meant to give everybody a taste of free-dom, so I wasn't out of line compared to the couples who didn't even know each other.

"When we got back to the mansion, I did, however, let him kiss me good night before we went to our rooms. He was a great kisser, and he wasn't shy about stealing more. He got a little rough, and that's when the light in my darkness began to dim.

"The next morning, Jake took me for a ride in his B-17. He helped me up through the same hatch he had come out of, plopped me down in the co-pilot's seat, wrapped me up in a sheepskin jacket, put headphones on my head, started the engines, and we roared down the runway like it was the simplest thing in the world.

"I was holding on like I was about to die, but it was the most thrilling, edge-of-the-seat, exciting, frightening experience of my life. That B-17 felt like my dad's locomotive with wings. They weren't built for comfort, mind you, and the plane shook and squeaked and swerved and bounced and lurched like you wouldn't believe. You have to remember this was 1943, and I had never flown in an airplane before. When he leveled off at ten thousand feet, everything smoothed out and it was the most glorious feeling of freedom. Clouds look completely different when you're flying over them. I looked over at him, and he was every inch a commander ruling the air.

"He took me up to Duluth, flew over the coast of Lake Superior, flew over the deep woods, and then back to the airfield. I could hardly catch my breath because of the wonders I was seeing. Everything that had been two-dimensional suddenly became three-dimensional, and I was stunned by the effect.

"The landing was a little scary, but Jake never flinched. He celebrated my maiden flight with several more kisses and then offered to give me a tour of the airfield operations. We made it to a hangar with a set of overnight rooms with beds the airfield kept for visiting pilots who were flying across the country.

"That's when he took me inside one of the bedrooms, closed and locked the door, forced me onto the bed, and raped me."

She said it so matter-of-factly I wondered if I had misunderstood.

"Oh, Mom," Nancy said, reaching over, trying to hold my mother's hand.

My mother didn't allow it. Instead, she sniffed the air, smelled smoke, and quickly pulled the oven door down. She yanked out a cookie sheet of charred rolls, gave a huff, scraped them into the trash can, and began again, all without missing a beat.

"You kids are disturbing my focus," she said as she started measuring out another cup of flour.

"Mom!" Nancy stood up and almost yelled. "Jake raped you?"

My mother finally stopped, took a deep breath, and looked at us both. "Technically, yes. He dropped his pants, forced himself on me, and I was no longer a virgin when he was done."

"The crummy bastard! And he's rubbing your face in it a year later?" Nancy said, steaming.

"Well, hold your judgments, because there's more to the story," my mother said. She deliberately turned the electric mixer on to knead the dough, which pretty much killed the conversation. Nancy finally pulled the plug and threw the power cord to the floor.

Mom calmly set the mixer to the side. "Jake forced me to have sex with him on Tuesday afternoon, and I felt terrible afterward. He also felt bad, and spent plenty of time apologizing and making excuses like he had been in the Pacific so long, had never expected to get carried away, didn't mean to do it, etcetera.

"Dumb ditz that I was, I believed him and told him I understood. However, he certainly seemed to have enjoyed it a lot for not meaning to do it. It wasn't like I hadn't enjoyed some of it either, after he had gotten started. Sex is powerful, and the first time is pretty overwhelming even under ordinary circumstances. Afterward, I had the standard 1940s female mindset: maybe I hadn't resisted him like I should have, that I'd led him on, that my kisses had inflamed him beyond his ability to control his emotions. And I *had* let him kiss me, twice. Maybe I had given him the wrong impression."

She gave a huff.

"I finally realized that I was the only one feeling guilty, no matter what excuses he came up with. But it was the 1940s and there was a war on, which was an excuse used for a great number of wrong things being done. I wondered if he had sex with every infatuated female he met."

"My god, Mom, what did you do?" I asked.

"There wasn't much I could do. We laid there for a while, me trying to get my clothes back on and him acting like he'd just done me a favor. He had a talent for being nonchalant, but I had just crossed a line I'd had since junior high, a line based on fact: You're either a virgin or you're not. I was, and then, suddenly, I wasn't.

"But, again, there's more to the story. We drove back home and life seemed to continue unchanged from his viewpoint. He acted no different than usual, whereas I went up to my room and cried buckets."

"Did you tell anyone?" Nancy asked.

"Not a word. I stayed alone. Until late that night. That's when I went to his room and made him have sex with me again."

My sister and I were beyond stunned.

My mother plugged in the electric mixer again, finished building the dough, used a roller to flatten it out, spread the butter, sugar, and cinnamon, rolled it into a cylinder, and sliced even-sized slices onto the cookie sheets, again.

Before she put the pan back into the oven, she stopped and looked at us. "We're all adults, right? We're old enough to deal with reality, right? After coming in from the airfield, I went to my room. But the longer I stayed in my room, I realized my first reaction was not about being violated, but that I had expected more from it.

"I had dreamed about having sex for years, like all other girls. I had thought about it, imagined it, and had all the thoughts young people have. I expected to someday be physically loved by a man who was filled with passion for me, but all I got from Jake was forced sex in a back room at the hands of a sailor passing through town.

"I exchanged my guilt for anger and felt short-changed. I wanted to charge down the hallway, confront him, make him feel bad, make him feel guilty for ruining my dreams, make him feel…something."

"How about making him realize he had committed a personal crime against you?" Nancy chimed in.

My mother huffed again. "Remember me talking about being suddenly swept up in being rich, in being bolder than I really was, and growing my ego? About feeling privileged and entitled? Before I knew it, my ego had gotten me down the hallway, and when I charged into his bedroom, he thought I was going to slap him a couple of times.

"But my anger didn't make it past the door. I literally shoved him on the bed and crawled on top. I'm ashamed to admit that a small part of me wanted to show him that I could be a better lover than he'd found the first time. Remember I said being a little rich girl was intoxicating? Well, here you go— I acted like I was drunk.

"One thing led to another and we were soon at it again. The second time was better than the first, and it satisfied some of my anger, which, of course, was immediately replaced with even greater guilt.

"So, my educated children, if I was seduced against my will the first time and then I was the seducer the second time, who gets the blame?"

Leave it to my mom to turn rape into a logical debate.

"Mother!" Nancy said, clearly agitated. "You were raped! Period! Case closed. You can't change the rape-*er* into a rape-*ee* just because you felt guilty or had an inflated ego. He raped you in that hangar, and what you did the next time doesn't matter. You should have taken a knife with you to his room and cut that scumbag's penis off!"

"Okay, okay, I see a long argument coming," I said. "I want to know what happened next. Did it go further?"

Mom looked at us and took a deep breath. "I guess you'll be disappointed to know that we did it again on Thursday."

Nancy groaned and covered her face with her hands.

"It was inevitable," Mom continued. "On Wednesday, I acted as normal as possible. Lady Gunnarson held yet another luncheon social for her club to show Jake off, and we all went to a war bond parade in the afternoon. Thursday was another day for us at the Red Cross while Jake gave a noon talk at a YMCA and another one that night at a downtown men's club. We all had a nice dinner together afterward.

"That night, Jake came to my room after everyone else had gone to bed. I was hoping he would come. I'd had time to face my inner demons, and he'd had time to realize the damage he had done. I think both of us had lost our defenses, so it was easy for me to act like a mature woman. He held me for a while, we talked, and I cried on his shoulder. When we finally had sex, it was more like the love-making I had always dreamed of. It was relaxed, sweet, natural, and passionate, like two people who loved each other."

My mother was struggling and finally looked at Nancy.

"You are entirely correct," she said. "He raped me and he shouldn't have. He violated me without a second thought of what I wanted or didn't want, and he physically forced himself on me to do it. But things happened so quickly that by the time I was strong enough to hate him for it, I had become part of the whole mess.

"Remember that not being in love didn't mean you couldn't be captured by someone? I didn't love Jake at the beginning of the week, and I didn't love him at the end of the week, but we'd become entangled in each other, and everything about life after that moment changed. I didn't know what to do.

"I wanted to erase it all, but I couldn't."

Mom slid the buns into the oven, set a timer, and we all went back to the dining table.

Chapter 15

I thought Jake was an opportunistic stud on the prowl, and I couldn't help imagining Mom as just another notch in his jockstrap. Maybe she had been flirting and maybe she had acted too loose, but that doesn't give a man the right to rape any woman. And Mom was right—he knew what he was going to do before they climbed into that airplane. Flying among the clouds was just his version of foreplay.

And let's not forget that she was his brother's fiancé. Are you kidding me? Did he have no shame?

"Was it actually over?" I asked. "Did Jake just fly away? Was there discussion of the future? Did you talk about Dad and whether you should tell him? Did he even acknowledge Dad? Did you promise secrecy?"

Those were a few of my questions. Nancy had a longer list.

My mother finally held up her hands under the avalanche of questions. "I know this is new territory in what you know about your mother, and I know you now think Jake was a horrible person, but I'm telling you the gritty details because I promised your dad I would be brutally honest about the war. The important thing is that what happened between me and Jake was all within a single week. I never saw him again, nobody else knew, and your dad never found out, so it was up to me to handle it.

"Now, both of you look at me," she said firmly, looking from Nancy to me. "As significant as the events were, it's been forty-plus years, and Jake has been dead for almost all of it. Jake, me, your dad—we're all past any pain, any remorse, any damage. If any terrible things were going to result from it, they've already happened. It's been a long time, so don't think that you need to do anything. I don't need saving or consoling. You two need to take a breath."

Okay. What had she asked—were we all adults? I had said yes and honestly thought there was nothing I couldn't handle with maturity and wisdom.

So much for that idea. I felt like I'd been hit with a sledgehammer. And about the forty years gone nonsense? Mom had had to live with the secret of being raped for most of her life—which should count for something. I hoped Jake had suffered a slow and miserable death.

"Did Senior or Lady Gunnarson ever have a hint of what was going on?" I asked. "I mean, you must have been together at meals or in the evening with the family. It's hard to imagine that the giddiness you felt at the party, at the dance, and around the mansion didn't show a big change after Tuesday night. Senior could probably have cared less, but Lady Gunnarson was too much of a socially oriented woman not to pick up on it."

"Maybe Lady Gunnarson was just a poor, naïve Norwegian princess," Nancy said in a voice that still held a level of disgust.

"Oh, she wasn't Norwegian," Mom said, anxious to talk about something else. "She was raised in Chicago of good Midwestern stock. She was also, by the way, ten years younger than Senior.

"I always thought she was part of a business deal when

Senior was buying a locomotive. Louisa's father was also a railway tycoon, but he owned transcontinental railroads, not locals. He and Senior met up somewhere along the way, the way rich men do, and when Senior was expanding his Minnesota railroad, he needed another locomotive. Mr. Bennett came up with one, they worked out a deal, and lo and behold, Louisa was suddenly included in the agreement.

"I hope I'm kidding, but this was around 1910, and she and Senior were married a couple of months later. Junior was born the same year."

"Who's Louisa?" I asked.

"Too many cookies have clouded your brain," Nancy said.

"Louisa was Lady Gunnarson's first name?"

"Her full name," my mother nodded, "was Louisa Angelica Bennett Gunnarson. It could be neither of you have actually heard her called by her first name."

"Was she really that formidable? Or queenly?" Nancy asked.

Mom looked toward the ceiling and then moved her head back and forth before she answered. "She liked formality, I think. However, I wouldn't be surprised if it wasn't Senior who started calling her Lady Gunnarson. Having a titled wife would get him into more social and political circles."

"You didn't mind working with her while Dad was away?"

"We got along okay. If one of us was ditzy, it was me. I rarely called her 'Mom' or used any other endearments for her, but she was kind and patient and orderly in the things we did. She kept a big calendar on the wall in the kitchen and jotted down every event with its time and place. When we had socials, she always penciled in who the host was and kept a list off to the side of who was being celebrated or introduced or recognized. She kept her finger on the pulse of her social circle. My part was wearing the clothes and pretending to be her loyal daughter.

"By the way, after Senior died, Louisa moved to New York City. Do you know why she moved?"

We both shook our heads in the negative.

"She was good friends with Eleanor Roosevelt and went to be part of her support staff when Eleanor worked with the United Nations Commission on Human Rights."

"You're kidding," I said. "That was pretty important stuff."

"She thought so, too, but she was up for it. Of course, by the time she had decided to move, Junior was already figuring out how to sell the mansion. It took him a while—I think it's a museum now—but once she had moved out, Lady Gunnarson, who went by Louisa after Senior died, had no place to go back to. She died in 1957 in New York. You might remember her coming to stay with us on a few occasions. She loved you kids to death because you were her only grandchildren."

"How well did you get along with Senior?" I asked.

"I didn't like the man, but he had a policy that females were to be seen and not heard, so I didn't have much inter-action with him. I'd always take a different hallway to not have to pass his office."

The timer went off and she went to the kitchen. We both listened while she moved the buns to the cooling racks and then returned to her chair in the dining room.

"Okay," Mom said, "I want to go back and finish up my story about Jake's visit. By Friday, I had faced up to reality. First, I had crossed the hard line of no longer being a virgin. Second, I had slept with my husband-to-be's brother. Third, maybe the first time was excusable, but the second time was all me, and the last time was black-and-white infidelity.

"But no matter what, Jake was an important fly boy who would be back in the war in a couple of days, and I had to get back to writing letters to the man I was going to marry. Yes, we had gotten emotionally entangled with each other, but neither one of us considered it meant anything for the future. Saturday morning, family and friends all crowded around the airfield as he took off for New Jersey, and he disappeared into the clouds."

"But he started writing letters to you?" Nancy asked carefully.

Mom nodded. "Not right away. It was six months before I got his first letter, so I thought he was just checking in. When the letters continued, though, I knew he was still thinking of me. I never expected to write him back, but I found myself writing to him as much as I was writing to your dad. You asked me if I fell in love with Jake and I answered truthfully—I didn't. But we had a bond that grew over time, a bond I never quite knew what to do with. I didn't love him, but I missed him, in spite of what he did to me. And he knew it."

"That's what he was talking about in his letter!" I had suddenly made the connection. "His letter was more than a year later, but he's still referring to that one week. You were the 'magic' he was talking about. He was in love with you, wasn't he?"

Mom bowed her head and took a deep breath. She looked up at Nancy first. "I was never in love with Jake. But after flying in combat for a year, Jake had talked himself into thinking that I was. I still felt connected to him in some way, but he was desperately lonely and now wanted to have someone he could dream about having a future with. I understood, I really did, but it wasn't going to be me. Imagining him as my brother-in-law was bad enough.

"I stopped writing him. The last letters you read were the last ones I got."

"That sounds consistent with his being a worthless scumbag," Nancy said. "So much for the war hero."

"Well," Mom said, "maybe if you had been there, you might have more sympathy. You cannot comprehend what the war was doing to people. Jake may have become a bad guy, but he hadn't always been one, and I don't think he would have remained one if he had lived. Wait until Dad tells the whole story and see if you don't think differently."

I interrupted. "Jake called you Peg. Dad never called you Peg. Did other people call you Peg?"

Mom shook her head. "Not after high school. Some of my high school sorority sisters had called me Peg, and I liked it. In one of my talks with Jake one night, I asked him to call me Peg. It felt like a different identity."

She looked away. "I was already thinking that Margaret was my Gunnarson name—the name I used as a proper lady. By the end of that week with Jake, I didn't feel like a proper lady anymore. I clearly had another entity inside of me, someone unknown, darker, someone untrustworthy. Peg was what I began calling my 'other self'."

"Peg was your alter ego," Nancy said in a softer voice.

"Yup. Peg was on the inside, where no one could see her or hear her. I imagine it was one way I was coping with the mess I had made. But I want to say—I need to say—that even with this feeling of suddenly being split in two, I still loved your father very much, no matter which one I was. He was, in fact, all that mattered anymore.

"Dad was a steady, bright, handsome, happy, funny, gracious man and was every bit the man Jake was, just different. He loved me, there was no question. And I loved him. I loved your dad then, and I love him even more now. We had a quality of love that grows over time. There was never anything temporary about your father's love.

"That's where Dad had an edge over Jake. Jake was definitely a lone wolf. He might have made a faithful husband for a while, even if he thought he was in love, but his sense of adventure, his need for moving on, his need to find challenges, would have caught up with him, and he would have needed to escape."

"How about you?" Nancy asked. "I mean, did you feel the same toward Dad? Did you think you shouldn't marry him?"

Mom brought the cooling racks full of buns into the dining room. She rolled out two strips of waxed paper on the table and put the racks on top.

"I suppose this conversation is my punishment for raising kids whom I always told, *Oh, sure, you can ask any question you want.* However, I agreed to talking about Dad and the war with no limits, so I guess I asked for it.

"To answer your question about not marrying your dad: absolutely. As soon as Jake left and I was alone, I thought I'd committed every sin in the Bible. I was on my way to hell, and any attempt of excusing it would only make it worse. Meaning, of course, that I certainly couldn't marry your father. It would have disgraced him and his family. The afternoon seduction at the airfield was one thing, but my two nights with Jake were full-blown, deliberate transgressions. Only a truly wanton woman would do that."

"Rape, not seduction," Nancy corrected her in a neutral, lawyer-style voice.

Mom looked at Nancy with an expression encouraging her to drop the subject and then continued. "I cried over two or three letters I wrote to Dad confessing I had slept with a man, telling him everything was over, that he hadn't agreed to marry a sullied woman, I was releasing him from our engagement, I was sorry, and I would never enter his life again. It was all my fault, and simply disappearing sounded like a good strategy. By the way, my letters never said it was Jake. It was one thing to destroy my life, but I couldn't destroy the two brothers, no matter what.

"I never mailed the letters and I'm glad I didn't. My heart was still bound to Dad. I was still very much attached to him and very much wanted to spend the rest of my life with him. What I really needed was to confess my infidelity and cleanse my soul, but I didn't have anybody to confess to. I was too embarrassed to go to my parents, and I certainly wasn't going to go to either Senior or Lady Gunnarson. They would never have accepted my apologies, and certainly would never have accepted a loose woman into the family, even if she had been compromised by their own son.

"So I buried all of my guilt and shame and didn't *do* anything. You have no idea how much I suffered while the rest of the world kept on turning. I attended the same social functions, helped at the same places, gave the same speeches at the rallies, kept answering Dad's letters in a cheery voice, and life continued. Maybe I was looking good, but on the inside, I was falling apart. I needed cleansing. I needed forgiveness. I needed to not have anything to hide.

"The longer I did nothing, though, the less unstable I felt. Sometime after Christmas, during which I suffered the most, I gradually accepted the position that it had only been an unfortunate, unexpected, but understandable situation and hadn't really hurt anybody. Thank God I didn't get pregnant. More time went by, and I stopped hating myself.

"I took a philosophical approach. However it had happened, I was now a sexually experienced woman who could settle down to a normal life, loving a husband who would never know he was not my first sex partner. I was perfectly confident my 'entanglement' with Jake would simply dissolve away under your dad's love and I would be fully committed to being his wife in every sense of the word.

"This was at the beginning of 1944. Dad was still in England, Jake was brand new to Europe, D-Day was five months away, and there was still a lot of war to go."

Chapter 16

"That means the letters we've read from Dad and Jake were written after your encounter with Jake," I said.

"Yes. Sorry I messed the timeline up."

"Okay, then," Nancy said with a summary attitude, ready to move on. "1944 would get Dad finished with England, get him sent to Normandy in July, then out of Normandy and into Belgium and Holland and back to Belgium around the end of the year so that he's at Bastogne in mid-December. Meanwhile, Jake is training pilots in England, gets into bombing missions in Germany, and then hurts his arm and switches back to flying fighters in support of the ground troops by the end of December."

I was impressed.

"That's right," Mom said. "You've read everything up to when Dad leaves Paris and goes into Belgium for the first time, so let me summarize a bit so we can get back into sync. He likes Belgium. The fighting is heavy, but always to the east, close to the German border. He goes to Holland for a short time, where he does have a picture taken of him in front of a windmill, and then returns to Belgium and gets to the town of Bastogne.

"All this time, the weather in northern Europe was turning into winter—ice, snow, and fog, with the coldest temperatures on record. The descriptions from your dad of what it was like living in snow-covered tents and ice-filled foxholes, and driving around in unheated vehicles are brutal. Thousands of soldiers were treated for frostbite and frozen feet.

"I'm sure the weather didn't help, but your dad's letters began taking on a darker tone, a more negative outlook on the war. There was more conflict inside of him, especially when the Battle of the Bulge pushed the intensity of the war off the charts. He became cynical of the costs of the war, how the Army treated its soldiers like cannon fodder, how many people were dying, and the inefficiency of the military processes. He talks a lot about driving through bombed-out villages and towns and seeing the constant parade of people who were either surrendering or escaping from the land being fought over, or who were refugees with no place to go. He was really disturbed by the people standing in the snow, begging for food.

"Well, anyway," Mom continued. "I kept writing, he kept writing. I'd send him small boxes of cookies or cakes with newspaper or magazine articles, and he'd send his thanks. America was getting tired of the war, and there was a lot of communal sadness because it was getting close to the third or fourth Christmas a million soldiers had missed. Every day, the newspapers published lists of those killed or wounded, and they would oftentimes take up a whole page. Lots of gold stars were showing up in windows. It was getting harder for people to attend the war bond rallies and Red Cross drives. It reminded them too much of the war, and they were tired of thinking about it."

She took a deep breath. "Then, well, things hit a wall for your dad. After the Battle of the Bulge ended in January of

1945, when his unit had been placed in Patton's Third Army and they had moved across the Rhine River, I got this."

She reached into her apron pocket and pulled out the first of the two letters she had removed from the stacks. She passed it to me. The letter was three densely written pages, with the sheets stapled together.

"It's not V-mail, and there's no date," I said.

"No. Your dad wrote the letter and gave it to an injured soldier who was being shipped back home. The soldier mailed it after his ship docked. The censors never saw it. It's also the first letter he ever sent that wasn't dated. I want you to read it aloud."

Margie,

I've lied to you. I've lied over and over, and now I can't lie anymore.

They told us not be too truthful about our experiences over here, that our loved ones weren't accustomed to war, would worry too much, or would be hurt by the events we described, so we should talk only about positive things when we shared our experiences and feelings.

But there are things you need to know. I have learned to hate.

In England and even in the first week after we landed at Omaha Beach, the war was pretty exciting. I had never experienced something this big and important, and it was interesting and exciting and nerve-racking and absorbing and scary as hell. I had never experienced the range of emotions that I'd felt. I had always wanted to be a warrior, to be a hero, to fight evil on a grand scale, but I had never felt it to be personal. I hadn't yet seen piles of dead bodies, and I certainly hadn't watched anyone I cared about die. I hadn't felt it on the inside.

When we got into the fighting, things became relentless. My unit stepped up. We did our duty with the utmost care because men died if we didn't get it right. It became oppressive, running the radar every minute of every day, and within a week, everyone was worn out. And yet, we were happy to finally be doing something real and important, something that made a difference. Thank God for everyone I met. I like these people. I like getting to know them and spending time with them and relying on them like a unit should. I've never been a member of a team like this.

But we were being targeted by evil. The noise, the smell, the cold, the wet, and always the fear—the constant fear of somebody shooting you, or dropping a bomb on you, or machining gun your tent. None of those around me died, and yet we'd hear every day of hundreds of soldiers only a mile away being shot at and bombed and machine-gunned. We hardly moved during the first two months because the enemy never gave ground, never relented, never stopped being savages. I'd lie on my cot every night listening to the artillery and the bombers, wondering where the truck I just heard was going and how many bodies it would bring back.

No matter what I saw, it kept happening over and over. Line after line after mile-long line,

Germans, Slavs, Ukrainians, Russians, Czechs, and Italians being herded to the beachhead to be taken to POW camps.

Convoys of trucks taking replacement soldiers forward to the infantry units in combat. Always. More cargo planes, fighters, bombers, tanks, artillery, and trucks, trucks, trucks—trucks full of ammunition, trucks full of food, trucks full of water and fuel. Always. There were Jeeps with stretcher racks on them, and ambulances rushing the wounded from the fighting, and then truck upon truck of dead bodies zooming by on the way to the GRU at the Division Headquarters, and then more crosses. Always.

Sixty-five hundred a day. That's how many were killed in Normandy every day. Sixty-five hundred dead soldiers, every day. That's almost fifty thousand a week. Every one of them had a mother and a father.

Why are young men obligated to go to war? Why do they have to be the first to die? The night before D-Day, the bombers had missed their targets in the bluffs above the landing beach. The German emplacements and defenses had not been knocked out, and when our soldiers landed, that part of the invasion turned into a bloodbath. Thousands died, and enough blood was shed that the sea turned red and bodies kept washing ashore for days. In the Normandy breakout planned by General Bradley, bombers missed their targets and bombed our own boys, and hundreds died. The British lost hundreds of their own soldiers from their own bombers and artillery missing their targets. Every day, young men died because of mistakes.

And what about Carlos Ortega? I was talking to him one day and he was dead the next. Everything about him was snuffed out like a candle. When will those people who start wars understand they're not just killing people, but they're destroying everything that was someone's past and everything that would have been their future? Carlos had a lot of candle left.

I thought I understood war. I honestly wanted to. If someone wants to put you into slavery, or wants to take away your liberties or your family, or wants to possess you or what is rightfully yours, I understand the need to fight against them. But I live at the bottom of the ladder, and on every rung above me is someone who takes an order and passes it down to me. I'm not fighting for me, I'm only doing what the order says.

The people above me want me to kill the enemy, but I haven't yet pulled the trigger on my rifle.

Every day, all day long, as soon as Patton's Army crossed the Rhine, there were even longer lines of surrendering soldiers. A POW camp north of us had seventy thousand Germans sitting in the snow-soaked mud. If this is war, why keep them alive? Lock the gates and let them starve until they eat each other. Or shoot them and get it over with.

SS officers have been captured and they, too, march in long lines past us. Their eyes are full of hate. They stare at me because they do not want me to exist. Why? Who am I that they hate me so much? I don't have time to find out, so let's just shoot them all.

Normandy, Paris, Belgium, Holland. All full of people killing each other. Captain Hornfeld told me I hadn't been here long enough, that I hadn't learned to be a professional killer, that we all have to be professional killers to win the war, that we needed to see the war as personal.

It hadn't yet become personal to me.

A major came by our tents looking for volunteers. There were so many people being killed around Bastogne that the GRU needed help, needed people to help them gather the dead. If I was dead someplace out there, my mother would have wanted someone to help get me back home, so I volunteered.

My truck alone brought back twenty-seven men who had died that morning. The mix of blood and frozen mud and ice and snow smells worse than you can imagine. Several men had been blown apart by grenades or mortars or artillery shells or land mines, so we put what we could into sacks, trying to get the right parts together.

I was within a mile of the front, and the stench was so bad it was hard to breathe. Herds of bloated cattle had lain in the fields for days. Dozens of dead horses had been pushed into the ditches, where they swelled up and then split open. A lot of the German artillery is still pulled by horses. So much for the German war machine.

I saw bombs exploding in front of me. There

were constant zings and booms of howitzers and cannons firing from each side. How can men listen to them all the time, feel the ground shake all the time, feel splattered by the mud as it's slung through the air? Why don't more people run away? What keeps them from going crazy?

I had wondered what I would do if I ever got close to the fighting. Now I know. I got back in my truck and got the hell out of there. I guess you wouldn't win any wars if you had only me. If that makes me a coward, Captain, sorry.

Remember my flyboy brother Jake? Mom told me he quit the Navy and joined the Army Air Force to fly bombers over Germany. I heard he wanted to fly fighter planes again, so he was assigned to fly fighters against the German ground forces. He was based out of an airfield north of us. I listened to his voice on the radio as he flew his way to shoot at tanks or truck caravans or railroads. He sounded fine. He must be one damned good pilot. He and his P-47 Thunderbolt. He named it Maybelline.

Jake gave us a call, saying he'd fly over enemy locations the radar couldn't see because they were behind hills and would dump out bags of aluminum strips above them. The radar would get returns off the metal strips, giving us the distance and direction we needed to give the coordinates to the artillery. It had been done in other places, but I was against it—he'd be flying low over enemy territory, and that's too dangerous just to acquire targets that might be gone by the time we got the coordinates to the artillery.

He decided to do it anyway. I could have stopped him and I should have stopped him but I didn't stop him. My radar was responsible for keeping up with him, and it was me who watched his blip on the screen.

He flew a Piper Cub spotter plane along a line of armaments and encampments on the other side of the hills in front of us. Every now and then, he'd empty a sack of strips over a target and we'd get a big signal on our screen.

We marked the location on a map. His idea worked. He was on his way back when his blip on my screen went out. He was shot down.

Jake is dead.

I was responsible for Jake dying just like Jake was responsible for Lilly dying, and the war finally became personal. I can now hate and not feel guilty. It's time for me to kill, whether I am good at it or not, whether I want to or not, because now it's my family Hitler has murdered. I'm going to get my rifle, start walking east, and kill every Kraut I meet. I don't have to be a professional killer, I just have to pull the trigger. The man in front of me and the man beside him. It's my duty to kill them all.

I burned all your letters. I didn't want anyone else to read them. I wanted to leave nothing for people to find.

I love you. I've always loved you. You are the greatest thing to ever happen to me, but I'm not who I used to be. You don't want me now.

I won't make it back. I'm sorry.

*Don't tell Mom or Senior, or even Junior what
I did.*

Let them think I died a hero.

Teddy

Chapter 17

There was silence as my mother walked back into the kitchen. Nancy and I followed. There were still tears in my mom's eyes when we sat down.

"Uh," I muttered, not knowing what I should say. "Did he grab a gun and go shoot Germans?"

"Eventually, yes."

"Did he do something dramatic?"

"Yes, he did."

"Did he tell you what he did?"

"Not until the videotape."

"Okay, okay," Nancy said, looking at me with exasperation. "Instead of guessing your way through it, let her talk. Jeez! Mom, what did you do when you got the letter?"

"I cried a lot," she answered. "There wasn't anything else I could do. It was my punishment from God. It was hard to believe Jake was dead, but it was harder to think of Dad being dead. Jake took risks. You expected he'd someday fly into a blind alley he couldn't fly his way out of. But Dad was deliberate, cautious, and very smart. He wasn't the kind of man to fly off the handle, and he certainly would never have walked into a situation if it was guaranteed he'd be

DONALD WILLERTON

killed. And the idea he'd learned to hate was counter to everything he felt about life.

"Every day for a week, I sat at the front window, watching the gate to the house, dreading the moment when a car with a big American star would drive up and an Army chaplain would get out and hand Lady Gunnarson the letter stating that her second son had been killed, and maybe another letter stating that her third son had been killed. I hoped I would be in the house with her when they came, but I could not bring myself to tell her what I knew. I had earned my suffering, she had not. So I continued my routine, doing as I had done, being who I had been, never confessing that I had been made hollow.

"But the Army chaplain and his car never came that week, and a day later, this showed up in the mail." She took the second envelope from her apron and gave it to me to read aloud.

Margaret,

I am so, so sorry. I was crazy. What the last week must have been like for you is beyond my imagination. Please, please forgive me. I should have never sent the letter.

Jake is alive. He was shot down, but local Germans pulled him from the wreckage and turned him over to the SS. The German underground got us the information that he's wounded, but alive enough to be taken to a POW camp.

I'm going after him. My silliness about striking out on my own and killing Germans

130

was stupid, but I can make up for everything now. I'm going to find Jake and bring
him home. I know what my duty is.
    Ted

"If your dad had been in front of me, I would have killed him myself," my mom said. "Sending one letter saying Jake was dead and that he was going to go shoot everybody until somebody shot him, and then sending another saying that Jake was alive and he was so sorry. For the amount of sadness and grief I endured for that week, I could have strangled him."

"That's why there's another stack of letters," Nancy said.

"Yes. He wrote me two or three more times. To his credit, he continued apologizing, but it was a long time before I got myself straightened out. He hadn't told me where he was, and I didn't know when he had written the letters, so I didn't know when or where Jake had been shot down.

"Then, after all that, something happened at the last of March and everything changed."

Chapter 18

"The letters stopped. I kept writing, but never got anything back. Almost a month went by, and I was sure he had been killed, but a letter from him came the last week of April, with no explanation of why he hadn't written. He sounded different, his Army address had changed, and he never mentioned Jake. He said that he had been transferred to a different unit and was working in a different area. His letter sounded rushed, shorter, and it was like he was confused.

"Before I got another letter, Germany surrendered. Victory in Europe Day is what, May 7? May 8?"

"May 8, 1945," I said. "The Germans surrendered on the seventh, but it wasn't until the next day that they signed the papers. We can assume he didn't go after Jake, right? Germany had almost a thousand POW camps. He would never have found the right one. And even if he did, it would have taken an army to get to any one of them."

My mom shrugged and looked as if she didn't have much more to say. "You can look through the unread letters from your dad," pointing to the remaining stacks back on the table. "You should. The ones after March don't say much and they're a lot shorter, and he didn't put a date on any of them. Never talks about Jake, never talks about his radar, never mentions his crew members or describes any battles or troop movements, never really talks about what he's doing or where he is, or why his address changed. For as little as he said, there was always a sadness to his words. I wondered if he was sick or wounded or had gone crazy. I wish we had known about PTSD because I'm sure he had it. Somebody should have known enough to get him out of there."

"He might have become part of the Occupation Army," I said. "When Germany surrendered, Eisenhower had more than a million and a half soldiers in Germany alone, and a total force in Europe numbering three million. When the fighting ended, some of the divisions in the field became occupation troops, charged with maintaining law and order and establishing the Allied military presence in the defeated nation. As neat and efficient as that sounds, it only took a couple of hundred thousand men to get the job done. That left millions of troops without anything to do.

"The military set up training classes and recruited American universities to set up for-credit courses. They established thirteen hundred libraries, set up baseball, basketball, and football teams that played each other, ran movies at the Army bases, and sponsored buses that took GIs on tours throughout Europe. Meanwhile, they were shipping thousands of GIs back home every day, as fast as they could, either to England or directly to the States. They even commandeered two German luxury liners and turned them into troop ships."

"Alright, already," my sister said, interrupting my history lecture and giving me another exasperated look, "Dad came home, lived a full life without telling his kids anything about his time in the Army, and then finally made a videotape revealing why."

Yes. His last six months started with the incident of Jake

being shot down. It must have been in late February or the first of March, I think. Your dad must have written the *I'm-going-to-kill-them* letter about then, and the apology letter would have come a week after that, making it around the middle of March, I guess.

"Let's go sit down. I'm tired of standing up."

She had dumped a half-bag of confectioner's sugar in a bowl and whipped it into a glaze. I carried the bowl to the table, and she used a spoon to drizzle a narrow stream of sweetness over each bun on the cooling racks.

Chapter 19

My mother was silent until she had finished sugar-striping each bun. She was obviously tired, probably as much from the weight of the memories as from the efforts of baking.

I was tired, too, but my anxiety was off the charts, and I could hardly sit still. I had heard things far beyond what I could have imagined, and if the tape had even more trauma, I couldn't guess what we were in for.

"It's time to play the videotape," my mother said softly. "I've seen it and I'm not up to seeing it again. Not now, anyway."

The letters were still strewn around the table as she took the tape from the trunk and handed it to me. "I'm going to make myself a cup of coffee and go sit in the sunroom for a while. I need a break."

MY DAD WAS FASCINATED with technology and through the years, we put up with his reel-to-reel tape recorders, cassette players, laser disks, the rise and fall of Beta format, VHS tapes, and CDs. Thankfully, he was never one to skimp on quality, so we used the VCR in his office because it had comfy, overstuffed chairs. The player took the tape my mom had given me and began playing.

The cabin he went to, a couple of hours away from Boston on three acres along the shore of a backwoods lake, wasn't really a cabin. It may have had rustic architecture, but it still had five bedrooms, six bathrooms, and a custom kitchen. Even more than our attic at home, the cabin was our escape route to worlds unknown.

I recognized the desk Dad sat behind. It was an old wooden behemoth placed in the center of an office that had a typewriter, a TV, a sound system, and various bookshelves full of magazines, books, and games. Company reports were not allowed here. The wall behind him was covered with photos from the trips we took during our summers and school breaks. Mom and Dad were always taking us somewhere so we could 'experience the culture', meet new people, and see how other folks lived.

He looked thin but good in a striped sports shirt, and it was all Classic Dad once he started talking.

"I want to first apologize for not having pictures or illustrations. If there were more time, it would be fascinating to research the places I went to, the people I met, and the roads and trails I traveled. I especially regret not having maps.

"However, I can only do what I can do. With not many more minutes, I'd rather spend them with you. I've already spent too much time over the last month trying to remember every step I took, whom I met, what we said. If I was going to do this, I wanted to be thorough and not leave anything out. Having kept everything secret for all these years, now was not the time to falter. I hope I did a good job and that there's enough information to allow you to appreciate my journey.

"Over the past forty years, I've read every book even faintly related to the event I'm about to tell you about. What can I say? If my descriptions seem surprisingly historical or full of excess detail, it's because I stole the information from some book. And the dialogue? Well, I took poetic license with all of it, so if the words sound like Shakespeare, I doubt we really talked like that. I wanted everything to sound and feel real. It was certainly real to me.

"I also beg your forgiveness if my delivery gets choppy. I'm miles away from your caring hands, and my feeling good comes and goes. I brought my pain medicine, but it usually puts me to sleep, so I'm going to use it sparingly. I'll record my story as my energy allows, and Jim has promised to stitch everything together so it looks good and you won't have to sit through constant interruptions.

"Okay, I guess it's time to begin. Let me give you the context.

"I was in or around Bastogne from the last of November until the third week of December, '44. The German offensive started east of us in the Ardennes Forest around December 16 and moved our way. They didn't reach Bastogne until the nineteenth. My radar unit was already withdrawing to the west, wanting to set up about twenty miles away. The offensive peaked around the first of the year, and we had beaten them back to where they had started a couple of weeks later. My unit joined up with the Third Army the last of January, moved east, crossed the Rhine River, and then followed Patton as he proceeded to run all over southern Germany.

"Jake was shot down in the last week of February. I wrote you that night. A few days later, I heard that he wasn't dead but had been wounded and captured by the SS, and according to the German resistance, had been taken to a POW camp. Because Jake was a captain, and a pilot, I knew he'd be taken to an officers' POW camp. I don't know why the Germans had separate camps for enlisted men and officers.

"When I found out Jake was alive, I spent every moment I could at the aircraft control center, listening for any information about which POW camp Jake might have been taken to. I also tried other headquarter units. Pretty soon, everybody knew my brother was the pilot who had been shot down. That gave me a lot of contacts.

"Patton's Third Army, meanwhile, was racing through a hundred miles or more of German homeland, so the General kept us on the move. Eventually, the front elements of the Third Army crossed a bridge over the Main River into a town called," he glanced down at his notes, "Aschaffenburg. As with any river crossing, the front elements set up a defensive perimeter on the far side of the river and waited for the rest of the Army to come across the bridge behind them.

"I was in the control room the next morning when an artillery sergeant pulled me outside. His artillery unit had been ordered not to fire into a certain sector over the next three days. To learn what was up, his Captain had dropped by headquarters, and while there was nothing official, the chatter was about the resistance getting information to headquarters about an officers' POW camp outside a town named Hammelburg, some fifty miles east of Aschaffenburg. Patton had ordered a special task force to go behind the German lines and bring back the American officers in that camp.

"According to my maps, that was almost directly in line with where Jake had been captured. If he had been wounded, they would have taken him to the closest officer POW camp that had a hospital. That was all I needed to hear. I had become obsessed with finding Jake and would have believed anything that had the slimmest hope to it, which is saying I had gone crazy. I became convinced Jake was at the camp and set out to join the task force, which was not exactly easy to do.

"But I had an advantage. Back when I had worked for an infantry captain, repairing the company's radios, whenever I wasn't riding around in his command Jeep, no one paid any attention to me. Nobody thought twice about a captain having a radio repairman with a combat unit, so if I could make myself look like a radio repairman who had been assigned to the task force, I could slip right in.

"That's where my story begins, and I will try to tell it as if I were still there."

Chapter 20

I grabbed my tools, stuffed my shirt with D rations—ugly-tasting meal bars, but three would keep a man going for a day—put on a combat jacket I'd taken off a dead infantry-man, and drove off in my unit's Jeep when no one was looking. The roads were packed with convoys, but I snaked my way through until I was in the line of vehicles crossing the bridge to Aschaffenburg.

My sergeant friend had found out that Company A of the 10th Armored Infantry Battalion was heading up the task force, so I asked the MPs on the other side of the bridge for directions to their headquarters. They pointed me toward a smaller town to the south called Schweinheim. I actually didn't want the headquarters. I wanted to find the task force. I figured if one were being organized, there'd be tanks and trucks and a lot of activity near the command center.

I was lucky. Halfway between the two towns, a number of Sherman tanks were having several jerry cans of fuel poured down their pipes while I counted five M3s, which were smaller tanks, sitting together alongside the road. Next to them were three self-propelled assault guns, called tank killers, which are Sherman tanks adapted to carry a massive artillery gun with a shell big enough to penetrate the armor of any tank used in the war. Maintenance people were wiping grease over the American stars on the front and sides of each vehicle and then throwing dirt on the grease to make it look like mud. Without the big stars, they didn't look American, which is what you'd want if you were going behind German lines.

Scattered among the tanks were groups of half-tracks—armored vehicles with regular truck wheels on the front and tank-like tracks in the rear, equipped with 50-caliber machine guns mounted behind the driver. Behind its armored walls in back, each had space for a dozen men or more. Around the half-tracks were groups of GIs cleaning their pistols, rifles, BARs, and machine guns while others were eating, sleeping, or slinging boxes of ammunition into vehicles. Like the tanks, everything was having its military markings covered up.

Sending out task forces wasn't unusual. Commanders put them together for raiding parties or special missions, like to protect a bridge, or to protect engineers while they built a new bridge, or to destroy specific pillboxes or road block-ages, or to rescue groups of men who had gotten separated from their units. I always thought you'd want task forces to be small, fast, and flexible, but what I was watching was not a small operation—ten Sherman tanks, five smaller tanks, three self-propelled assault guns, several Jeeps, and what must have been at least thirty half-tracks. Altogether, more than three hundred men and fifty vehicles which, to me, seemed like a small army. I hoped they wouldn't notice one more guy.

I hid my Jeep in nearby trees, expecting to retrieve it in a day or two, and then slipped around the groups of men waiting to load up. They'd be rolling in an hour, probably right after nightfall, so I needed to get onboard something and hunker down so I would look as if I belonged.

The half-tracks were jockeying for position, and one of them was loaded not with people but with boxes, fuel cans and maintenance stuff for the tanks. That's the one I wanted. I jumped on the running board, asked the driver if this was the task force going to the POW camp, told him I was ordered to join up, then jumped off before he could answer. I climbed in the back and settled in among the boxes next to another guy who was a vehicle maintenance tech. I introduced myself.

He gave me a strange look. "You sure you want to be in on this? Sounds like it's going to be a bumpy ride to hell and back, and I wouldn't think we'd need a radio guy."

"I just go where they tell me. Where are we headed?"

"Captain said we're on the way to a POW camp about fifty miles from here, all of it behind German lines. We're supposed to free the camp and bring everybody back. You ain't got a weapon?"

I had forgotten to grab my rifle. "Nope. They told me we'd be going so fast, I wouldn't need one. If something happens, I'll throw a radio at 'em. You know who's in charge?"

"Captain Abraham Baum. I've been with him since Brittany. He's a good man and a helluva leader, but he don't ever go backward. If I were you," he pointed to the submachine gun strapped to the wall behind the driver, "I'd grab that grease gun when the shootin' starts. Throwin' a radio might get one German off your ass, but I expect we're about to meet a few more than that."

I HAD NEVER SEEN General George S. Patton but had heard a lot about him. Several men at the airfields and around the flight control rooms told stories of his tank battles in Africa and Sicily, passed on descriptions of the ivory-handled six-shooter he wore at his side, quoted him from speeches where he told remarkable stories of courage and perseverance, and cited every instance when a soldier had peed his pants as the General was chewing him out.

There was no denying he was a genuine intellect, a well-read historian, a philosopher, and a strong believer in the Bible. He spoke a number of languages and had a God-given talent for putting words together that were inspiring, humorous, and usually filled with profanities. He was a firm believer in true leaders not watching things happen, but making things happen. Patton believed war brought out the best qualities in men.

Once having determined an objective, Old Blood and Guts put all of his energy into pursuing that objective, and he tolerated no weaknesses from the men under his command. He was one hard-charging sonofabitch, and the German commanders were flat-out scared of him.

Once in Germany, General Patton immediately spread the radar units across the front to be the eyes and ears of the chess board in front of him. Having determined our areas, we'd find airfields that had been either built by us or taken over from the Germans, find the high ground, set up our radar, and start finding targets, giving the controllers a wide view of German artillery emplacements, mortar crews, and crossroads, as well as any remaining Luftwaffe.

Then Patton waged war. Between the end of the German offensive in Belgium in January, 1945, to the end of March, Patton's Army took sixty-five hundred square miles of German territory, liberated three thousand towns and villages, captured one hundred forty thousand enemy soldiers, and had killed or wounded ninety-nine thousand more. He was an unstoppable force, and Eisenhower and his staff were elated with his progress. Patton was almost winning the war all by himself. If he hadn't run afoul of politics and been shorted on fuel, he probably would have.

It also might have helped if he hadn't decided along the way to send a task force to free a bunch of officers from a German POW camp outside a little town named Hammelburg.

CAPTAIN ABRAHAM BAUM had assembled the task force on a hill outside of Schweinheim to give everybody a good view of the town's main street. That's the street we'd be going down to connect to a road looping north, close to Aschaffenburg, which then connected to highways taking us to the POW camp.

The maintenance guy and I were standing in the back of our half-track, watching the town center. It didn't look like much of a town, and finding the highways taking us east didn't appear very difficult on the map I had brought along. I learned later no one was familiar with where we were going. Planes hadn't flown any reconnaissance over it, recon patrols hadn't scouted out the German defenses, no one knew if the bridges in front of us were still intact, and the commanders who sent us out didn't even know exactly where the POW camp was located.

That's called going into battle blind, but we were going, and the first problem was getting through Schweinheim: It was still held by the German army.

Whoever was running the show didn't want the task force to waste its time and resources fighting through the town. They assigned B Company of the 37th Tank Battalion and B Company of the 10th Armored Infantry to start clearing our path at 1700 hours so the task force could get to the highways and on to Hammelburg before daylight.

Fighting through the town had turned into a nasty business—lots of resistance, smoke, German artillery coming in, constant gunfire and chatter from machine-gun nests, and bodies mounding up along the sidewalks. The American forces had come up against Major von Lambert, the commandant of the SS officer candidate school. He executed soldiers and civilians alike if they abandoned their posts or even considered surrendering. This made his soldiers tenacious and stubborn, fighting the GIs every inch of the way, shooting anti-tank rounds from every corner and pouring sniper fire from the upper windows of buildings.

Six hours later, long after it had gotten dark, Captain Abe Baum and his task force were still sitting on the hill, watching in frustration.

It was midnight when Baum made the decision that he couldn't wait any longer. We'd already be running in daylight before we got halfway to our objective, but the Captain had no choice: He had been ordered to go.

He gave commands for the vehicles to sprint through town, fighting only if somebody tried to stop us. He rode his Jeep up and down the task force vehicles, yelling at every-body to get ready to move, not to slow down, not stop to shoot anybody, just keep the hell going forward as fast as the vehicles would go.

The five light M3 tanks went first, then the Jeeps with Baum, other officers, medics, and a recon platoon, then the ten Shermans, the assault guns, the half-tracks with men, and the maintenance vehicles, where I was. At his signal, we flew down the hill and onto the main street of town with a thunderous roar, shaking the ground with our steel treads. The vehicles had been told to not turn on their headlights but every tank should be blasting its siren as we raced through. It was like the rebel yell of the Civil War, striking fear and panic in the enemy in front of us.

I don't know how the enemy was reacting, but it was scaring the hell out of me.

A few minutes later, we were through.

. . .

HAMMELBURG WAS a town of about six thousand in 1945. A postcard-perfect town with a tall Gothic cathedral and a town square with a Renaissance-style fountain in front of the town hall, it bore the markings of a thousand years of Germanic rule, going all the way back to Charlemagne. During World War I, they built an extensive military training center two miles south of the town. Part of the training center was a POW camp with forty to fifty stone and wood barracks, plus some brick command buildings for the German staff.

At the beginning of World War II, the POW camp was increased to serve two distinct populations, divided by a small hill: an enormous *stalag*, short for *stammlager*, housing thousands of captured Russian, French, American, English, Canadian, and Australian enlisted men, and an *oflag*, short for *offizierslager*, eventually housing more than fifty-five hundred Allied officers over the years of the war.

With rows and columns of more crudely constructed barracks, the oflag had a water tower at one end and a perimeter of barbed wire fencing connecting twelve guard towers, each with a machine gun unit. The individual barracks were heated by a single coal stove, woefully inadequate for spaces crowded with forty or so two-tiered bunks.

The first World War II officer POWs at the Hammelburg site, named Oflag XIIIB, were four thousand Serbian officer-elites captured in 1941 when Germany invaded Yugoslavia. One of the officers who would eventually join the others in the camp would be the son of Soviet Premier Joseph Stalin. By January 1945, however, American and British officers captured during the early days of the Battle of the Bulge had arrived in camp. The Serbs were moved out of their barracks into a different area, segregated by barbed wire.

In February, another group of twenty officers joined them and then, in March, eight hundred Allied prisoners were moved from Oflag 64 in Poland to Hammelburg. They had been forced to march three hundred miles in forty-five days. The ranking officer of this group was Colonel Paul Goode, and the executive officer was Lieutenant Colonel John Waters. Waters was captured on St. Valentine's Day, 1943, in Africa, and had suffered in POW camps in Africa, Italy, Poland, and now Germany. As they were now the ranking officers, Goode and Waters became the senior leaders of the American prisoners.

By the time Task Force Baum was screaming its way through Schweinheim, more than fifteen hundred American officers were shivering through another cold night, never expecting it might be their last night in captivity.

Unfortunately, that was a problem. General Patton had told Captain Abe Baum to expect three hundred.

Chapter 21

No one knew any of this information at the time, of course. All I knew was that my body was being jackhammered against the steel floor of the half-track, tossed and turned and bumped and slammed and vibrated by the repetitive grinding of the tracks against the road while being repeatedly thrown against the armored wall as Captain Baum pushed our convoy down the highway with a deadly urgency.

Task Force Baum came out of Schweinheim on a side road, looped up by Aschaffenburg, then headed for Highway 26. It would take us east until it connected to Highway 27, which would take us directly to Hammelburg. Captain Baum continually checked his map by flashlight, and when we came to a sign with a big "26" written on it, we gave a whoop and felt like we had accomplished our first objective. Every driver turned his vehicle onto the new highway and put his accelerator to the floor.

We didn't know we'd never see "27."

But everything was working. We were like a black caterpillar racing down the pavement. Captain Baum constantly rode his Jeep up and down the convoy, calling out instructions to the drivers, telling men of the upcoming twists and turns and road signs. I had not witnessed much leadership in my unit because we rarely had critical situations, but I was impressed with how well Baum assumed responsibility for every vehicle and every man under his command.

Every so often, a tank would swing off the road and run over telephone poles strung with communication lines between the German towns. Baum soon ordered a half-track of men to stop after the poles were down and use cutters to sever the wires, guaranteeing no information could be exchanged.

As the morning light slowly grew around us, Baum moved the more heavily armored Sherman tanks into the lead. Sometime later, the front tank driver, Lieutenant Weaver, noticed a German truck convoy on the road ahead, led by two tanks, and called out their location on the radio. I yanked the grease gun out of its holder and got the maintenance guy to show me how to use it.

Unfortunately for them, the German convoy did not recognize us as enemies, and we were on them before they knew what was happening. Our lead tanks let loose with their cannons, and the rest of us sprayed the troop trucks in a continuous volley as we raced by them. The cannons blew the turrets off the tanks while the enormous hail of bullets ripped the fabric of the truck covers to pieces and turned their gasoline cans into balls of flame.

I had never shot at anyone before and found myself pleased as the grease gun kicked in my hands and the German trucks careened into the ditch. Soldiers were leaping out of the back as they tried to escape our bullets, and one's cap flew off. I watched as locks of blond hair swished sideways.

It was a convoy of young women. German flak girls. By

this stage of the war, all able-bodied men were fighting at the front, so the German commanders used young women for their flak gun crews. The average age was probably sixteen. I had finally killed my Germans, but this wasn't what I'd expected. The image of blond hair spilling against the asphalt would stay with me for years.

It was 0900 when we paused outside the large population center of Lohr, allowing everyone to catch up and prepare to turn onto a road going north. We did not know it at the time, but in the town of Lohr was the command post of General Hans von Obstfelder, who had just been appointed the *Befehlshaber*, or commander, of all ground forces in southern Germany. He had received reports throughout the night of the task force's progress, with the first report coming from Schweinheim itself more than twelve hours before. Expecting the task force to be the first in a wave of Patton's tanks, he was surprised when no other parts of the Third Army were found to be following.

Task Force Baum was suspiciously alone.

General Obstfelder ordered a squadron of reconnaissance planes to maintain constant surveillance of the Americans, then ordered the Highway 26 bridge over the nearby river to be wired with explosives and large mines to be buried in the approach to the bridge. If the task force attempted to go across, the bridge would be blown while they were on it.

I HAD EXPECTED to use my own map to keep up with where we were but soon stuffed it into my shirt, gripped the grease gun closer, and hunkered down instead. More scared than when I'd ridden with the infantry captain, I was certainly not feeling like a combat soldier and had an overwhelming feeling of regret. How could I have been so stupid? I wanted to save Jake, but I was almost guaranteed to get myself killed, and that wouldn't help either of us.

We had turned northeast at Lohr, finding ourselves on a road that closely paralleled a railway track. The convoy gradually caught up with a slower train moving north on the track with both passenger cars and freight cars. Our lead tank put a round directly through the locomotive's boiler, and the 50 calibers poured hot lead into the rail cars. By the time we passed what was left, it was a shamble of smoking metal and burning cars with dead troops hanging out the windows. A few miles later, we peppered a large number of military cadets out on a school practice field, leaving a few dozen bodies on the ground before any of them could make it to their stacked weapons.

We were no longer a covert operation, and I guess Baum was trying to destroy anything that might shoot at us on the way back.

The road turned directly east, and we halted on the outskirts of Germunden, a small town on the north shore of a big loop of the Main River and one of the few towns to have a bridge that crossed over. Getting across that bridge was the key to getting to Highway 27 leading to Hammelburg. If it had been destroyed, or was blocked, the day was going to be a lot longer than everyone had planned.

Baum sent the three Jeeps ahead to check the bridge and any defensive positions that might have set up by the town's garrison. The platoon's lieutenant was soon back, reporting that the bridge was still intact but that the entrance to it had been mined. He and the others in the platoon used several smoke grenades to cover themselves as they removed the mines by hand.

As they did, the German garrison on the other side of the river laid down heavy fire on them. Baum was a stubborn and violent marauder, but he wasn't stupid. Getting to Highway 27 meant crossing the bridge, so that was a given, but he wanted to avoid a major battle. His plan was to send tanks in front of us to keep the garrison busy so the rest of the force could get over and get past the Germans. We'd then run like hell to get out of the town.

He put the medium tanks in front, ordered a platoon of infantry to follow them, and gave the signal for everybody to make a sprint for it.

It was a trap.

A garrison of soldiers had been hidden on the task force's side of the bridge, planning to ambush the back end as the front end of the force went across the bridge. They knew how to take advantage of their single-use *panzerfaust*, the German equivalent of our bazookas. Whereas a single GI carried one bazooka in a platoon, German squadrons carried upward of twenty panzerfauste spread among them.

But someone got too anxious. As the lead tank of the task force made it halfway across the bridge, a large anti-tank gun across the river blew it into a ball of flames, followed by the bridge suddenly exploding in a huge cloud of water, concrete, and steel, killing our soldiers, sinking another tank, and leaving nothing but river between the opposing shores.

A minute after beginning our sprint, we had lost two tanks, two officers, and eighteen men. Captain Baum was gushing blood from his knee and hand from the splatter of a panzerfaust explosion. The wounds were serious, but Baum had the medic put on quick bandages and struggled back to his Jeep to grab his map.

The only way to keep going forward was to turn the convoy around and escape up a country road taking us north and connecting to a different route going east. Turning around was not so difficult for half-tracks, but tanks can't maneuver in narrow streets—they would have to reverse up the road, all under the garrison's machine guns.

It took several minutes, most of which had me staying

low behind the armor of my half-track. But when the shooting got quiet, I was finally able to peek over the top to see our convoy running north out of Germunden on a smaller road. We were headed to a small village called Burgsinn, which intersected a mountain road going through a forest, which would turn southeast into the valley of Hammelburg.

Chapter 22

Life in Oflag XIIIB meant unending disease, cold, and hunger. Dysentery was the scourge of POW camps, causing men to have prolonged diarrhea. Forced out of their bunks four or five times a night to relieve themselves in the building with rows of latrine seats, they often didn't make it and left trails of foul-smelling feces along the way.

With only one meal of watery soup a day and sometimes bread, the prisoners endure stunning weight loss, making them shadows of what they had been. Pyorrhea, the degradation of teeth and gums, was induced by the lack of vitamins in the diet and prisoners routinely had their teeth fall out. There was no medication available to relieve bed sores, gangrene, trench foot, swollen joints, rashes, or everyday hurts, nor did they have more powerful medicines needed for wounds.

The cold was an ever-present evil. The small stove in each of the barracks gave off little heat, and the ration of coal or charcoal was meager, causing some prisoners to remove wooden slats from their bunks to burn at night. One officer put together a secret crew to crawl under the barbed wire fence to pillage an empty barracks nearby, gutting the interior to bring back anything that burned.

But it was the hunger, the continuous, gnawing, craving for food, that pervaded every minute of every day. Each barracks might get a ration of dark bread in the morning, one loaf for every five prisoners, or maybe for eight, or for twelve. For supper, there was one bowl of soup, sometimes containing tiny bits of horse meat. Prisoners learned to supplement their soups with anything that could be grabbed or caught—grass, roots, rats, or cockroaches.

The German guards would occasionally distribute Red Cross parcels containing food and tobacco, but it was rare for the parcels to be given directly to individuals. The guards preferred treating the parcels as a common mess, putting all the parcels together and allowing representatives of the prisoners to distribute the contents. The guards would punch holes in any of the canned goods to check for contraband and to prevent hoarding, sometimes causing the contents to spoil before they could be eaten.

Sleep in the oflag was a continuous battle between human bodies and fleas, lice, and bedbugs. Thin mattresses of straw were soaked with sweat, dirt, blood, and waste, making the smell no small obstacle to falling asleep. Searchlights from the guard towers constantly played across the compound, robbing the men of any chance for continuous rest should they fall asleep in the first place.

Men died on a regular basis. Prisoners were forced to dig graves and carry each body in a plain wooden coffin to the hole dug in the ground. At graveside, the body would be taken from the coffin, thrown in the grave, and the prisoners would carry the coffin back to the compound, ready for the next occupant. Burying fifteen men a week was common, twenty not unusual.

. . .

I HAD BEEN awake for two days and felt weariness like I had never experienced, but I was the lucky one. Most of the men in the task force, including Captain Baum, had been pulled directly from combat, having had nothing but short naps in the previous three or four days before being assigned to the mission. Ignoring the maelstrom of noise, shaking, and stink keeping me awake, many fell asleep any moment there was no fighting. Most of them missed the crossing of the small bridge at Burginns, turning us east and puttig us on a small dirt road ten or twelve miles above Hammelburg.

How Baum stayed awake, I'll never know.

The Captain had only an old highway map, forcing him to capture and intimidate local villagers to identify adequate roads for snaking the convoy through the unknown country. The threat of being killed for being a spy or aiding the enemy made it hard for German citizens to cooperate, but a few eventually helped.

General Obstfelder had alerted all military units within a large radius of Hammelburg that the Americans were coming. The town had always been a strategic location, and the countryside was littered with encampments, schools, training grounds, and ranges. By the time Captain Baum saw Hammelburg in the distance, every road leading to it was blocked by somebody dedicated to keeping us from going there.

But we made it. We lost men, tanks, half-tracks, and all our spare fuel, but we were finally crossing a wide field below the oflag, shielding ourselves behind the Shermans as we soldiers warily stepped through the grass. There were small groups of Germans firing at us, but the fighting was less than expected. We kept up a steady fire as we crept forward. Suddenly, the front tank roared up an embankment, broke through the tall fences of barbed wire, and halted inside the POW compound, surrounded by screaming prisoners who couldn't wait to touch something American.

Chapter 23

A second tank veered off and rolled down the line of barbed wire fence making up the camp's front wall, and all firing stopped. The haggard infantry climbed up the embankment to find themselves mobbed by hundreds of prisoners, while the vehicles pulled into a group below.

I wanted to stop and rest and enjoy the elation of those around me, but my own mission was just beginning. During the last eighteen hours, as I was being shot at, screamed at, splattered with blood and bone, terrorized by the noise, the screams, the explosions, and the stench of exhaust and gunpowder, I was cursing myself for being on a violent and chaotic mission without any proof whatsoever that Jake was even there. How could I have been so stupid?

But now I was here, surrounded by frantic bodies with rotting teeth and sunken cheeks, wobbly legs, foul smells, all giving fervent hugs and kisses. I would have been crushed if they had been healthy men, but most were closer to skeletons. One by one, pushing my way through, I got past the crowd and up the line of barracks.

"Jake Gunnarson, Captain, do you know him?"

"Jake Gunnarson, he was a pilot and was shot down a month ago. Is he here?"

"Captain Jacob Gunnarson, a pilot, where can I find him?"

"In the hospital," someone finally said, and my heart skipped a beat. He *was* here! And alive, though I had assumed he'd be out of the hospital by now. It had been a month. I hoped they were wrong, but it was as good a place to start as any. I had only minutes to find him and I set off at a fast trot.

The hospital wasn't hard to find. I made it up the steps in a flash and opened the door. Doctors in surgical smocks, plus a handful of uniformed assistants and most of the patients, stood at the windows, either whooping and yelling or staring in disbelief, stunned at the commotion going on at the other end of the compound.

Jake was lying on a bed opposite the crowd, and I almost screamed. Moving along the beds behind the raucous people at the window, I wondered why my brother wasn't standing and cheering with them, why he was still lying down.

Then I understood. Jake wasn't standing because he had no legs.

I took off my helmet and rubbed at the dirt and exhaust on my face as the man in the bed stared up in disbelief. He must have thought someone was playing a joke on him.

"Hey, big brother," I finally forced myself to say. "You ready to go home?"

His smile was twisted as he shook his head in disbelief.

I struggled to think of something clever to say. "I was in the neighborhood and saw that it was visiting hours."

He started laughing, slowly at first, but then hysterically as his face squeezed into furrows and squints, and he finally broke down in sobs. I moved closer, knelt beside him, and put my face next to his, my tears falling with his. He alternated between wiping his face, pounding my shoulders, and grasping my head. When his shuddering finally quieted down, he took deep breaths as the tears streaming onto his pillow slowed.

He pulled up an edge of his pillow to wipe his eyes. "Well," he finally stuttered as he gave me a last pat on the cheeks as I stood, "you'll have to pardon me for not getting up."

His sheet was draped at the foot of the bed, revealing both of his legs cut off a few inches above the knees. The remaining stumps, a little longer than mid-thigh, were wrapped in bandages stained red, brown, and pale yellow, probably—hopefully—from disinfectant. The bandages stood out against the thin sheets as strange terminators of his body. They looked awkward and misplaced, as my mind imagined the rest of his legs being hidden in a fold of the sheet.

I was embarrassed by Jake's overt emotions but more startled by mine. His sad state shocked me into realizing I hadn't thought about his wounds at all. I still had him as the vibrant, healthy, capable brother I remembered, marvelously resistant to the normal injuries that afflict the young. I might have imagined a broken arm or leg or a head wound from the plane crash, but nothing more.

My naiveté and his missing legs left me gaping. I tried to regain my control by looking away, glancing around the room, pretending to take inventory of what I saw.

The hospital looked old but well-kept. The Geneva Convention required the Red Cross to do inspections, so the Germans kept the hospital presentable by using the slave labor of prisoners. Any shine on the floor came not from polish but from the continuous buffing of rags and water against the wood. Floor wax had gone to war in some other place.

The doctors and assistants, all gowned, appeared professional, as if they knew how to be careful about germs and infections and the spilling of blood. They eyed me suspiciously as I stood next to Jake. I wasn't looking very clean myself and realized I'd left a trail of mud as I walked in.

I felt unsteady, my stomach churning, vomit surging up my esophagus. Some of it was from having just gotten off a roller coaster ride packed with roaring fear, panic, exhaustion, bullets, blood, and death, but most of it was simply the shock of Jake. I forced my eyes downward to look at the blood-tinged bandages around his thighs, then up past his Army-issue underwear and the soiled undershirt exposing his arms as thin and boney. When I focused on his face, I saw his cheeks fallen in and his eyes circled by darkness; he was a ghastly shadow of the brother I once knew. His face was full of pain and despair.

He was silent, his tears beginning again, watching me as I looked at him. There was pity and embarrassment in his eyes for me to see what he had become.

I took a deep breath. "Jake, I've come to take you home."

"Is that what all the commotion is about?" he asked in a choked voice and then blurted out, "The Army has come to save me? We're being liberated? Hot damn! Yeah, get me the hell out of here! I want a beer! Somebody get me a beer!"

I wanted to smile, but I was not yet able. He was trying to be Jake, but it was hollow and forced. "It's true," I said. "We've come a long way and had a hell of a time getting here, but here we are."

I sat on the edge of the bed, he shifting his stumps to the side, and told him a quick month's worth of news about the war, what Patton had done and how he had ordered a task force to come to the camp and bring the officers back. I roughly described the route we'd taken, and the unexpected battles along the way. I ended with a glowing account of him being back in a real hospital, bound for a ship taking him back to England. After that, it would be a short hop home.

His face hardly changed expression. He lay in silence, staring at me. I had been there only minutes, appearing out of nowhere like a spirit of Christmas past, spouting all sorts of rousing proclamations when I finally realized that prisoners of war, above all else, learn to disregard hope.

What his expression did say was that he felt pity and sorrow and an overwhelming tiredness. It wasn't the concept of being liberated—he had hoped for it every day he'd been lying in bed. But now, for him, liberation had a different meaning: even if he were free from the camp, he'd never be free of what he had become.

There was no reason to hurry to get to a life holding so much less.

It was getting dark and I stood to look through the windows. "We've got to get you wrapped up in something and shoot you full of painkillers so you can stand the shaking of the half-track. It took us eighteen hours to get here, and they're refueling right now. We've got to go. I'll carry you. You look like you've lost a lot of weight, so it won't be a problem. I can do it, but we've got to go!"

He took a deep breath and pointed at an old chair across the room.

"Blessed Teddy, pull that over here and sit down. You're making me nervous."

I grabbed the chair and put it next to his bed, but I could hardly sit, turning back and forth, jumping up to glance out the window, rubbing my aching head, impatiently waiting for Jake to grasp the urgency of the situation. We had to get him up and prepped, so I could get him to the half-track before my place was taken. It was a horrifying thought that we might be left behind. We had to go.

"Ted, stop fidgeting. Yeah, you rushed right in here and

you think you're going to rush right back out with all these happy guys. Trust me, it'll take a while. You said you came for three hundred? Well, there are fifteen hundred guys out there who think they're all going home. It will be a while before they find out they're not.

"So," Jake said, "sit down."

I plopped hard onto the seat, leaned forward, and dropped my head into my hands. I was so damned tired. "But, you and I," I said, turning my head to get a kink out of my neck. "That's why I came. I'm taking you home."

Jake shook his head, looked around the room, watched the doctors returning to their patients, and listened to the chatter among the patients and the raised voices outside. "And I appreciate it," he said calmly. "I do. I would like to go home, sure enough. But I wouldn't make it. Even if we had Patton's command car with those little starred flags on the fenders and Hitler himself was sitting in the seat next to us, I wouldn't make it.

"The first reason is, in case you haven't noticed, I don't have any legs. See, when my plane was shot down, she dove right into a tree. It pushed the front of the plane into my lap, trapping my lower legs against the engine. My legs weren't shot off or torn off—they were burned until there was nothing left but charred pieces of bone."

Vomit was working its way into my throat.

"The villagers nearby were upset with my screaming, so they pried the door open and pulled what was left of me out into the dirt. They carried me to somebody, probably the town butcher, who hacked off the burned parts and wrapped me up using some of that stuff they use to wrap cheese in. Some kraut got my flying jacket during all of this, and I hope the bastard takes care of it. The SS came and they at least got me to a first aid station where I got morphine and somebody wrapped my legs with regular bandages.

"When I got here, well, let me tell you these doctors are really good. Can't pronounce their names because they're both from Yugoslavia, so I call them Doc One and Doc Two." Jake pointed down the room. "The tall one is actually a dentist, but he must be a helluva dentist. Anyway, I got here and everything below the knees was a mess of burned skin and muscle and tendons and blood vessels and dirt and shit. Whoever did the hacking must have done it with an axe.

"Both doctors decided it was best to start over, so they amputated above each knee and did it the textbook way, cutting and tucking and tying everything off and then leaving enough skin to wrap around the good part and sewing it up like a cushion. They packed it hard and wrapped it hard, and I've been here ever since. They threw my pants in a fire—there wasn't much left of them—and gave me a new shirt to put on and pants from a sucker who had died on the table, so now I almost look brand new when I put them on.

"They check me every day, change the bandages every now and then, and everything has stayed where it was supposed to. Some of it's even growing together. I've had some infections and a fever or two, but I must be pretty good at not dying.

"Now, that's the good part. The bad part is living in this hellhole. It looks pretty good right now because we had a Red Cross inspection last week. They forced a squad of prisoners to clean and polish the floors. When that's not happening, I'm lucky if I can keep the cockroaches on the floor from crawling in bed with me. We don't get much food here, or medicine, or clean water, or even sterile gauze, except whatever the doctors can trade for with the guards. And way too little morphine! Let me tell you, we ought to sink the family fortune into pharmaceuticals when we get back. Tell ol' Senior to forget about trees and railroads and go for medicine. I'd give a truckload of money right now for an IV of morphine.

"It's tough watching people die. Some of the guys have been in POW camps for two or three years. There's no hope for the human body after treatment like that. Crummy food and not enough of it, while the drinking water usually has something swimming in it. I can smell the latrines when the wind comes out of the south. I never feel good, even ignoring the absence of legs. I hate it here. I'd give anything to get out of this cesspool.

"So, okay, enough crying in my beer. The point is, little brother, I've lost most of my muscles, I'm as shriveled as a prune, and *I ain't got no legs!* I'm not going anywhere."

Chapter 24

It wasn't fair. Captain McCall, back at the ranch school, had spent the early 1900s as a forest ranger in the northern part of Arizona and claimed his experiences had shaped him into all a man should be: resourceful, steady, knowledgeable, skilled in every regard, hard when needed, soft when required, able to be a politician, an elite, a lawman, a pathfinder, and even a wilderness guide. He and his troop of forest rangers were the kind of men who saw new horizons, while having practical souls crafted in every dimension by a life in the great outdoors. He had been their leader, and it was with immense pride that Captain McCall admitted he had been equal to all the tasks he'd encountered.

In my first year at the ranch school, Captain McCall created this game. Well, not so much a game as a challenge. I told you he was big on American frontiersmen like Davy Crockett, Kit Carson, and John Fremont. Well, McCall would have been a lot happier if he'd lived in the early 1800s when most of America was what Lewis and Clark wrote about.

His frontiersmen stories were the foundation for his

outdoor skills training—how to hunt, how to trap, what you could eat in the forest, how to start a fire without matches, how to move through the woods, how to navigate by the stars, how to read a map, how to find water, etcetera. It was mostly about survival, but some of it was simply how to live in the woods.

He came up with this idea: What better way to see if we had been paying attention than to drop us way out in the woods to see how we fared?

It sounded like a jim-dandy idea to him, so he mixed the platoons together to put younger boys with older boys and then divided us into groups of six. We could choose five items to take with us, in addition to our boots, hat, knife, shorts, and poncho, but no flashlight, no tent, no sleeping bag, no compass, no matches—and no food.

He loaded us and our small bags of gear in a truck and drove all over the nearby remote Forest Service roads, periodically depositing each group of six in what seemed to be the deepest wilderness.

Our objective was to make it back to the ranch within three days. It was a good ten miles from every drop point, and the only thing he'd do to help us would be to point in the direction of the ranch when he dropped us off.

And if surviving in nature weren't enough, on the second day, he'd send out Indians to track us down and eat us.

Well, okay, not really. It was just the cowboys from the ranch dressed up like Indians, with warpaint on their faces and feathers stuck in their hats. They'd try to find us, and we'd try to elude them. I actually think they knew where we were all the time, but the illusion was still sobering to a bunch of kids. It was all in good fun and it served its purpose: The skills we had been taught were true survival skills, they weren't learned just to put stars on our report cards.

Of course, Jake took to the challenge like he'd been born to it.

Strong, athletic, a natural leader, outstanding at survival skills—you name it, he had it. His group was never caught and always made it back on time—rested, grinning, and usually with something to eat.

I, on the other hand, was a mid-school fatty, big, awkward, and introverted. I hadn't been through survival training, yet, but enjoyed the experience; the older boys kept me from doing stupid things. We didn't get caught only because the cowboys worked hard at *not* finding us.

I would have gotten good at it if I'd stayed longer. I left the ranch after Jake was dismissed, only participating in the challenge my first year, but the difference between being fourteen and being eighteen is considerable, especially in the mind. By the time I graduated high school back in Minneapolis, I yearned to go back and try it again. I knew I'd make it through this time in great shape, maybe even better than Jake.

When I heard Jake had survived his plane crash, the memories of what I'd learned at the ranch kept coming back to me. I hadn't learned enough to *be* proficient, but I still watched the ones who *were* proficient. From the time I got to the ranch my first year until I left, I'd ridden horses every day, went on camping trips in the high mountains, and learned the basic skills. When I was back in Minnesota, I'd gone on wilderness canoe trips in the Boundary Waters, climbed the highest peak in the state, and sailed on Lake Superior. By the time I graduated, I was eight inches taller, and all the mid-school flab had changed to muscle. A couple of months of Army boot camp and I was in the best shape of my life. Give me three days and I'd make it home from anywhere on the planet.

Fate meant for me to prove my skills. By half-track, by

tank, by Jeep, by escaping my enemy, by whatever it took, I could get Jake back to the American front.

Which is why it was unfair that Jake now refused to even think about my taking him back to the American side of the war. He didn't believe I could handle him and the chaos both, even if we had a few tanks on our side.

But we wouldn't be going back the way we'd come. During our running away from the Germans, I learned Captain Baum's plan. We'd shot at everything coming up Highway 26, causing the German army to lay out every ambush possible to catch us on the way back. But we wouldn't go back on Highway 26, we'd go due south out of Hammelburg, running like crazy to find the Seventh Army. Finding them had to be a lot easier than finding the POW camp. Patton had alerted the Seventh to watch for us, so they'd probably send out advance units to help us make the last few miles.

All Jake and I had to do was get in the damned half-track. If the going got rough and the task force had to leave the vehicles and make a run for it, then Jake and I would set out on our own, just like the frontiersmen had done. I'd strap him on my back and take off into the darkness. It had been fifty miles coming through Schweinheim, but the Seventh Army to the south had been moving toward us. I was sure they'd only be thirty miles away by now, and their advanced units would probably be closer. I could do thirty miles, no sweat. Three nights. Give me three nights and we'd be knocking on Seventh Army headquarters.

Along the way, we'd elude the Germans the same way we'd eluded the Indians.

THE HIGHEST-RANKING POW officer of the oflag was Colonel Paul Goode, and as such, he was considered by the Oflag XIIIB Commandant, General Gunther von Goeckel, to be the officer in charge of the American prisoners. When it was obvious Oflag XIIIB would be overrun by an American task force sent by none other than General George Patton, von Goeckel did an interesting maneuver: He surrendered Oflag XIIIB to Colonel Goode.

The reason lay with the three thousand or so Russian soldiers who were prisoners of war in the enlisted camp. Every German POW camp had a standing order that if the camp were ever threatened with liberation by some foreign force, the commander was to immediately take all of the Russians to a more protected POW camp, preventing any Russian prisoners from being liberated. It was given the highest priority.

As much as the Germans feared General Patton liberating the American officers, they feared more what thousands of freed Russians would do to the German countryside and its inhabitants. It was all wrapped up with Hitler betraying his alliance with Stalin and attacking the Russian homeland, intending to capture it as well as Eastern Europe. Hitler failed, but along the way his army had murdered millions of Russian people, both civilian and military. It caused the Russian people and its army to bear a deep, deep hatred for Germany.

General von Goeckel had been ordered to take the Russians to a POW camp farther to the east, but he needed time to do it and had no spare soldiers to fight off the task force. If the oflag was no longer his, his men wouldn't need to fight the task force and could be used to slip the Russian prisoners out the back door while the Americans were at the front door. He assumed the task force had no interest in liberating the Russians and wouldn't interrupt their being taken away. He also presumed the Americans wouldn't be interested in chasing any of the German soldiers who were slipping away with them. For the four thousand Serbians in the other part of the oflag, he had already given the Serbian royalists the keys to the gun cabinets and told them to manage themselves.

He wouldn't worry about the enlisted Allied soldiers in the stalag, either. Whatever General Patton intended, it could not have included freeing the larger part of the POW compound. Whatever would be left of the task force would not be able to manage the thousands of multinational prisoners who would walk out with them. Additionally, he was sure Patton's goals did not include capturing and holding anything. The task force, at most, had to be a hit-and-run maneuver to free only the officers and take them back to the Allied lines.

All in all, von Goeckel wasn't exactly sure what Patton had intended.

The surrender of Oflag XIIIB was quite a turn of events. Captain Baum, his tanks, and his men, including me, were already shooting at the Germans from below the camp when the commandant made his decision to surrender. It was now up to the Americans in the oflag to tell Captain Baum to stop shooting. Lieutenant Colonel John Waters, Colonel Goode's executive officer, volunteered to carry an American flag raised on a pole and walk toward Captain Baum and the task force to tell them the news.

But not everyone had been informed of the decision, and as Executive Officer Waters and an American contingent were walking through the front gate with their flag, Waters was shot by a young German guard. The bullet broke the bone in his right hip, deflected to chip the end of his backbone, and exited from his left buttock. Several of Waters's friends rushed him to the hospital, where he was immediately put into surgery.

The imminent doctors who had worked on Captain Jacob Gunnarson were now working on a new patient, but this patient had a secret that made him far more valuable than any flyboy from Minnesota.

. . .

I WAS EXHAUSTED. Arguing with Jake was always a depressing experience, especially when he was right. I had planned on his and my going with the task force wherever they went and whenever they were going. Surely, General Patton would never have sent a task force into a place if he hadn't planned on getting them back out again. But having experienced several encounters with an enemy who was surprised by our presence, how much more intense would the fighting be if the Germans had a day or two to prepare for our exit? On their roads? In their country? When they had us surrounded?

What in hell was Patton thinking?

While I was sitting, listening to the increasingly subdued noises outside, glancing up through the window to see the daylight growing dim, watching Jake use a towel to wipe his face and then drink water from a canteen to swallow some pills, a side door opened and two men carried in a stretcher. On the stretcher was John Waters, fresh from surgery. He was still sedated, but the surgery had been successful, and the men took extra care to move him from the stretcher onto the bed two down from Jake.

"That's a good man," Jake said, bending his arm up and placing it beneath his head. "That's Lieutenant Colonel John Waters, the XO for this place. I'm used to dealing with senior officers who have been pilots. We pilots are fundamentally a bunch of sissies when it comes to shooting or stabbing people up close or even hiding in foxholes. It's not in our blood. We'll fly into clouds of shrapnel, drop a bunch of bombs on some city, and then call it a day so we can get back and go find a pub. Getting shot down is always a fear, but you always assume it's going to be some other plane.

"Since I've been here, I've been surrounded by infantry and artillery officers, talking about their jobs and what they did, swapping stories, listening to how people think about themselves, how they got here, what they care about. It's a whole different breed of leadership to command the soldiers working for these guys. It's gotta be tough to order an individual to walk straight toward some-body shooting at them, knowing the probability is always 100 percent that one of you is going to get wounded or die.

"I don't know how to express the difference in the kind of leadership it takes to do that. Different grit, I guess. Maybe different kinds of courage or ruthlessness or plain stupidity for running toward the bullets instead of hunkering down and waiting for the other guy to run out of ammunition.

"Ol' Johnny there was captured while he was fighting down in Africa, two years ago. Two damn years he's been in POW camps! He was the first one to introduce himself when the SS carried my ass in here. Real nice guy for being a looten kernel. He made it a point to ask my name, where I was from, what unit I was in. He was impressed that I was a flyboy in the Pacific before I moved to the Army Air Force. He and I swapped some good—"

Jake suddenly went silent, his face screwing up as if he were thinking hard.

"Well, sonofabitch!" he cried. "You said that General Patton himself ordered up this task force?"

"Yep."

"Well, now, that's mighty interesting. Johnny has been in this place less than a month. He and around eight hundred others came from some POW camp in Poland that was about to be invaded by the Russians. They marched them here hard and fast, from what I understand.

"And didn't you say that the Third Army had just crossed a big river, so they're fifty miles or so from here?"

"Yep." I couldn't see what he was getting at.

"Patton's not particularly famous for liberating POW camps, is he?"

I shrugged. He was famous for running his tanks roughshod over the enemy, but I didn't know anything about his attitude toward POWs.

Jake was chuckling, which made me worry. I hadn't seen anything humorous in quite some time. "There's your reason for the task force," Jake said, pointing at the motionless body. "That man over there is General George S. Patton's son-in-law. He's married to Patton's daughter, Bea."

I must have been more tired than I thought. How'd that guy end up in a POW camp that Patton was liberating?

Oh, shit. It was the other way around. Patton chose to liberate this particular camp so he could get his daughter's husband back on the American side of the fighting. "You're kidding," I said to Jake as I looked carefully at the man. Surely you don't send three hundred men and fifty vehicles fifty miles into enemy territory just to get one particular prisoner."

"Not if you're a three-star commanding general over a hundred-thousand-man army," Jake said. "He's probably been telling his daughter he'd do it if there was ever a chance, while she was probably peeved he hadn't already done it.

"Colonel Waters there told me about George and Bea and what it's like to be in the Patton family. He'd worked his way up through West Point and the various ranks of the military fair and square, so he's earned everything he's got, but I'm sure it never hurt to have a father-in-law named George Patton."

I had to think this out. It didn't seem right to me, but I had just been shot at for eighteen hours. Things might look different if you were a father-in-law directing an entire war and your two-years-in-POW-camps son-in-law is suddenly only fifty miles away. It might have seemed a simple thing to do. It might have even seemed an easy thing to do.

On the outside, maybe even the right thing to do.

There was suddenly the roar of a tank starting up, and a big commotion began at the end of the compound. I stood to watch out the window. It was early evening, dark, but the camp's floodlights had come on, and I could tell what was happening.

Task Force Baum was preparing to leave.

"Sounds like your ride is honking the horn. You'd better get going," Jake said.

I watched the other end of the compound where people had been milling around. The lead tank was backing out of the compound while someone standing up in the back of a Jeep was yelling instructions. I paced back and forth, watching them, wondering what to do. My brain was telling me to get up and get out, go, go, go. I could be out of this mess and back in my nice, warm tent in a couple of days. Back where we hardly touched our rifles, played horseshoes, and had two cooks to prepare hot meals. We had cots to sleep on and would typically make it through the night without a single person trying to kill us.

I even told myself Jake would be okay. He'd stay in the hospital, and someday soon, one of the American armies would waltz right in and take him home. I didn't have to do it. I didn't have to do it. I didn't have to do it.

"Nah," I said, finally leaning my arms against the window sill, watching the tanks and half-tracks lining up, each one crowded with men hanging all over it and a large group of walkers gathering behind. I'd heard Baum had been told he'd have to steal German trucks and gasoline to transport the three hundred prisoners. That might have been possible when George told him to do it, but it wasn't now. The Germans were using everything they had to evacuate the Russians, leaving Baum with nothing.

"Nah. My butt is going to hurt for a week the way it is. If that guy over there is General Patton's son-in-law, then I'm probably in the safest place in Europe right now. I think I'll stick around for a while."

Jake looked up at me without surprise or disappointment. He shook his head, thought about it, and then pointed to a bag under his bed. "Get me my bag, will you?"

I pulled it out and put it where his legs should have been.

Jake struggled to reach it, opened the drawstring on top, and pulled out a rumpled, dirty shirt. The bottom half was covered in grease, burns, and blood stains, but the top was clean enough. It still held his rank insignia.

"Well, if you're bunking next to me, and I don't think the doctors will mind because they'll put you to work, then you need to look like an officer. The attendants are also from Yugoslavia, and they're pickier about protocol than most people. Here, put these on."

He fussed with the shirt and then tossed me his silver captain's bars and an Air Force pin with a set of wings attached to a propeller. I poked the bars into my collar and the set of wings above my pocket.

"Congratulations," Jake said. "You've been promoted."

Chapter 25

The hospital staff immediately put me to work changing sheets, making beds, carrying patients, and mopping the surgical room. I caught a short nap when business slowed down. It took my mind off what was turning out to be quite a predicament.

The task force had spent hours sorting everybody out, getting the wounded treated, giving out various excuses for not taking everybody, fixing vehicles, reloading guns, and finally loading up. Baum had given the POWs the choice of crowding onto the vehicles or walking behind. After he had the vehicles in an acceptable condition and the people ready to follow, they turned the vehicles off and waited for night to come. He hoped to slip away in the darkness.

Through it all, I was busy helping with men wounded by a solitary German soldier who had gotten anxious, crept through the forest, and taken out a tank with a panzerfaust. It was through them that I learned what was going on.

The task force was now an undermanned force going up against a slew of seasoned enemy commanders who held all the cards. Captain Baum didn't know the country, much less the roads, so he sent out tanks and Jeeps to probe the different roads to the south and report back what they found. He wanted to avoid ambushes, roadblocks, direct confrontations, or anything threatening to bottle him up, and he did not want to stop and fight if he could help it.

It took a few hours of precious time for the probes to test out the possible routes for escape, sneak up to observe intersections, and check out any German preparations. It was rough going from the beginning, and regardless of trying to be invisible, every probe was attacked wherever they went. The last road that appeared to be a potential breakthrough point cost a tank because it was ambushed— several German Panzer tanks had been hidden up a hillside.

All the vehicles sent out to probe the area were crippled or destroyed, men were killed or captured, and Baum, at about two in the morning, decided they could not leave during the night. He moved what vehicles and men he had left into a meadow two or three miles west of the oflag to wait for morning. He told the soldiers to drain the fuel from each vehicle and put it into eight half-tracks, plus the remaining tanks. At 0800 hours, Baum would lead the force in a tight cross-country dash, heading south, hoping like hell to find the Seventh Army. He had been ordered to lead the task force back to the American lines and he was going to do it.

Without anyone having to tell them, the mass of prisoners who had convinced themselves to walk behind the vehicles, understood they didn't stand a chance of keeping up. They abandoned the idea and walked back to the camp, Colonel Goode leading them with a white flag so no one would think that Baum was dividing his force. That left only the remaining men of the task force and the POWs who were crammed into the half-tracks or hanging on the outside of the tanks.

At eight the next morning, Captain Abe Baum told a

tank to turn over its engine. An instant later, the meadow erupted in smoke and flames.

Baum's meadow had been a German army training range. For years, every square foot of the area had been mapped, every distance recorded, every feature noted. When the first tank was started and its thunderous roar echoed around the hills, it was the signal for the Hammelburg area commander, Oberst Hoeple, to send a barrage of shells from tanks, mortars, and artillery directly into the vehicles.

The meadow lit up like a field of fireworks, followed by German troops who had been secreted around the area's perimeter. In minutes, every vehicle was disabled or destroyed, and every man was dead or forced to surrender, except for a few who fled into the woods; they were quickly hunted down by dogs. The task force no longer existed. The wounded and captured were soon marched back to Oflag XIIIB, while the dead were piled into trucks.

More wounded were rushed into the infirmary, and the hospital became chaos. Of the two hundred fifty men ready to dash to freedom, only a hundred survived, and all but one of them, including Captain Abraham Baum, had been captured.

Baum was severely wounded, shot in the groin by a grinning German soldier. As he was carried in, German officers were searching for the American who had commanded the force. What they would do with him was uncertain, but the doctor working on Baum took no chances, pulling the armored patches and his rank insignia off his jacket, shirt, and helmet. Baum was written down as a returned prisoner and hidden away in a room where medications were stored. Thankfully, Baum had already tossed away his dog tags, which showed he was Jewish.

I listened to the stories told by the wounded with horror and overwhelming sadness. The task force had failed. If the reason for the task force had been to rescue John Waters, it had not only failed to get him back to the American line, it had also gotten him severely wounded.

As far as I could see, there was only one benefit: the Germans were leaving. The military leadership was sure Hammelburg and the surrounding area were now circled in red on some American General's map—certainly on Patton's, but maybe also on Eisenhower's. This meant the whole damned Allied Army might soon be moving toward Oflag XIIIB.

Believing there was no time to lose, the Germans began vacating the area. By foot, by car, by truck, by train, by any means that could be found, the High Command hurried to move their military resources from the Hammelburg area closer to Berlin. The country around the camp, as well as the camp itself, was not important enough to keep.

Through the windows of the hospital, I watched a mass exodus as vehicles from the countryside crowded onto the roads. The camp itself assembled large formations of non-officer POWs and marched them away under heavy guard. The Russian prisoners, already being evacuated, continued to be ushered out until they were all gone. The Serbians remained where they were.

General von Geockel immediately took back the command of the oflag but had decided not to enforce rules, sanctions, or punishments. He expected the American Army was headed his way, and it would be only a few days before the camp would again be overrun by American tanks. He wanted to look like he had been a gracious host.

It was raining rumors in the hospital. One side said the Germans would eventually slaughter everyone who was left because they'd done it before. Another side said the Commandant and his crew would slip out during the night, abandoning everything and leaving every prisoner inside their enclosures. A third argued there were too many towns in the area to be left without protection, so a heavy battle would ensue whether the High Command wanted it or not.

A fourth believed a train would show up, and everyone who was left, including the wounded American officers, would be loaded on board and sent east to a different oflag. And yet a fifth opinion was that the Germans would just sit down and wait for the Third Army, or the Seventh Army, or whomever, and then surrender. Better to surrender to the Americans than to the Russian Army that was getting closer every day.

No matter the option, with the Germans leaving the area, one of the Allied armies would probably be along shortly. There was no hurry in anybody's mind except mine. Jake wasn't looking any better, and both his stumps were increasingly swollen, maybe from infection, maybe because of the increased load on the doctors, or maybe because of the depletion of medications. Maybe his body was just tired from lying down for a month.

Whatever it was, I made a modified Plan A: strap Jake on my back and make a run for it. Von Goeckel was refusing to show his face in the hospital, and his staff officers were skipping their inspections, so I doubted anyone would notice we were gone.

No one had even bothered to fix the fence torn down by the tank. If everyone who had left with the task force hadn't been able to make a good escape, who would be dumb enough to try it now? Jake and I would have a clear passage out of the oflag.

As for Jake, his legs getting worse made him think he was dying, and damn it, he truly resented the idea of dying as a prisoner of war. It wasn't right. He was a decorated war hero, he'd served in the Pacific, he'd served in Europe, and he'd trained pilots in both places. To him, dying in a hospital bed in a prisoner of war camp was like dying in jail.

If he was going to die, he wanted it to be in a battle where he had a chance to win.

I preached at him long and hard, and he finally agreed to my plan. Using my map, I plotted a southwesterly route that I hoped would get us rescued the soonest. Travel at night, hide during the day, and expect to find the Seventh Army in two, maybe three days. Just like in McCall's challenge.

The doctors objected, of course. They thought Jake would be strong enough to make it, but why risk it? He was certainly strong enough to wait right where he was, so why make so much effort for something that was likely to fail?

I'll admit I made a bad decision, but I wanted desperately to be the one to rescue Jake. That's what a good brother would do, and maybe it would be a little payback for McCall.

When I refused to budge and Jake got behind the idea, the doctors gave up and accepted that we wanted to die. They rebandaged Jake's legs, plugged him into an IV to get him hydrated, and gave me a handful of disposable syrettes of morphine, some sulfa packets and a double-handful of clean bandages. They found him a cleaner undershirt, a dress shirt without holes in it, a combat jacket, and then helped fashion a sling out of a bedsheet. It wrapped around Jake's butt, tied around my waist, circled up and over his back, and then hung from my shoulders like a backpack. It didn't feel that uncomfortable. He hardly weighed anything at all, he felt snug against me, and I was reasonably maneuverable. It hurt him to splay his legs out, but there was only so much that could be done.

We'd leave as soon as it got dark. I had a good sleep the night before and napped a couple of times, so I felt as physically ready as I could get. Mentally, not so much. I had argued with myself all day. Watching the frayed ends of the task force drift through the hospital, I struggled to squash my fears, finally convincing myself it was the only thing to do. Once convinced, a feeling of assured victory and expected euphoria flowed in me, and I was ready.

My weakest moment was when I stepped over the downed barbed wire of the front fence and scrambled down into the field. As I settled into a good pace, I thought of Jake reaching down and helping Lilly up and onto the back of his saddle.

Chapter 26

The moon didn't give enough light to keep me from stumbling over rocks and roots, but Jake was easy to balance and I plodded my way down the fields and along the drainages of the valley to work ourselves out of the military ranges and into a countryside crisscrossed by fences.

The sling left Jake's arms free. Putting them around my neck or grabbing onto my shoulders allowed him to lift himself and relieve the pressure on his butt and backbone. I had folded a wool blanket and stuck it between us as an added cushion. In a rucksack hanging off Jake's shoulders, we had food from Red Cross parcels given to us at the hospital, three handfuls of D rations, a couple of rolls of gauze bandages, and two canteens of water. Centered on my chest, I carried a bag holding the map, a compass, a flashlight, the sulfa packets, and the morphine syrettes.

We didn't carry a weapon. Not only would a pistol or a rifle been heavy and awkward, but having either meant we expected to fight our way out of something. Jake and I had agreed that fighting would be useless. If we were found by German soldiers, it would be better to surrender and hope we would be returned to the camp. I also left my helmet behind. Jake refused to leave his pilot's hat, so I stuffed it in the rucksack. To keep our heads covered and warm, we both wore Army-issue wool stocking caps. It was another attempt to look non-combatant.

Fully convinced we'd find American troops to the south, I planned our route to take us a maximum of thirty miles over three days. But even with fewer German soldiers in the countryside, we couldn't take the risk of being discovered. We couldn't walk through open fields or close to roads and especially had to avoid houses and such, so our strategy was to walk on the outside edge of the fields and pastures, typically right along the edge of the forest. Staying close to the forest also helped us hide within its shadows. We felt safe enough, but the number of steps probably tripled over what we would have walked along a road.

It didn't take long before Jake felt heavier each hour, making my steps slower. As enthusiastic and positive as I had been, my strength wasn't lasting as long as I'd expected, not to mention that once my back began to hurt, the aches became unrelenting. He was my brother and not a sack of potatoes, but I was still hurting.

But as many aches as I had, Jake had more. Uncomfortable even without doing anything, his joints were killing him. He'd been lying in a bed for a month, not using his back muscles or arm muscles and especially not flexing his pelvis. His thighs were splayed out around my waist, the wounds pulled and pushed and pinched against his bandages, his butt sagged, and the edge of the sheet cut into his hips, not to mention that everything was constantly being jostled by my movements. He tried not to complain, as did I, but we were both throbbing with pain after only a few hours of walking.

We gritted our teeth, kept going, and finally stumbled to a stop when we detected a glow on the horizon. We were at the top of a field next to a line of bordering trees. Finding a flat spot, I sat down as softly as I could, leaned back, lowered the sheet off of my shoulders, and let Jake unwrap himself. I carefully untied my waist-band and then rolled over onto my face. Every muscle I had felt like an open wound.

Jake lay on his back, groaning as his body had yet another new position to adjust to. We suffered in silence until he finally looked over at me. "You okay there, Chief?"

I flopped onto my back, not sure if my muscles were still attached to my bones, and stretched whatever I could feel. "Remember when we got into arguments when we were kids and I accused you of riding my ass too much? Well, I had no idea."

Jake laughed, but it came out as a series of half-moans. He was lifting his stumps up into the air, swinging them back and forth, up and down, then working his arms and shoulders. "How far do you think we've come?"

I guessed we were eight miles south of the oflag, though I must have walked almost twenty.

"What do we do now?"

I wanted to do nothing but lie there. However, the morning light was growing, and I needed to get us hidden. The bunched vegetation between the field and the forest was dense, but going in under the tree branches three or four feet, the thickness of the leaves, dirt, and loam had kept the build-up from reaching the forest floor. Wrapping the blanket around me to wade through the mess, I found a nearby patch of ground where Jake and I could lie down for the day. No one in his right mind traveled through this stuff without using trails, so our hiding place seemed well concealed from innocent intruders.

Jake, the sling, the blanket, my chest pouch, and the rucksack were soon nestled beneath the tree limbs. I had gathered enough leaves together to give us a cushioned bed. I would have preferred to lie on the blanket, but we needed it to pull over us during the day time. Even with the thick forest around us, we couldn't risk not having camouflage.

Another session of exhausted stretching followed. While I groaned, Jake propped himself up with the knapsack and watched the sunlight flood the forest as he devoured some of our rations. He put the sling and rucksack between us, took out a syrette and gave himself a dose, straightened the blanket over the two of us, threw leaves on top to blend us in, and then pulled it over our heads.

Worn out, I slept until late afternoon, almost ten hours. Finally, the aches and pains tortured my body beyond what I could stand and I opened my eyes. Pushing the blanket off, and stretching as I rolled silently side to side, I brought my legs to a bent position to relieve my back pains. After a minute or two, I lay still and listened to Jake's fitful sleep. His breathing was labored, and I could see sweat on his forehead. I was sure he was hurting worse than I was.

With the map as a guide, I now guessed it might be four nights of travel before we got to Allied territory, a day more than I had planned for.

What if the Seventh had moved southeast, away from us instead of toward us? What if the German defenses had held? If I was already worn out, how many more nights would I last? Did we bring enough food for four nights? Somebody my size doesn't make a good thief, so it would be hard to steal food. What about finding water?

What if we were caught? What if I was killed and Jake was not? Would he be cared for, executed, or tortured? I thought of some Nazi jerk tying him to a tree limb by his hands and walking away. I hoped I would already be dead because I'm not sure I could have lived with that.

We could still turn back. It would take one night to get back to the oflag, and we wouldn't have to stay in the forests since we knew the German army had left. Back in the hospital, Jake could rest all he wanted.

"Don't even think about it."

I turned my head to see Jake looking at me. "What?"

"I can see it in your expression. Besides, big brothers always know what their little brothers are thinking. You were thinking we should turn back."

I admitted he was right, but how did he know? On the other hand, he always won whenever we played cards, so maybe he had intuition and I had the face of Dumbo. "We could make it back by morning, you know. We wouldn't have to stay in the trees and we would go faster. Once back, we could sit around—uh, lie around—and wait to be liberated like everybody else."

"Forget it. I'm not going to die in some kraut prisoner-of-war camp and get thrown into some grave on top of somebody else's putrid body. Piss on 'em."

"Well, you're not going to die in any case because you're too damned stubborn. How are you feeling, anyway? You got a fever?"

He relaxed his head against the leaves. "Ah, I'm all right, though I could really use a shot of bourbon."

I sat up, grabbed my chest bag, and pulled out a syrette. "I've got some bourbon right here. Leg or ass?" He moved his right stump toward me, and I stuck it through his pant leg and squeezed. I recapped the syrette and put it back into the bag. No reason for leaving something for the search dogs to find.

Jake took some deep breaths, whispered "Oh, yeah," and drifted back to sleep.

I listened as his labored breathing smoothed out and then gobbled down a meal bar and the remaining water in my canteen. I lay back in the leaves and tried to think about things a little longer. We had passed no houses, only a few pastures, and one or two dirt roads but according to the map, we'd soon be crossing a highway and then a stream. The highway I didn't worry about. We had seen no traffic the night before, so the darkness of night should give us all the cover we needed. The stream, however, would be different.

Trying to wade or swim would be impossible, coupled as we were, and I wanted to avoid getting wet. It was cold enough without also being soaked. That meant we needed a bridge, and bridges were typically located inside towns. I had no strategy for handling towns, other than avoiding them.

We'd have to be creative when the time came.

Chapter 27

I had carried our gear and Jake out of the trees before I laid him on the sling, tilted my back on top of him, put my arms through the improvised sleeves, tied the waist cinch, and rolled over so my front was on the ground. That pulled him onto my back. I carefully pushed myself onto my hands and knees, grabbed a limb, and stood up.

I felt like I'd put on a walrus. I handed him the rucksack to wear, took a deep breath, and stepped off downhill as I again adjusted to walking in the darkness. The sleep and idle time had gotten me out of my depressed thoughts, and I again felt like I could accomplish what I'd set out to do. I had sucked up a couple of cans of pretend-meat and some kind of dried fruit, and if I could ignore feeling like I'd been whipped with chains, I was ready.

A couple of miles should get us to the road, and the stream a mile farther. The map was only a road guide and didn't show houses or farms or anything, or topographical features. It didn't much matter, as we'd be back following the tree line, no matter what.

Okay, eight more miles, maybe ten. Move silently, move quickly, don't give up.

. . .

IT WASN'T an hour before I felt my energy draining away.

"Tell me a story."

"What?"

"Tell me a story. Listening to you will help me keep my mind off feeling stupid."

"What kind of story do you want?"

"I don't know. A world traveler like yourself must have lots of stories. Didn't Mom tell me that you destroyed the entire Japanese navy?"

Jake chuckled. "I wish. I did bomb a Japanese carrier during the battle of Midway, though. You know anything about the battle of Midway?"

"Genuinely nothing. I was paying attention to other things."

"Everybody thinks the Navy was out sailing around for the day, found the Japanese fleet, sent over some dive bombers, and destroyed them all. It was actually a lot more complicated.

"Admiral Yamamoto, the guy who attacked Pearl Harbor, regretted not getting more of the Pacific fleet when he had the chance, so he thought about trying it again a year later, in 1942. Hitting Pearl again wasn't going to work, so he chose Midway Island. Midway is between Pearl and Tokyo and had become one of our most important military bases. We had a lot of facilities there, a good harbor, lots of supplies, a great runway, and a submarine base.

"Yamamoto figured if he took Midway, the US Navy would send all of its ships to get it back, and when they did, he'd ambush us with the Japanese fleet and wipe out everything we'd sent.

"Not a bad plan, but he didn't know we'd broken the secret Japanese communication code and were listening to everything he was planning. In the early morning of June 4

—this is in 1942, remember, two years before D-Day—one of the main Japanese carriers has moved into position and sends fighters and bombers to attack the island. The US fighters are already in the sky, waiting for them. Our boys took out more than half of everything the Japanese carrier had sent.

"Then we got lucky. A Japanese scout plane sees one of our carriers and radios back to his carrier, the one that just launched the planes to attack the island. Should the carrier commander continue to focus on his attack on Midway, or should he send his reserve aircraft to bomb our carrier?

"His problem is this: The reserve aircraft are equipped for bombing the island, but attacking a carrier requires different bombs, so all the planes would have to be unloaded and then rearmed. That takes at least an hour and a half. Well, the commander hesitates, then hesitates some more, and then decides to attack the carrier. He orders all the planes to be rearmed, which means he had no planes to defend his own carrier.

"However, because he had read the messages, Nimitz knew the day before that the Japanese fleet was attacking and had sent out search planes to find the specific locations of all four of the big Japanese naval groups. Rear Admiral Fletcher, head of the task force that includes the carrier *Yorktown*, knows where all the Japanese ships are, so he launches his carriers' aircraft against not only the Jap carrier that had already attacked Midway, but all the others as well."

"Do I need to be writing this down?" I asked. I was starting to sound like a locomotive going up the incline of a small hill.

"Sorry," Jake said with a small laugh. "I love talking about the strategies involved. Let me jump to the end.

"When the Japs attacked Midway, they had been at war since the end of the 1930s. Since Pearl Harbor, their Navy had essentially been out on the ocean the whole time. Their ships are getting old, they can't replace their ships like they need to, they can't replace their planes like they need to, and they especially can't replace their pilots like they need to.

"When a reconnaissance plane found a carrier of ours, they didn't have enough recon planes to find the rest. The attack planes sent to Midway were running out of fuel when they tried to return and were ditching in the ocean. They were using old techniques to manage their aircraft attacks, and the fighters they did use were low on ammunition.

"The Japanese fleet was essentially hobbled, and when you throw in the hesitation of the carrier commander, who has suddenly allowed his carrier to be unprotected, you can see that the US fleet is finally catching a big break.

"Two squadrons from the *Enterprise* split up to attack two carriers, the *Kaga* and the *Akagi*. We catch them while they're fueling fighters on deck, so the Kaga is set completely on fire. *Akagi* is hit with only one bomb, but it goes directly down an elevator shaft and blows up the aircraft below deck. They had already been loaded with their bombs, so a bunch of them explode as well, and it cripples the whole ship.

"Meanwhile, planes from the *Yorktown* attack a third carrier named *Soryu*, and *Enterprise*, late that afternoon, takes down a fourth, the *Hiryu*. During the next few days, we sink a few more destroyers and heavy cruisers. We had, in one battle, destroyed a significant part of the Japanese navy."

"So, were you eating donuts all this time? Sitting it out with the boys back in the coffee room?"

I could feel Jake's whole body grin. "I was hoping you'd ask. Remember I said it took only one bomb to destroy the *Akagi*? Well, that one was mine. I dropped it right down their throats. It was pretty much accidental, of course, but I forgot to mention it when I made my report."

It was my turn to laugh. "A hero after all!" I said with a low voice. "So why in the world did you want to get out of the Navy?"

"Oh, well, I didn't for a year. When I dropped that bomb, I was a fledgling pilot who had been there for only a couple of months. But when it hit, I was suddenly hot stuff with immense talent, and they assigned me to train pilots. I was flying high, and all that glory went to my head.

"But here's the deal. I didn't tell you about the attack that occurred the day *before* the Japs hit Midway. A PBY, that's a plane made to land on water—big sucker—spotted the Japanese transport ships carrying the troops meant to occupy Midway. They notified the airfield at Midway and the airfield launched a bunch of fighters, dive bombers, and nineteen B-17s to find those ships and send them to the bottom of the ocean. When they found them, the B-17s dropped their bomb loads and reported that they hit four ships.

"But they didn't. The pilots of the other aircraft around them reported that not a single B-17 hit anything. I had flown a B-17 during summer training at an Army Air Force base in California and loved it. It fit me like a glove. I saw it as the biggest weapon we had in the US arsenal for long-range bombing. Sending nineteen of them up—*nineteen* of the damned things—and not one of them hitting what they were aiming at just pissed me off. Not only could they not deliver their payloads, they couldn't even tell the difference between a hit and a miss.

"I knew the Allies in England were ramping up the bombing of Europe, and I thought that if the B-17 pilots in my part of the ocean were missing their targets, a lot of American foot soldiers were going to die because the pilots above them couldn't hit their targets. Right then and there, I decided that if I ever got the chance, I'd quit flying small planes in the Navy and go teach the Army Air Force guys to fly the big ones.

"It took me a year to get up the courage to leave what I had grown to love, but I finally found an opening. By the way, going from the Navy to the Army was not easy for a simple, low-life flyboy like me. Guess who made it happen?"

I had to think for a moment and then I grinned from ear to ear.

"Is he kind of fat?"

Jake laughed a good and honest laugh. "Yup! I got ol' Junior involved. That guy may be worthless outside a boardroom, but he does have contacts. A couple of months after I asked him if he could make it happen, I'm shaking my Commander's hand and flying to the other side of the globe."

Listening to Jake helped keep me going forward. It was good to hear him talk again. It had been a long time since we'd been alone together. He must have known how messed up I was when he was kicked out of the ranch school. I had missed him terribly, and I wasn't going to stay there without him. I wished Jake had never met Lilly.

Until I met Margie. Then I understood that being smitten takes matters out of your hands and scrambles your brain.

I kept my eyes on the ground and the surrounding area, my feet plodding ahead in a good rhythm and my breathing controlled, while Jake told me more war stories. Some of them were hilarious. He must have been an incredible instructor, and I bet every pilot he trained thought he was the greatest pilot ever.

In a couple of hours, I found a short rock wall and sat down for a breather.

"Okay, your turn," Jake said. "You're not working very hard. You tell me a story."

I huffed a short laugh. "I don't have any stories."

"Ah, come on. Everybody over here has something to tell."

"Not me. I'm just a flat-footed GI who spent a year in England, missed D-Day, runs away from any real combat, does the same thing over and over every day, and then plays horseshoes when things are quiet. I'm not like you. I'm a technician, not a soldier. I just watch blips on a screen."

"Well, pardon me, Sad Sack, but some of those blips were the Luftwaffe trying to blow my ass out of the sky, so you saved me plenty of times."

I laughed quietly. "Okay, so my blips meant something. But you know, just between me and you, I wish I had landed at Omaha on D-Day."

"Are you kidding me?" he said. "You'd have to be nuts to want that! Remember the ocean turning red with blood? I saw some of the footage they used to train the Marines to make amphibious landings in the Pacific and Omaha Beach was a bloodbath."

"Oh, I know. I would have been face down in the water a few seconds after running down the ramp of a Higgins Boat. But still, going down the ramp is something people are going to talk about for years. I might have been killed, but people would remember me dying for something. That ramp was hero business.

"What you don't realize, Jake, is that your career has been hero business. Chasing carriers, stopping invasions, shooting down planes, teaching pilots and bomber crews, dropping bombs in spite of clouds of flak around you— that's all hero business. And God bless you, by the way, and all your buddies.

"I'm not cut out for the grind of war. I've tried to understand it and why people in the world seem to be so anxious to be in one. I'm not a warrior and I don't like things that don't make sense. I've been staring at little blips on a green screen for almost a year. There were some exceptions where I got close to the front, but I never even pulled a trigger until I machine-gunned a truck full of teenaged girls. This war is going to be over one of these days, and I'll get my participation medal and maybe a service bar or two, and then I'll go home and have to tell my kids that the only enemy I ever shot was a bunch of women."

"Well, damn it, don't tell them that part," Jake said, growing gruff. "What have you got to be so bitter about? You're smarter than the rest of us and are protecting guys like me, as well as a few thousand more on the front who would have seen a lot more bullets and shells coming their way if you hadn't helped them shoot down enemy planes, or destroy artillery, or take out a few mortars. The air war has let us win this thing, shithead, and your part helped make it happen."

It was time to get going again. It took a lot of energy to argue with Jake, and I don't think he understood what I was saying anyway. I wasn't sure I knew what I was saying, either. "I'm sorry. I don't mean to be morose or disappointed, and I especially don't mean to be ungrateful for all the bodies I've stepped over getting here. I just wish I had stories like yours."

"Yeah, well, I wish I had a couple of legs."

WE HANDLED the highway crossing with no problem, but the stream forced us to make a decision. It was maybe twenty feet wide where we first approached it and it looked like it had a mild current. I used a stick to judge the depth, and it was at least a couple of feet deep close to the bank, meaning it would be deeper farther out. Too deep for us to wade, too far across to attempt swimming.

The countryside on the other side of the river looked like stretches of level fields separated by fences or stands of trees, and narrow farm roads with occasional houses. We must have worked our way into a valley, which was welcome, with more inhabitants, which weren't welcome, and no forest-covered hills we could fade into, which might be fatal. There was enough moonlight to highlight a tall church steeple in a village to our right, a couple of miles or so away, but the village was dark and opaque. We couldn't see if the river ran through the town, but there had to be a bridge either in the town or next to it. The question was how in the world would we negotiate a town without being seen.

I knelt on my hands and knees beside the stream while Jake reached over and filled our canteens. We drank as much as we could, refilled them, and then checked the map again. We could continue south or even veer west, putting us out in the open as we crossed the valley. We could see a dotting of trees bordering the fields, so we knew we could use them for cover, but we'd have to time our movements to not be out in the open when dawn came.

"We could go back to the forest and work our way farther east, hoping for the valley to narrow," I said in a low voice.

"We could," Jake replied. "That's opposite of where we want to go."

As he talked, he was breathing hard. At the beginning of our journey, I could feel his muscles and arms and hands as he alternated hanging on, or turning, or tightening up to flex his butt or shoulders, or moving to be closer to my head if I said something. Lately, I hadn't felt anything more than his thighs quivering against my back. He was getting worn out.

"You need another shot?"

"Well, gosh, if you really want me to have one," he said as he suddenly braced himself against the bottom of the sling and reached over my shoulder to get into the bag on my chest. He twisted the cap off a syrette and shoved the needle into his thigh.

We both waited until his quivering subsided and he sagged a little deeper in the sling.

"Man," he said as he rested his head against my neck,

"forget the damned trees and go for drugs. Let's keep going. There's nothing east that's going to get us closer to home."

I turned along the river bank, following the downstream flow, hoping it would take us westward to some kind of crossing before we reached the village. We moved around some brush, up through an open gate, and a few hundred yards farther until we came upon a stone cottage. The house backed up against the stream with a waist-high stone wall running at a right angle from the stream out a hundred feet or so to the road we had crossed a while back.

I crouched behind the wall to stay out of sight, put my hands on my knees, and slowly crept along, finally making it to the end of the wall. Turning ninety degrees, it followed the road along the front yard of the house. It was a solid wall, sometimes covered with vines, and if we followed it, there might have been enough vegetation covering it to blend against the stones. Jake's sling, however, as dirty as it was, would still show up in anyone's headlights.

We chose a second option: crossing to the other side of the road and hunkering down in a drainage ditch running alongside. It wasn't more than a yard deep, but if a vehicle came along, I could squat down and the night would hide us. It seemed the best choice.

I had begun steadily walking the ditch bottom when a dog started barking.

It was already difficult to hunker down while carrying a hundred pounds, but I probably set a new Olympic record for the hunkered-down dash in the next five minutes. I still don't know where that dog was, but it never stopped barking until we couldn't hear it anymore. I tore down that ditch like my ass was on fire, and I bet I shook some of Jake's teeth out. It scared the crap out of both of us, but by the time I collapsed, gasping, he was laughing hysterically.

"Let's not do that again," was all he could manage to say.

Dashing down the road's drainage ditch had unexpect-edly led us to an intersection with a smaller dirt road with a wooden one-lane bridge over the stream. We had seen no one, and except for the dog, had found the area empty. We quickly staggered down the middle of the bridge, feeling like we owned it. When we cut away from the road and continued cross country, I noticed that Jake's pants were soaked with fresh blood. His sutures must have torn during my sprint.

"We need to rewrap your bandages," I said.

"Yeah, well, it doesn't look too bad. Let's find camp first."

"Okay, but I think we've earned an early quit for the night. Let's cross a couple of fields and then I'll find us some place to settle down."

The next hour was a slow trudge across a field with culti-vated rows of what looked like winter wheat, followed by a short grass prairie. The moon was covered by clouds, and nothing could have seen us. It made for much better walk-ing, and I was able to straighten up and stretch into a better stride. The stands of trees along the borders of the fields were more substantial than what we had first thought, so it was easy to find a good enough stopping place.

We made it. The second night of our journey was over.

Chapter 28

"We're doing well," I said. "Not a single Indian has tried to eat us."

Jake gave a halfhearted chuckle followed by a cough. Our camp for the day was in a stand of trees off to the side of a field with only a single house in the distance. The clutter up against the tree line was thinner than the day before, and I pushed limbs out of the way until I made it to a small clearing next to a thicket. I carried Jake in. Using my hand to sweep aside a layer of loose dirt and rotted leaves, I spread out the sling and scooted Jake on top. He held his hand over the flashlight so that it lit only what was below his waist.

At the hospital, after wrapping bandages around his legs, the doctors had pulled on his pants and then folded each of the trouser legs up and under the belt until the cuffs could be folded over and secured with big safety pins. It made a protective pad under the wraps, but it also made the folded pants a perfect catch basin for blood.

I undid the safety pins and flopped his pant legs down. Pulling his pants off, and using them as pad under his stumps, I gently unwound the bandages. His wounds had opened, as I'd feared. The large flaps of skin had scrunched to one side, exposing the sutures on the muscles, blood vessels, and ligaments. It looked awful, but the smell was worse.

Don't ask me what a good wound smells like, but this one smelled sour. I was afraid another infection might be setting in.

I gave him a dose of morphine, waited a moment for his pain to subside, and then cleaned the wounds as best I could. It was a bloody mess, and I had to turn my head and take deep breaths to fight the nausea welling up in my throat. After getting him tidied up, I shook sulfa powder over the stumps, rewrapped them with clean gauze and our extra bandages, and tied everything tightly, hoping to pressure off the seeping blood. I used the old bandages to scrape and rub the blood from the insides of his pant legs and slid them back on, pinning everything back into position.

Jake had been grimacing on and off as I cleaned him up. When I was done, he leaned back, exhausted. When we came to the next stream or river, I'd wash the old bandages and get them ready to use again. If we camped close to water, I'd wash his pants, the sling, and try to get some of the blood off my own clothes. Until then, we'd both have to put up with the stiffness, the smell, and the muck.

We both ate something and then found ourselves tired, but not sleepy. We had trekked about six hours and still had a couple of hours before dawn. I spread the blanket over us while Jake bunched the rucksack under his head. I shifted myself closer to the curve of a tree so I could lean against it, then pulled him up beside me. I'd had enough of lying flat.

"Okay, Willie," Jake said in a low voice. "You don't have stories. But you have to have memories, right? You been here how long, eight or nine months?"

"Nine from the beach. A year and a half in Florida and England."

"Okay, well, there ya go. You have to have some memories of things that happened to you. If you won't tell me stories, tell me memories. What do you remember most from the time you left home?"

He still wasn't getting my anguish. It wasn't glimpses of things that were bothering me most, it was the increasing day-to-day progressions of depressed feelings keeping me disoriented. Maybe I was losing my mind. I wasn't a soldier, and I certainly hadn't become a professional killer. Maybe I was embarrassed by all the dead bodies I kept seeing, thinking that every one of them could have been me.

"Well, okay, here's one. I was in London on a five-day pass. I had two guys with me and we'd been taking in the usual sites, but on the way out of town, we put up at a small tavern that rented rooms above it. The owner and his wife were both in their seventies. They'd owned the tavern and the inn for most of their lives. They had two sons, one in the RAF and the other in the Coast Guard, and several grand-children. The wife served the tables while the husband and a couple of cooks kept the kitchen going. A couple of grand-daughters helped out with cleaning the rooms upstairs. The tavern was a favorite around the neighborhood, so it was always busy.

"The husband took off before midnight every night and reported to the Home Guard, spending the night helping people into shelters if the sirens went off. He returned home at sun up, slept until ten, and then went back to work in the kitchen. His wife closed the tavern at midnight, went to bed, slept six hours, and then got up to cook breakfast. The two of them continued the rest of the day and evening. They did it every day of the week.

"They had to do this because the war took their sons away. But they hated no one. They didn't even resent working so hard. Even so, they just got by. So, even with all the work, all the restrictions, and all the worry about the dangers their sons faced, they didn't have a mean bone in their bodies. They just made do with what they had.

"They sounded happy enough. They never doubted England would win the war, that righteousness would prevail, and that living their lives the way they did was service to the king and queen. I want to say they had faith, but faith implies they had made some decision along the way. There was no decision point for them; their conviction was ingrained in them. In the hard times, and during the Blitz when it was *very* hard times, they simply endured. They endured with grace.

"Most of the Britishers I met were like them. You and I were raised to think we had to negotiate our place in the world, to find what we wanted and to take it, to make things happen, and if we got it, we deserved it. If someone got in our way, then we went over them. This old couple wouldn't have understood that attitude. They accepted who they were, what they had, what they did, and how they did it, and it gave them a peace I still don't understand.

"Here's another one. When my unit drove out of the belly of the landing ship at the beach, we were directed to a large waiting area. The area had been created for the unloaded vehicles because there was only a single road we could use to get onto the highways above. Our beachhead was miles long and there were dozens of other LSTs letting vehicles out. Two troop ships were unloading, and a dozen Duckies were going to and from various ships that were unloading away from the shore. All sorts of stuff had been sorted into different piles as it waited to be moved to storage places inland. It was a circus, and the beach master's crews were working their butts off.

"It looked like it would be a while before we'd be called to go up, so I got out and walked over to something I had spotted up near the bluffs. Did you know there was a big storm during the last part of June? A big, bad storm, the worst in years. It destroyed the two harbors that the engineers had built out of the caissons towed over from England. Anyway, the storm beat the devil out of the beach, and the surf got up to the bottom of the bluffs. When it did, it washed a lot of stuff up from the sea floor that had been lost on D-Day and the days after.

"Okay, well, the storm whipped all that stuff up, plus the usual seashells and sand, and created a bathtub ring along the shore. I saw something sticking out of the mess. I walked over and found a banjo. It was mostly covered by sand, but the strings were still on it. I pulled it out and shook the sand off.

"That somebody would jump into a war with a banjo strapped to his back just struck me as funny. Some guy expected there would be time left over from killing people so he could play his banjo. Amazing. Maybe he'd carried his banjo with him into other wars, but I can't get away from thinking that soldiers are supposed to be consumed by war, that they get sucked up into something making a mess of them on the inside, and they have to change into monsters to get through a war in one piece. But I don't see monsters playing banjos at the end of the day. I don't understand.

"I walked farther along the mess and found clothes, rucksacks, books, maps, the little Bibles the chaplains handed out, postcards, broken rifles, weatherproofing used to protect guns, rusted knives, a soccer ball, boots, photographs, a checkerboard, helmets, helmet liners, glasses, goggles—all covered by little sand crabs scurrying around. I picked up a pocket notebook in an oilskin envelope and looked through it. It was some GI's address book. It must have had a hundred entries. How many people was he going to write?

"That's what I remember of my first day in the war."

I couldn't see Jake's face in the darkness and thought I'd gone on long enough that he was asleep. He wasn't.

"I never saw any stuff like that," he finally said. "I made everybody else have memories. I never saw anything but fire and smoke and shit in the air from twenty-five thousand feet."

"There was another time I remember," I said, suddenly rushing to tell more. "I told you about working for a Grave Registration Unit and digging the frozen bodies out of the mud at Bastogne? That wasn't all I did.

"Everything was a mad house, it was freezing, and there was snow and ice all over everything, but there were enough radar people to cover me, so I volunteered to drive an ambulance. I thought I'd make more of a difference working with them than watching blips.

"They gave me a three-quarter-ton hard-shell ambulance that still had blood all over the floor in the back. I made several trips back and forth down muddy backcountry roads and cow paths to get to infantry units on the front or close to it. I did that for three or four days.

"What I remember is pulling up next to aid stations in buildings with half the roof missing, or with only two walls left standing, or another one with just a bunch of tarps stretched between apple trees in an orchard. The ground was shaking from artillery and the noise was deafening, but in the midst of it, bundled-up medics were patching wounds, putting on tourniquets, tying slings on arms, moving live bodies onto their tables, or dead bodies off of them. Everybody was standing in mud and I bet their toes were frozen, but they kept on working.

"Everyone I saw, talked to, or helped was dirty, hungry, exhausted, cold, scared, and sometimes wounded, but not one of them was a quitter. But it was their job, and those guys kept on moving. They thought that if they didn't go forward and kill the enemy then we wouldn't win the war. I'd take the wounded infantrymen from the medics, help lift them into the ambulance, and rush them back to the hospital. And the next day, those same guys would be wrapped up in bandages, standing out front, limping, or with their arms in slings, flagging me down, asking me to take them back to the front, back to the bullets and blood, back to people dying."

I started to sob and suddenly couldn't control myself.

"WhydtheywantmetotakeembackJake?Why?"

Jake was grabbing my arm. "Okay, okay, settle down. I'm listening. You're telling me, okay?"

"TheywantedmetotakeembackJake. Ididntwantto! Theyweregonnadie!"

Jake's covered my mouth with his hand. "All right, you don't need to shout. I'm right here."

"WhydtheywannagobackJake?   Nothingbacktherebutdeath!"

"Okay, little brother," he soothed. "Settle down." He held me as I wept. "I had pilots who kept signing up for Germany missions. People do that. Some people do that."

"I don't understand," I said, trying to calm my breathing. "They were wounded, they coulda just gone home, just gone home. Why didn't they wanna go home?"

A cowbell began clanking in the distance, meaning some farmer was moving his cows in for milking.

"Let's get some sleep, okay, little brother? We're pretty tired, so we should sleep, okay?"

Yeah, okay, okay. Sleep sounded good. I felt a prick in my arm and watched Jake squeeze a syrette.

Yeah. Okay.

Chapter 29

The cushion of leaves didn't last long. My butt was freezing against the hard ground for most of the day, but I was feeling better. We slept on and off during the morning and afternoon. I was able to turn and stretch and shake out some of the hurt, while Jake could only move his arms and neck and twist his torso to stifle his pain. He tried rolling over onto his front, but he almost fainted from the pain of his spine suddenly bending opposite from what it was used to.

His pants were again showing fresh blood spots, but they were small. I had no way to put more pressure on his wounds other than tourniquets, which felt like the wrong thing to do. Lying still was the only thing that would improve him, but he needed days of it, not hours, and we didn't have days.

Eating had become a nonevent. We were both starving by the time we made it to camp each dawn, but gobbling whatever was in the cans took only a minute or two and it went so fast that taste made no difference. By evening, we were starving again. We had various cans left, plus some candy in foil envelopes and some ration bars. I was sure we

were both dehydrated. We needed to get more water sometime soon.

"Do you ever think about the ranch?" I asked in a soft
voice.

It was the end of the afternoon, a couple of hours
before it would be dark enough to travel. We were covered
by our blanket, quietly munching on D bars.

"Not much," Jake said.

"You think about Lilly?"

"Oh, well, that's a different question," Jake said, sliding
one of his arms under his head. "She was all I did think
about after Arizona. Joining the Navy at college took away
most of my thinking time, and I was pretty quick into the
Pacific after that, where I was mostly occupied with
throwing up over the side of a ship until I got my sea legs. If
I did think of her, I didn't really think about her, you know,
like remembering our talks, but she was still in my mind."

"Did you ever get over feeling guilty?"

"Probably not, but I learned to live with it. Lilly was my
awful mistake, my error in judgment, my instance of perfect
stupidity. I remember her every time I screw up, like I'm
keeping a scorecard. One column has my mistakes, my
stupid actions, the costs for not doing things right, while
another column has the things I did right. The bad column
is always twice as long as the good column. Every time
something goes into either column, I have to answer to Lilly
about it."

"I don't have a scorecard like that," I said. "I'm pretty
sure I don't want one."

Jake turned his head toward me. "I don't mean to be
melodramatic. I just wish I could stop mentally filling out
the scorecard. Maybe if I had more good things than bad
things, I could settle up with her and stop remembering."

"Isn't growing up supposed to make you stop the scorecard business?" I asked. "You need to forgive yourself, big

brother. You were barely eighteen at the time, right? Just a kid for all practical purposes. Taking Lilly up the mountain was an error in judgment. Nothing fancy, nothing special, nothing unusual. People have made errors in judgment since the beginning of time."

"Well, forgiving yourself is easy to talk about but a lot harder to do," he replied.

I heard his labored breathing and watched the flexing of his back muscles as he tried to stretch away his aches and pains. I knew his neck hurt by the way he kept moving it from side to side. It had been hours since his last morphine shot, but I wanted to wait either until he asked for it or when we were ready to leave. I hadn't counted the number of syrettes left, but we didn't have many.

"What about Captain McCall? I hated him for what he did. He did you wrong."

"I did me wrong," Jake replied. "Captain McCall responded in the only way he could. I don't think he thought much of Lilly, or any woman, but I had embarrassed him. I was his prize pupil, and when I was up on that mountain, he expected me to behave like Kit Carson. I ended up behaving like Bozo the Clown. All those years of skills training and survival techniques, and I acted like I'd never heard a word he was saying. He needed to blame everything on a misaligned character or a personality flaw so his teachings wouldn't look invalid. Throwing me out was overboard mean, but he didn't know what else to do.

"I've learned to live with that, too. I've grown up. I'm damn near twenty-six. And I've made good decisions in circumstances far more critical than Lilly's. I'm not haunted by memories or anything. I just wish I hadn't had to make all those bad decisions to learn how to make good ones."

"What did you think of Margie?" I asked. "My fiancé."

I'm sure Jake wondered where I got that question, but I'd been waiting for the right moment for a long time.

"She's a good-looking blonde, right? Maybe a redhead? I passed through Minneapolis when I was ferrying a modified B-17 from Los Angeles to Langley Field in Virginia. Stayed two or three days, which was long enough for Lady Gunnarson to throw a little party. It was a good thing I didn't tell her I was coming, as she only had time to invite a hundred or so people.

"She did have time to bring a tailor to the house to fix everything wrong with my uniform, though. A nip here, a tuck there, and then I had to go on display. Lady Gunnarson was not to be denied her right to show me off to her social club ladies and their eligible daughters.

"I hate to tell her I've gained twenty pounds since the party, helped by my regular visits to local English pubs. The ol' uniform was looking pretty tight the last time I put it on. After a month of being starved in a crummy hospital, I guess I don't have those twenty pounds anymore. I certainly don't know what the tailor's going to do about shortening my pants.

"So, I might have met your wife-to-be at the party."

He had deliberately lied. "Uh, you know she was living in the same house as you? Maybe you noticed her at breakfast?"

Jake laughed. "Oh, that one. Sure, I remember. Good-looking girl. She seemed fine. 'Course, Lady Gunnarson had a complete schedule mapped out for the both of us, so I was going one way while she was going another. I think I saw her at supper one night."

"I heard that you saw her a little more than that."

Jake turned his head to look at me. "What exactly did you hear?"

"Lady Gunnarson, as you like to address our mother, wrote me a letter about the two of you really hitting it off. Caused quite a stir. She said I should ask about you and Margie when we got back."

He turned his head back to looking ahead. "I don't remember a lot. There was a war on, ya know, so I'm not sure what she's referring to. Maybe she meant me taking her up in my airplane."

"In the 17? You took her up in a B-17? I guess Margie forgot to mention that, which is easy to remember because she forgot to mention you coming home at all. For you to suddenly fly in and take her up in the clouds, you'd think she would have said something about it. Maybe she was just too dazzled."

He laughed quietly. "Well, I don't know about her being dazzled, but it certainly tested her molars. They don't make bombers to be comfortable, ya know. I think she enjoyed it. We went up to the tree country, took a look around, and then flew back."

"Which reminds me," I said. "Your mother mentioned how proud she was of you. You made her look good at the Wednesday social you attended. Do you remember the Wednesday social?"

"Not at all," Jake said. "Your mother had me strutting at several functions while I was there. In fact, I'm pretty sure I left on Tuesday."

Another lie. "Well, you must have come back on Wednesday in time for the social because both you and Mrs. Avery were there and she was very impressed with you, too. A true hero. She was sorry her husband missed you at the airfield. You remember Paul and Paula Avery? Paula's famous for her roses. Wins the county fair every year. Paul Avery owns Avery Oil. The company operates out of Minneapolis and owns, among other things, the state contract for supplying aviation fuel to the airfields around the twin cities. You would have met him on Saturday when you flew in. He provided the tanker truck for refueling your plane."

Jake took a few moments. "Yeah, okay. I met him in

the office when I checked in. He needed me to sign a voucher for the fuel. Nice guy, if I remember. I was late getting to him because of the crowd. Do you know there were kids who wanted my autograph? That's something I never had to worry about in the Navy. There were so many people on the tarmac when I landed, it was hard turning around. It would have been bad form to run over somebody. Never saw so many people waiting for a nobody like me."

I gave a small laugh. Jake was never good at acting humble. "I've met Paul. Seems like a real nice guy. Mom said that Paula said he was very impressed with your airplane. He's been a pilot forever, and when you flew in, he wondered if you'd take him inside to check out the cockpit."

I rolled over on my side, facing Jake.

"He was going to ask you on Tuesday, the day you took Margie up in the plane."

We had the blanket over our heads since it was still light out. I couldn't see his face clearly, but I could hear his breathing becoming uneven.

"Tuesday? I'm sure I took her up on Monday. He must be thinking of somebody else."

"Could be, though I doubt there were many 17s at the airfield since he said he'd never seen one up close until you landed. I'm pretty sure you took Margie up on Tuesday. See, he was in the tower when you took off. He figured you'd want the tanks topped off when you came back, so he ordered a refueling truck for the afternoon.

"He was still in the tower when you got back. Besides needing for you to sign another voucher, he was going to ask if you'd show him the plane. When you landed and taxied over to the tarmac, he left the tower in time to see you and Margie dropping through the hatch and heading straight to one of the hangars.

"He checked the hangar but didn't find you, so he

checked the others. He looked all over the airfield and didn't see you again until he saw you drive away an hour later."

"Yeah, well…uh…Margaret wanted a tour," Jake said as he started stretching his arms and back. "You'd be amazed at how ignorant women are about airfields and flying and what it takes to handle all the air traffic. I showed her the repair shops and took her over to the tower, so ol' Paul must have been ahead of us or just behind, and we never met up. 'Course, I wasn't paying a lot of attention. I remember the airfield was awfully busy, so there might have been a lot of people going different places. Maybe it *was* Tuesday when I took her up."

"I guess Margie forgot to mention you and your activities in her letters."

"Well, it *was* a year or two ago. I don't even remember last week."

"You must have liked her."

"She's a babe, for sure, but I didn't see her that much. Mom was keeping her busy most of the time, doing the Red Cross and all the War Bond meetings."

"Yeah, those were on Thursday. Jake, you've lied to me, and you're lying to me now. I'm not your kid brother anymore—I can tell when you're lying. Mom described the whole week and you spent a lot of it with the woman I'm going to marry. But you didn't know Paul Avery was looking for you at the airfield, so maybe you weren't where you thought you were. I want to know about the hour when Avery couldn't find you. If—"

There was a sudden mechanical rumble in the distance. I immediately stopped talking and we both went on high alert. The noise was getting louder, and it became clear it was a train. I slowly lowered the blanket as Jake and I both rose up enough to peek over the leafy clutter around us.

Two hundred yards past our stand of trees, a railroad track paralleled the end of the field. We hadn't noticed it.

Elevated a few feet above the cultivated rows, a train was working hard to make progress.

It was a German supply train pulling a string of flatcars with tanks, half-tracks, artillery pieces, covered trucks, and large tarped piles of what was probably munitions. After the flatbeds came troop cars. At least two hundred men, I guessed.

We silently watched as one train car after another rolled by.

"It's going the wrong direction," Jake said quietly.

"What do you mean?"

"The tanks are clean and it's heading west. Those are replacement troops with new equipment. The front must be somewhere ahead of them, and must still be pretty far away. What we want to see are trains going east, looking all shot up, meaning the Americans are close and the soldiers are running away from the action."

If troops were going west, they were resupplying the front, which meant the number of Germans between us and where we wanted to go was increasing. Our escape route just got more difficult.

"Damn it," I said, watching the train as it chugged into the horizon. It was disappointing, and we both felt it. I laid back and pulled the blanket back over my head. To say I had been optimistic in my planning is being more kind than I deserved. I thought that if we started out from Hammel-burg with a certain number of miles to get to the American front, the front would have moved toward us as we were moving toward it, making our overall trip shorter in time and effort. I had honestly expected to be rescued within three days of travel. Maybe I had grown too used to Patton's way of doing things.

"If I had my P-47," Jake said, "I would have made a major contribution to the war effort with that train. Line her up with the tracks, push the buttons, and rain 50 calibers of hell on it from one end to the other. It's a lot more fun than dropping a few tons of bombs from twenty-five thousand feet while getting my ass shot to pieces. Let me look at the map again."

I wrestled the rucksack up from between us, took out the map, and handed it to him. He folded the blanket back and spread the map out in the air above him. He put his finger on Schweinheim, where the task force started and where the Third Army crossed the Main River. He traced the highway and the rivers and then made up some logic about where the train was going, where the Seventh Army should be, and what we needed to avoid.

"Scoot over to the trees and look for observers along the track. The German High Command doesn't trust the locals to watch the tracks anymore, so they send out observation units to go up and down the tracks looking for booby traps set by the resistance."

It sounded like a command, so I threw the blanket back, checked the area around us, and then got up on my knees. I looked back at him. "Jake, I want to talk more. About Margie, and you, and the hour you spent at the airfield."

"Sure, sure. We'll talk all you want, but right now, we need your eyes on that track. We don't want to be walking into any observers out there. They're probably pretty bored and would love to find some American ass to shoot at."

I crawled to the first tree, looking around for any movement, and continued around the other trees until the tracks were out of sight. It was getting dark, and by the time I got back, Jake had packed the rucksack, gotten himself on top of the sling, and was ready to go.

Chapter 30

We'd had good weather since we left Hammelburg, but the evening brought storm clouds with gusty winds and rain that lasted a good part of the night. Every now and then, the moon would peek through and give a ghostly glow to the landscape, but we were mostly peering through a gray haze or being beat on by raindrops. We draped the blanket over us, with me gathering the bottom to keep it from billowing open, while Jake held it out over my face. It became soaked but sheeted the rain enough to protect us. Fortunately, visibility was pretty much zero, so I walked upright and quickly, trying to make up for the night before.

The flat farmland gave way to low, rolling hills that may have been pasture in a previous life. It was a relief not to be sucked down into mud, but now I was sloshing through rain-soaked grass. I forced myself to maintain a steady pace, focusing on my feet rather than staring ahead into the sodden darkness.

The rain kept us from talking.

The storm dropped the temperature, and we both shivered as we picked our way through fields and circumvented the occasional farmhouse. The wind was blustery, sending wet spray into our faces. We folded up the collars of our combat jackets, the common soldier's uniform of waterproof canvas, and I had my Army-issue wool pants, which were not waterproof but shed the water and kept me warm enough.

The gusts were maddening, and being soaked to the skin was as uncomfortable as hell, but I, at least, was moving. Jake was never moving, and it wasn't long before he was shaking uncontrollably. With the soaked blanket across his back, even with his jacket buttoned tight around him, he was losing body heat and was just damned cold. His body kept up a constant quiver against my back.

I stopped asking him how he felt or if we needed to stop or if he wanted more painkillers. Even though I had given him his usual morphine shot to start the night's march, I was willing to give him more for no other reason than to deaden his misery.

We had crossed a half-dozen fields, walked down a few cow paths, and skirted a road or two when I decided we'd gone far enough for our third night. We had only walked three hours at most, so it must have been close to midnight when I started searching for a camp. I didn't want to—I was going at a good pace and felt like the hills were giving us an advantage—but Jake's condition worried me.

The rain was on and off, and haze was drifting along the ground. I wanted to stop, but lying on a sodden forest floor under a wet blanket while being pelted by raindrops was not appealing. If we didn't find someplace out of the rain, I wasn't sure if Jake could generate enough body heat to keep himself warm. We needed something with a roof. It wouldn't have to be much, but it had to keep the water off.

While skirting a road by sticking close to a long clump of bushes, I saw the faint outlines of a barn in the distance. I watched it as well as I could while I walked, constantly scanning the area for people. The barn looked isolated and empty, but the only way to find out was to get closer.

Against my better judgment but thoroughly disgusted with being drenched, I trotted across the road, slipped through an open corral gate, and hid behind an outside corner. I couldn't see the roof, but the vertical boards of the siding were old and mostly warped. I glanced through a broken pane of a window, saw nothing, and so took a longer look. In the dim moonlight, I saw no movement, smelled no fresh smells, and heard no noise. It was probably a casualty of war, abandoned when troops flooded the country.

I crept up to a crooked wooden door hanging by one hinge and cautiously peeked inside. I smelled musty hay but heard nothing. No scratching, no pawing, no snorting, no breathing—no sounds at all, except the rain on the roof and the splashes of water streaming off of it. I partially covered the lens of my flashlight as Jake pulled the blanket back, watching as I entered and circled the inside. No recent footprints, no wagon ruts, no sacks of feed, no harnesses, no ropes, no farm implements, no fresh manure. There were three open horse stalls, three or four feed bins, some large shelves covered in dust, one corner full of fencing materials and old wood, and an open area with a large, closed outside door, probably meant for a wagon. A ladder led up to a loft above us, but a couple of rungs were broken. It hadn't been used in a long time.

I declared myself a happy man with a ready-made shelter for the night that had enough space to hang wet things out to dry. We could get out of the wind and the rain and rake up some of the loose straw for bedding, which sounded like Heaven under the circumstances. I thought of building a small fire, sheltered so no light would leak out, but thought better of it. I settled for good enough.

I did the lay-back-and-roll-over version of unloading Jake, then wrung out the blanket and sling and hung them over the ladder rungs. I had to get him dry and warmed up as soon as possible, but there was little to work with. I chose the middle horse stall for a bed to give us the most protection from the drafts coming through the gaping door and broken window. Each of the stalls had piles of straw thrown into the back corners, so I swept what I could into the center stall.

Leaving my flashlight on the floor to give us enough light to work by, I took off Jake's jacket and shirt and redressed him in my shirt, it was reasonably dry except for the dampness from my sweat and the soaking cuffs. I threw his shirt and jacket over a section of the stall and pulled my jacket around him. I switched caps with him as his had become soaked from rubbing against the blanket.

His pants were bloody, but there was no way I could redo his dressings in the middle of the night. It would have released more of his stored heat, and that was a precious commodity under the circumstances. I carefully peeled each leg off, dripping blood on the stall floor, and wound new bandages over the old. I kept wrapping him up past his waist to give him insulation and propped him up in a corner of the stall on top of a mound of straw. I wrung out the blanket again, piled a few more inches of straw over him for a barrier, and then wrapped the damp blanket around him.

"Okay, that's about all I can do," I told him. He grunted in reply.

I packed my own surroundings with straw, laid Jake's jacket on top, and then tucked the wrung-out sling around me as best I could. I dug a meal out of the rucksack, opened a couple of cans, and helped Jake eat. His hands were shaking too much for him to do it on his own. He looked awfully pale, barely opening his eyes to see the spoon, and coughing as he shook with an occasional chill.

The sound of his coughing was dangerous. The barn and the surrounding corrals certainly looked abandoned, and I believed we could not be seen. But once the rain stopped, I wasn't so sure we couldn't be heard. We were still miles from any American presence, in the middle of a valley next to a paved road, so the likelihood of people walking or driving by during the day was not zero. I tore off part of the sling to make Jake a handkerchief to stifle his coughs.

Jake had struggled to swallow but managed to eat two cans before he turned on his side and curled up away from me. He still shivered, but not as violently. I gave him a shot of morphine, and he relaxed and fell asleep.

I only had three syrettes left.

Chapter 31

Jake was screaming.

After ripping open a packet of dried fruit from a Red Cross box and cherishing each small bite, I had drifted off to sleep, cold, frustrated, and disheartened. His screams jerked me awake. I found Jake leaning forward, his hands clenching the blanket, shaking violently and screaming at the top of his lungs. I turned on the flashlight and could see the whites of his eyes against the flint-shine of the sweat on his skin.

The medics call it *shell shock*, but it's nothing less than a man's soul coming unhinged, his inner fears trampling any courage or stability or control or sense of self-protection. I saw men dragged from Jeeps and trucks who were screaming, crying, sobbing as they were helped into battalion aid tents. Battle-hardened soldiers who were used to running straight into battle with guns blazing, ready to kill without mercy, would suddenly surrender to their fears inside their foxholes, dissolving like jelly. Bullets, bombs, explosions, shaking ground, friends dying, blood splattering, bodies torn apart. An overwhelming sense of abandonment and disorientation left them shaking and weeping.

That's what I saw in Jake's eyes.

I scrambled on top of him, covering his mouth, my body pinning his arms inside the blanket as he thrashed against me. His muscles were stretched as tight as rubber bands, and it was all I could do to keep him down. He struggled until he gave a final heave and fell limp, sobbing as if all hope were lost.

I rolled to the side but reached my arms around him to hold him in a close hug. It took several minutes for him to settle down and then, through his tears, his head only inches from mine, he confessed his secrets to me.

"I lied, I lied, oh God, I lied. To you, to Mom, to everybody."

It was hard to understand him, with his breathing erratic and his voice breaking.

"I didn't hit that carrier. Another pilot was on my wing as we dove. He dropped at the same time I did, but I saw my bomb splash. He dropped a hundred feet to my left and *his* went down the carrier's elevator shaft. Then his plane caught a shell and exploded into a ball of flame. Nobody saw him, nobody saw the drops, nobody knew it wasn't me. He died, I lied, and I got the glory.

"I got...I got the glory."

He began shaking again, screaming again, and I had to roll back on top of him.

"Jake, Jake! Come on, brother, stay with me now."

His panic finally subsided and he slumped farther down into the straw. His face was pale, like a man just out of a faint—lifeless, deflated, struggling because he could find no strength within his body. His voice lowered to a whisper, he sniffed, and I leaned in closer to hear what he was saying.

"I was bombing the Ruhr Valley out of an airfield in England when this lone Luftwaffe flyer came out of nowhere. Tore us to pieces. I turned around, two engines out, my co-pilot dead, my wheels messed up. I had to belly-in back at the base. A couple of hits had knocked the belly turret out of alignment, and the belly gunner couldn't get the carriage to line up with the hatch. He couldn't get out… couldn't get out. I didn't know—nobody told me. After we skidded to a stop, I saw his body smeared all over the runway."

Jake's tears were streaming down his face as he sobbed.

"I started screaming. Why didn't somebody tell me? He didn't have to die. I could've done something." He began huffing to catch his breath, trying to get the words out. "I kept screaming at the hospital, so they doped me up. After a week, I got back in a 17. I tried everything, but I couldn't get it off the ground…couldn't fly…like I couldn't remember how. Like I really had gone crazy."

Jake coughed, wiped his tears, and looked at me.

"They booted me. Nuts. He's gone nuts. *Mentally unstable*, they wrote in my psych report. Flying days over. Back to the States, kid, and they walked away."

Jake became more settled and his voice cleared up.

"They were kicking me out, but where was I going to go? I couldn't go home, couldn't show up a reject. I didn't have anywhere to go, and I didn't dare tell people why. So, I stole a Mustang off the field. I got it up in the clouds and suddenly everything in my brainpan fell back into place. When they saw I could do it, they let me fly escort for the 17s over the Channel every day for a week. Even if I was only flying escort, I wanted to stay with my buddies, help them stay alive.

"But my wing commander didn't care—he'd never trust me with a 17 again and was tired of me anyway, so he offered me up to fly fighters out of an airfield near the front in Germany, shooting up trains and convoys and tanks. That's where I was when you found me."

Jake closed his eyes, coughed, and began sobbing again. His next words were shouted in anger, then in pain.

"They gave me medals! Told me I was a wonder boy, a hero! But I had lied. I lied about the carrier, I lied about how good I was, I lied about being a good man. I was a jerk! A bum! I hurt people, hurt them bad. God took my legs because of it.

"I always thought I was a screaming locomotive. That was me, barreling down the tracks, a wild man from Minnesota. Get out of my way! Comin' through! Onward and upward! Never looking behind. Never. But now I look back and there's blood all over the rails, and I'm pulling boxcars full of dead bodies behind me. My locomotive is a train of death, and...Lilly...Lilly's at the very back. I see her staring at me, asking me why I killed her. I am...Lilly, I am...so sorry."

The last words came in a desperate, cracking voice that trailed off into silence like he had forgotten he was talking. His eyes stared past me. He stretched his neck, moved his head to the side, and his face slowly lost all expression. He closed his eyes and passed out.

I pulled the blanket up and tucked it around him. I guess even heroes go crazy sometimes.

Chapter 32

I woke up at noon. The sky was clear, the sun high above, the barn cool and dry, and the smell in the air was strong from the moist earth outside. There were birds chirping outside, which I hadn't heard in a long time. I felt warm under the straw and jacket, but the sling was still clammy, so I pushed it aside and welcomed the dryer air. I lay quietly on my straw bed.

Jake was turned away from me, his face toward the stall wall. I was relieved he was no longer coughing, and if he was as conked out as he seemed to be, more power to him. He needed all the sleep he could get. We had hours before we had to even think about leaving. Maybe we should stay another night? Probably do him good. That might mean finding a way up into the loft, but I bet we could do it.

I took a meal bar from the rucksack and nibbled it slowly to make it last. I was hungry, which made it taste better. The bars were about all we had left, and we'd need to ration ourselves to just two a day. I was also ready to talk. It was time to find out the truth.

Another hour passed before I checked on Jake. I called to him and gently rolled him onto his back. When I tugged at the blanket he had pulled up over his chin, I realized his chest was not moving.

I yanked the blanket off, raked back the straw covering him, and shook him. There was no response. I listened for his heart and found nothing. The blood from his stumps had soaked through his bandages, dripped through the straw, and made a puddle in the dirt. His body was cold and pale, his skin unresponsive to my touch. He had probably died sometime before dawn, maybe right after his fit of misery, and I had lain unsuspecting next to him for hours.

I jerked back across the stall floor and fell against the wood rails, finding it hard to breathe. My heart was pounding so hard my head began to ache. We might have been caught and executed, but I never thought he would die. How could Jake die? He was the strong one, the enduring one, the one who had lived life one dare after another. I had imagined us riding together, me on Sugar and him on May, on vacation back in Tucson, fishing in the lake high above the ranch, just him and me.

My throat stuffed up, and I struggled to swallow, to breathe. I straightened up and arched my back, trying anything to get more air, and then fell over on my side. I gasped, shook, and buried my face in my hands as I sobbed, wave after wave.

Our journey was over.

I WAS SO sorry he wouldn't make it home, wouldn't find the right girl, wouldn't marry and have children, wouldn't have a chance to find forgiveness. Maybe he would never have found forgiveness. Maybe he was destined to drive that locomotive all his life.

He talked one night about the ocean. He hated the ocean. He especially hated landing on carriers surrounded by ocean. The ocean was just too damned big, and if you went down, there was no walking home. He loved the high mountains, the lakes, climbing the peaks, riding May, being alone in the forest. It was the only time he mentioned the ranch without talking about Lilly. He loved being on solid ground. Let him off anywhere on solid ground and he'd find his way home. Solid ground won't kill you.

Not so with the ocean. Not so with the sky. Can't walk home if you step out of your plane when you're flying above the clouds.

It was the middle of the afternoon when I finally shook off the straw and got up. If I was going to go, I had to get things ready. I pulled Jake onto the non-bloody end of the blanket, hung his dog tags around my neck, peeled off my jacket and shirt, and put them back on. I left him in his undershirt and skivvies. He looked small and fragile, deflated, like an empty bag. At least he'd never feel pain again.

I carefully stripped the sodden bandages from his stumps and replaced them with others that were somewhat drier. I didn't think he had any more blood to bleed, so I didn't bother wrapping them tight. I pulled his shirt back on him, his jacket, and then debated what to do with his pants. They were a mess, stiff and stinking.

I may have been having an unconscious cultural response, dressing the dead for a funeral. I wanted to make him look better. If I had had the time, the water, the herbs, the oils that my ancestors had used, I would have washed his body, styled his hair, cleaned his fingernails and toenails, and shaved his face. I would have prepared Jake for the afterlife.

But I had none of those things. I had mud and straw and blood-soaked clothes. Going into the afterlife would be an ugly journey for Jake, but he had already joked about showing up without legs. Delaying the decision about his pants, I straightened out the blanket, draped it over him, and then stepped outside.

The area in the yard was hard-packed and barren, still wet with puddles, while the pastures beyond the corrals looked rich and uncut. There were a couple of fallen-apart troughs and some corral posts, all looking abandoned. There was a drainage ditch on the other side of the pasture beyond the corral. Hunkering as low as I could manage, I scrambled across the pasture and found the ditch still full of rainwater. I made my decision. I was going to fulfill my original duty and promise: I was going to take Jake home.

Which sounded noble enough but left me facing a reality with which I had grown familiar: It was impossible for *me* to take him *home*. *Home* was a few thousand miles away and there was a lot of war in between, not to mention an ocean. *Taking him home* now meant getting his body into the hands of a Graves Registration Unit. They would take care of his body and get him buried or sent back to the States.

Going back to Hammelburg was probably my best bet. The American Army had to make it there at some point because of John Waters. Patton wasn't about to leave his son-in-law behind. When the Army came, a GRU would come with them to gather the bodies of the GIs who had died during imprisonment or during the aborted rescue by the task force.

I snuck back to the barn, gathered Jake's stuff, and returned to the ditch to wash his pants, his shirt, and the sling. Soaking my own shirt as I brought everything back, I wrung everything out and then swung them around to get them at least somewhat dry.

When I thought I had done all I could, I pulled Jake's pants on, folded the legs up and over his belt, and secured them with the safety pins. There were no creases in the pants and certainly not in the shirt, but I did the best I could. I straightened them, zipped up his jacket, and fastened the snaps. I wished he still had his sheepskin aviator's jacket.

Jake was ready to go, but I hadn't decided if I should retrace the way we came, or just head north from where I was at, turning east later.

My answer came through the barn door, pointing a rifle at my chest.

THE TRAIN of the day before had indeed held reinforcements for the German front. The Seventh Army had bumped up against Patton's Third Army a hundred miles south of Frankfurt and was directed to go east toward Nuremberg while Patton went upwards toward Erfurt. In the face of both overwhelming forces, the German army could only stem the hemorrhage of their retreating troops caught in between by adding more troops and setting up skirmish lines while they retreated.

Jake had been right. Afraid of relying on the local villagers to help them, the High Command ordered observers to keep watch along the train tracks in case resistance fighters were sabotaging the rails. One of the observer units must have been guarding the same rail we had watched while Jake and I lay hidden nearby. They must have been on the other side of the track because I never saw anyone.

When the soldier with the rifle came through the door, I made no movement except to raise my hands and get on my knees while another soldier made a cursory inspection of the barn. They found Jake interesting, although I almost attacked the one guy when he poked Jake's body with his bayonet.

A car pulled off the road outside. An *oberleutenant* was met by one of the soldiers and brought in front of me. He had uncut white hair sticking out from under his officer's hat, a wrinkled face, and a uniform that fit poorly. He looked like someone who should have been sitting on a bench in the town square, joking with his neighbors, whittling on a stick.

The man looked me over, had a soldier hand him a flashlight to examine Jake in the dim light of the barn, and then pointed to the dog tags around my neck. I held up Jake's, pointed at his body, and then held up mine, pointing at me.

He first looked to see if we were Jews. There would have been an *H* stamped in the lower right corner, for Hebrew. He saw a *P*, which meant Protestant. He looked relieved and then noticed that our last names were the same.

He looked at my face and then at Jake's. "*Der bruder?*" he asked. I nodded.

"*Hammelburg Oflag?*" he asked. I nodded.

The man appeared cordial. Then I remembered he was talking to a captain. I had not removed Jake's captain's bars pinned to my shirt. They might have saved my life.

He motioned for me to carry Jake to the back seat of his staff car and to get in. One of the soldiers crammed in close to me with the oberleutenant's Luger held against my stomach. I tossed the rucksack onto the floor and climbed in. I cradled Jake like a child in my lap, his head falling back against my shoulder, while I watched the countryside. The damp of his pants made a circle of wetness in my lap.

I recognized the tower of the village with the stream and the one-lane bridge as we passed it. We were no more than a half-hour from the barn when we drove into Oflag XIIIB. All that time, all that effort and misery, and we hadn't made it more than a half-hour car ride from where we'd started.

I was weeping as we approached the POW camp, much to the amusement of the soldier holding the Luger—the older man made no notice. I cried not only because Jake was dead, but because, once out of my hands, I might never see him again. It would be hard to let him go. I had messed up. My scheme to free him from the camp and return him to our side of the war had gone awry and resulted in his death. I had failed in my duty, and I had broken my promise.

I thought of Lilly. I hoped Jake had found forgiveness for all he thought he had done wrong because I was now next in line. I had taken Jake up the mountain to free him from captivity and held only his lifeless body on the way down. It felt all too familiar.

The staff car pulled through the front gate of the camp, which no longer had a guard, circled the flagpole in front, and stopped at the door of the command building. The oberleutenant went inside while I was directed to get out and stand at attention. I replaced Jake's dog tags around his neck, tucked them under his shirt, put his wings and captain's bars back on his shirt, and held him in my arms as the commandant came out, more out of curiosity than anything official, I think.

He looked me over with a grunt, then pointed toward the hospital. If it had been a week earlier, before the task force had come roaring across the field, he probably would have shot me where I stood. As it was, I expect he wanted to demonstrate as much grace as possible from the Americans who were watching through the tall fences of the prisoner compound. It wouldn't be long before he'd be on the other side of the fence.

No longer accompanied by soldiers, I carried Jake to the hospital, where someone pointed me to the area near where the tank had crashed through the fence.

Above-ground graves had been created in the review grounds. Knowing the problem of decaying smells and disease, the doctors had directed the dead to be wrapped in whatever was handy, laid on the ground, and then covered with dirt from a pit dug nearby.

More than a hundred mounds had been made in the three days since Jake and I left. Everyone assumed that liberation was near and bodies stored above ground would be easier for the GRU people once they arrived.

As I walked to the site, I was given an old sheet.

It was a hard goodbye. I knew my brother had long departed to his journey's end, and only his abbreviated body was left. I laid him on the sheet, made two wraps, and then folded the excess across the top. I tore some strips of cloth off and made three ties around him. I patted him on the chest and covered him with dirt from the pit. It wasn't very secure, but it was all there was.

The patients and doctors standing at the windows of the hospital watching me said nothing when I came back. I sat on the steps and worked at getting the mud and dirt off my boots. When they were as clean as I could get them, I went inside. Mercifully, they found cleaner clothes for me and then offered to wash what I had on.

I wish everything could have stopped there. I wish I could have gotten on a bus, gotten myself to a ship, and come straight home to you. It would have all been over, and for me, there was no reason to continue. My war was done.

Chapter 33

"I've thought of a story for you." I missed him, oh God, how I missed him. I couldn't sleep because I ached over his absence, so sitting next to him was the only comfort I could find.

First in England and even more so in Normandy, I had learned to talk to people, those in my unit, the support people at the airfields, the controllers in the control room, and an assortment of people in other places. I could talk to people without treating them like game pieces. Senior would be disappointed. I could joke with the people from the South, or the North. I could make fun of them and their accents, and they'd joke back and make fun of my big feet or the size of my hands. The boys from New Jersey were a riot. When the going got tough and we felt the breath of the enemy on our faces, we all blended together and became the trained soldiers we needed to be. There was a war to win, and we responded in every way.

But there was nobody like Jake when it came to having a good conversation.

While we were gone, von Goeckel had moved the American officers and the captured task force members to other

POW camps near Nuremberg, marching them out under guard. The sick and wounded remained in the hospital, along with the medical personnel.

That left the oflag basically empty. The fence the tanks had knocked down had still not been repaired; there was no point. No one I saw would even consider trying to escape, and I certainly felt no temptation. I had had my chance and ended up back where I began. That left a meager group of us going through the motions of being prisoners. There were still some duties, but few enough that everyone did what they were told and then spent the rest of their time waiting.

I used my waiting time talking to Jake. I had told Jake I had no stories, but now all I could think of were stories, about people and places, about me. The two of us hadn't been together much since the ranch. I'd visited him in Duluth a couple of times, but we didn't do much more than swap family updates and tell drinking stories. This last week together had been special, even given the trauma. The people at the hospital had left us to ourselves, and we had time to visit. When our three days on the lam began, it reminded me of our horse rides up to the lake. Nobody but us calling the shots. Me and Jake against the world.

"Maybe this isn't a real one, but it's still something I wish I'd told you about." It was late afternoon, and I had brought a chair out next to his grave. Nobody thought it strange that I wanted to sit next to my dead brother, speaking to a mound of dirt, saying things to him I wished I had said when he was alive. Every soldier had lost a friend or a buddy or someone close and then had to leave before they could say a proper goodbye. Most never saw their buddies again, not their bodies, their graves, or even their markers. There was a war on, and those who were alive were always moving forward so there was no time for looking back. When men did have the time and wanted to remember someone, wanted to say a prayer or a goodbye, wanted to say some final words, wanted to say something they wished they had said when someone was alive, talking to ghosts wasn't unusual at all.

"Remember me driving an ambulance? I was out one day going around to the aid stations when some sniper shot me through the windshield. I didn't write Margie about it or Mom or anyone. He got me on the left side of my rib cage. The medic said the bullet slid along the outside of the ribs and didn't break anything, but it made a nasty rip about five or six inches long. It hurt like hell, but I liked the idea of getting one of those Purple Heart medals. I could show it to my kids.

"The medic wrapped me up and sent me back to the division hospital to check myself in as a patient. I drove myself. I wouldn't have gone, but I did need stitches, and I worried about getting an infection; aid stations aren't particularly antiseptic.

"After getting zippered up, I was there for the day, on a cot in the tent where they put people to rest and recuperate. It was stinky and crowded. No place to be if you wanted to sleep, let me tell you. The snoring reminded me of Senior's sawmill.

"There was a guy in the cot next to me who had trench foot in both feet and couldn't walk, so he was waiting for transportation to a hospital ship at Amsterdam. He tells me his name, which was Sergeant Terrence Maxwell Healy, and he's from Duluth. I tell him my name and he sits up and asks, 'Is Old Man Gunnarson your father?'

"'Well, yes he is,' I said, 'although I don't remember anybody calling him Old Man Gunnarson.'

"'I mean no disrespect to you personally,' he said, 'but if Old Man Gunnarson was standing next to you right now, I'd shoot him.'

"I wasn't sure what to say to that, but I was curious as to why, so I asked him.

"'My daddy worked at the Gunnarson lumber mill in Duluth for years. In 1933, the Depression had put most everybody out of work, so he was happy to have a job. Then that sonofabitch decided that with all the people looking for work, he was paying his workers too much. He cut the wages in half. Said that if anyone wouldn't work for that, there were plenty of men outside the gates who would be happy to take their jobs.

"'My daddy was fit to be tied, but he didn't have a choice, so he gritted his teeth and kept working. My mom was already taking in wash and couldn't do anything more to make up for the lost wages. The next year, that sono-fabitch decided the mill wasn't making enough profit, so he shut the place down. Announced it on a Friday morning, had some thugs escort everybody off the property, then locked the doors. Friday was payday, in the evening, but when it came time to pay the workers, nobody was home. He had skipped town.

"'Your daddy cheated my daddy and about a hundred other workers out of their pay, out of their jobs, and put most of them in a breadline. I was only twelve at the time and didn't understand why my dad was staying home instead of going to work. He finally found a timber job up north, cutting branches off trees before they were loaded on trucks.

"'That's where he lost his arm. Got caught when a log rolled over him. He was at the hospital long enough for them to make his arm a stub, then booted him out because he couldn't pay the bill.

"'My brothers and I went to pounding the streets every day looking for any way to make money. I dropped out of school and did what I could until I lied about my age and joined the Army. Up until 1940, I'd been sending my pay home, but with the war and all, the mill opened up again and they found work for my daddy that he could do with one arm, working for the same sonofabitch that fired him and stole his money, and still not making what he used to. At least my mom's working in a factory now and making good money.

"'So that's why I'd like to see Old Man Gunnarson burn in hell.'

"I didn't know what to say, Jake. I didn't doubt a word the man had spoken. Senior *was* a sonofabitch. He was set on making money and he didn't mind running over anybody to get it. He taught us that it was the way of the world. There were winners and losers, and we would be the winners if everybody else became the losers.

"You didn't believe him in the first place, but I did. I thought he was teaching us how the world worked and what we needed to do to be successful. I thought he was taking care of me. That made it hard joining the Army. I wasn't used to the wide range of people and thought they didn't understand the basics of success. I was all set to be ruthless and aggressive and to focus only on impressing the officers above me, on getting promoted. I even expected to get a field commission—like it was something I was supposed to get because I was Senior's son.

"Sergeant Healy shipped out in the afternoon, so I didn't have a chance to apologize. I wanted to. I was ashamed of how his father had been treated and the misery it caused his family. Senior didn't have to throw all those workers out, and he certainly had no right to steal their meager wages. He could have made do with a few less rooms in the mansion, or a few less cigars. I still don't understand why he had no regard for compassion or kindness.

"I've got to get out, Jake. I can't go back and keep being what Senior expects me to be. I *like* the people I've met. It took me a while because of the education difference and the fact that I didn't realize how little money most people have. But I've found lots of decent people here who have families they care about, jobs they work hard at and want to get back to. Most of them have fine lives without having a lot of money. They're good, talented, hard-working people who are making their way the best they can.

"They don't deserve disrespect or manipulation. Remember the pub owner and his wife? They were fine people, and they had convictions about what was right and what was wrong. It didn't take some boss or manager or even a queen to tell them what their values should be or how they should live. They treated people like they wanted themselves to be treated. Why can't I be like that? Why wouldn't I *want* to be like that?

"Nobody wants to be in a damned war, but why am I having such a hard time? Part of me wants to escape and go back home, part of me wants to stay and kill Germans, part of me wants to die, and part of me still wants to be a hero. Why can't I figure this out?"

ON THE NIGHT OF THURSDAY, April 5, the thunder of distant cannons was heard within the oflag. By morning, the thunder was much closer. An hour later, a couple of the remaining German soldiers lowered the German flag from the pole and ran up a bed sheet. Soon after, the Germans were piling arms in front of the command building. General von Goeckel appeared in his dress uniform, backed up by his staff, and stood under the waving bed sheet. He would patiently wait for an American officer to come and accept his surrender.

The patients who could walk came out to stand behind the barbed wire and then cheered when the unmistakable clank of tank treads was heard from down the road. A column of tanks from the 14th Armored Division of the

Seventh Army soon appeared and swarmed into the field, with thousands of infantrymen following.

The day the Seventh showed up, some major in a clean uniform walked into the hospital, greeted Lieutenant Colonel Waters with a hearty handshake, and spoke to him in a low voice. He rolled Waters over, looked at the bandages, shifted a couple to see underneath, looked in his eyes, held onto his feet for a minute, and had Waters squeeze his fingers.

He shook Waters' hand again and went out. A half-hour later, a couple of Piper Cubs landed in the field out front, two medics hustled out, and they took Waters away on a stretcher. They folded him into the backseat of one of the planes and both took off. I don't know what happened to him.

When the GRU fellows came, I showed them where the newly dead had been buried as well as the camp's regular graveyard. I helped them uncover the bodies and pointed specifically to Jake. Since I was next of kin and had the dog tags to prove it, they let me have his few personal effects, which included his captain's hat, the shirt he was wearing when he crashed, a V-mail letter and envelope found in the shirt's pocket, some change, a thin wallet containing a few bills and his military ID, plus his captain's bars and Air Force pin.

I stuffed it all into the rucksack.

The GRU men sorted through the bodies, scribbling what information they could gather from dog tags and from the hospital reports, if there were any, and putting whatever personal possessions they could salvage into individual bags. They then wrapped each body in a mattress cover and laid them side by side in the back of the truck. I thought about jumping aboard to stick with Jake a little longer but decided against it. Our journey was over, the rest of his journey was now his own, and he did not need me.

I returned to the hospital, helped strip the beds, threw the used bandages and cast-off clothing into a bonfire in the yard, and helped stack the mattresses to be burned later.

After the wounded had been loaded into ambulances and trucks, the doctors disappeared in a Jeep and took off. I grabbed the rucksack and jumped in the back of the last truck.

It was time to go back to the war.

Chapter 34

I stayed with the wounded as they were evacuated to the Seventh Army hospital. During the processing, it was discovered that I was listed as *Absent Without Leave* from my radar unit. I told them about the task force, Hammelburg, and the circumstances afterward, and that I would have gladly returned sooner if I could have. But the commanders were in the middle of launching a new offensive, and no one had time to listen. They put me under arrest and trucked me over to a temporary military prison in Frankfurt.

I was happy when my duffel bag showed up a week later because it meant that somebody, somewhere, knew that I was still alive. But I never saw my radar unit or heard from my buddies again.

A week or so later, I was returned to the Third Army headquarters for a trial. They'd figured out what I had done and they charged me with a number of crimes, some of which were considered severe, especially the one for treason. They didn't call the proceedings a trial, preferring to call it a Review Board, but it wasn't much of either. I was not allowed to attend but had to be there when they handed down their decision and punishment.

From what I was told, three Third Army colonels got together, were shown the list of accusations, talked a minute, and then decided the treason charge was unreasonable since it appeared I'd had no contact with any German official and was captured when trying to escape the POW camp. They let the other charges stand, desertion now being the big one. Of course, I did steal a Jeep, joined a task force to which I had not been assigned, went behind enemy lines, though I hadn't been ordered to, and then pretended to be a captain, so I had enough charges to look guilty under any circumstance.

They wrapped things up pretty quickly. They signed a court martial busting me back to private and then recommended a dishonorable discharge when my enlistment was over. There was a war going on and they didn't have much time to spend on justice. They also reassigned me to the Seventh Army, which I suspect came from the Third Army Command, meaning that General Patton probably wanted anyone who knew anything about the task force to be as far away from him as possible.

The important thing is that General Patton declared the task force events classified after the Review Board finished and after their report had been issued, so the report was not classified when the decision was finalized. I was given a duplicate of the summary page as my official discharge paper. Later on, when Junior had the report itself classified, I had to return the page. I took a photograph of the page before I returned it. I wanted evidence of their kangaroo court if I ever needed it.

I also never got my Purple Heart.

I was told to report to some infantry unit in the Seventh Army to help out the Red Cross. I think this is when I started writing to you again. Whatever I said in my letters was a lie. I couldn't bring myself to tell you the truth.

. . .

I WAS SITTING behind the wheel of a Red Cross truck near the Czech border when someone told me the war was over. I didn't believe it until the thunder of the artillery stopped and it got spooky quiet, making it even more suspicious that it was a trap. It took a few days before the scattered German outfits turned themselves in, then another day to get our combat platoons rousted out of the field and into company headquarters in a nearby town.

The town quickly became a crowded mess, with every-body shoving their way into bakeries, lounging on the side-walks, crapping in the bushes, squatting in abandoned buildings, waiting, waiting some more, everybody relieved to be done but still nervous that there might be some leftover sniper out there waiting to put a bullet in their skulls. It was another half-day before orders were given, columns were formed, and troops started walking toward an assembly point near battalion headquarters a few miles away.

The Red Cross was committed to giving out their remaining food boxes, coffee, and blankets to the locals, but I wasn't. I climbed in the back of a supply truck going west and settled down for the ride. I was anxious to be done with the war and thought I'd be on a ship going home in a week.

Once again, I'm wondering how I could have been so stupid; nobody was going anywhere. Divisions were assigned to be sheriffs in different areas of the country: at check-points, railroad crossings, arms and ammunition depots, aircraft hangers and airfields, bridges, city halls, prisons, banks, towns with no leadership, towns with no town left, and a dozen other categories of places where people were likely to dissolve into chaos. It must have been an enormous problem, figuring out how the Army would prevent up-risings, rebellions, strikes, civil unrest, gangs, looting, murder, rape, or other lawlessness without our looking like conquering Mongols.

Some outfits were given dangerous duty, like locating and removing mines, booby traps, unexploded shells, and mortars. No one batted an eye when they were authorized to use German prisoners to help. Served them right. Put those suckers out in front.

Then there were the "displaced persons" who crowded every road, every square, and every city: refugees, ex-POWs, ex-concentration camp prisoners, ex-political prisoners, released non-German conscripted soldiers, slave laborers from any number of countries, plus all kinds of poor, starving, and disenfranchised miserables scattered all over the countryside. Some needed medical attention, many needed shelter, most needed food and water, and every one of them needed an advocate in the system, someone to figure out what they should do and where they should go. Many didn't have homes to go back to, while others didn't even have countries to go back to.

I felt sorriest for the kids. They were less inhibited than the adults and were always begging for food; some of them obviously hadn't had enough to eat in a long time. Every time I turned around there'd be some scruffy little urchin pulling on my jacket.

And the old women. My heart went out to them. They'd be wrapped up with scarves tied around their sad faces and ragged sweaters, wearing the ugliest stockings I'd ever seen, begging, holding out their bony hands alongside the convoys as we passed through villages. They weren't as quick as the kids. We'd throw them leftover cans of rations, candy, or D bars, but somebody would push the women aside and grab whatever we had thrown, leaving the old ones weeping in their hunger.

For those not assigned occupation duties, the soldiers of the Seventh Army collapsed back to central locations around the bigger cities, establishing huge depots of tanks, artillery, food, ammunition, gasoline, and other leftover military materiel, as well as setting up large housing complexes. Tents as far as you could see, kitchens, latrines, showers, postal services, medical tents, lights, telephones, radios—it reminded me of England in the weeks before the invasion.

I found the infantry unit I was assigned to in a little town outside Munich and was shuttled around to a couple of the depots, where I helped stack endless drums of fuel and oil. The second week of July, I was called in by my friendly Lieutenant for a special assignment.

"First off, Private Gunnarson, I don't like scumbag deserters. I would have put you in front of a firing squad. But I don't make the rules of this Army, so I have to live with it. But now that you're finished being a pansy-ass with the Red Cross and lying around while other people do real work, I've got you something special. I am damned tired of looking at your sorry face every day, so you're going to be my special designee to help clean up some of the mess the SS left us. There's a Jeep outside to take you to your new assignment. Now get your ass out of my sight."

It wouldn't have done me any good to tell the Lieutenant what I thought of his nobility and where he could put it, so I did a quick salute, picked up my duffel bag, and went outside. I'd been treated like I had a disease, so it was no surprise he was anxious to pass me off to some other place to do some other kind of grunt work.

I didn't care anymore. My nights were still haunted with visions of Jake lying dead in blood-soaked straw while I did nothing but bawl like a baby, so nothing was going to make my war better. I wanted to just get it over with and go home.

I tossed my duffel bag into the back of the Jeep and plopped down in the front seat.

"You have to get in the back," the driver said in an apologetic voice. "The Lieutenant said not to let you ride in front."

I looked at him with mild disgust. He was about half my size and I thought about yanking him out of his seat and beating his ass into the mud. I had a lot of anger inside of me and I could have done it without breaking a sweat. But it wasn't his fault. He was following the orders of the guy above him, just like me.

I got up and stuffed myself into the back seat. Whatever they wanted me to do.

"Where am I going?" I asked the driver.

Swerving around tank tracks and tire ruts, the man answered, "You hear about the concentration camps we found? I guess they need some help."

That was all he knew. I had heard a few things about the camps. People didn't talk about them much, and what I had heard was honestly unbelievable. I thought somebody was making it up, and it didn't matter if they were. I'd do whatever they wanted, and I didn't have to like it. They had to ship me home sometime. I just wanted to be invisible until I was on a ship headed for the good ol' U.S. of A.

You'd think I would have gotten over being naïve by now.

Chapter 35

An hour later, having crossed from one side of Munich to other, I was let off in front of a large stone and iron gate with two military guards, both armed. If this was a concentration camp, I wasn't sure if they were keeping people out or keeping people in. They looked at my orders and thumbed me through the gate, telling me to turn left at the end of the street. I'd find a building south of the plaza with someone who would help.

Once I turned left, I thought I'd stepped into a ghost town with a bad smell. There were no GIs standing around, no trucks and Jeeps bounding down the roads and through parking lots, no scurrying junior officers, exhaust fumes or noise. There were no people at all. I didn't even see any birds.

I was standing in front of a large plaza with uncut grass, unkempt flowerbeds, trash blowing around in the wind, dirt piled in various corners of walkways and street corners, all bordered by crisscrossing streets and a number of brick buildings. A massive, two-story building sat on the far side with Third Reich symbols on top of ornate columns, and a few swastikas here and there. The brick walls looked intact, no machine gun sprays across the front, and no shell craters. None of the windows of the large building were broken, and the front doors looked intact.

Large buildings like this one typically meant importance, and importance meant good shower rooms, something headquarter units were always looking for. It was far enough out in the country that it was surprising it hadn't been turned into a central headquarters or something.

I turned left and walked to a building a hundred yards down with several Jeeps parked out front. I found someone at a desk in the entryway, handed them my orders, and asked where I should go and whom I should see. It took several minutes of slightly confused communications among a number of clerks. Apparently, few, if any, soldiers had ever walked in with orders assigning them to work at a place without specifying what their work was to be. They were wondering why anyone had sent me here in the first place.

I was finally shown down a hallway and into a large room of people working at desks and leaning over stacks of papers, a row of typists clacking away, file drawers lining one side, and a number of maps hanging haphazardly on the walls. It resembled the newsroom of a city newspaper. I walked in front of a desk where a soldier with glasses sat studying several pages laid out before him, with an over-flowing ashtray to the side. He was smoking a cigarette with a new pack and a lighter close by. He had the shoulder patch of a senior technician, which made him something other than the combat soldiers I had grown used to.

He glanced at my orders and then leaned back in his chair to look up at me. "You must have really messed up to get assigned here," was his only response. "Oh, for God's sake, quit standing at attention. I'm not an officer. Can you type?"

I said I could and he pointed me to an empty desk nearby. There was no typewriter, but he said he'd find one.

"Excuse me, uh, sir, but…uh…what is this place?" I asked.

His eyebrows shot up and he looked at me with an amazed look. "You really did get dumped at the end of the earth. Martha, this kid wants to know where he's at."

A small, pretty woman wearing a uniform with an insignia I didn't recognize looked up from the handful of papers she'd been reading. She rolled her office chair over to the man's desk and addressed me. "What's your name, soldier? Where are you from?"

"Gunnarson, ma'am. Private Theodore Gunnarson, from Minneapolis, Minnesota."

She looked at me, turned her head a little, glanced at the ceiling with a thoughtful look, and then looked back at me. "Gunnarson, hmm. Strong Norwegian name. Minneapolis, you say? Lumber? Railroads? Isn't there a Gunnarson who sits on the War Production Board?"

I brightened up. "Yes, ma'am. That's my brother."

The man's eyebrows shot up, and he glanced from me back to the woman as he gave a *humpf* through pursed lips. "This is Martha Hammer, and she runs this place. Martha is a walking encyclopedia. If she doesn't know it, it hasn't been discovered yet. Maybe we need to take our new man out for a tour so he gets the picture of what we're doing. You free?"

Martha stood up. "I'm always free for a tour, but I get to drive."

"Grab your bag, kid, and we'll get you checked in," he said as he lit another cigarette.

I MENTION the cigarettes because I never saw James Tobruch without one, with few exceptions. The definition of a chain smoker, he was well-known for lighting a new cigarette from the still glowing stub of his previous one. He didn't use the harsh ones given out by the Army in ration boxes or sold in the commissaries, but ordered his directly from the states, and only Chesterfield Regulars.

He stood up and offered a handshake. "Call me Tobruch. We're pretty informal out here, unless some officer we don't know shows up. I figure for what we do, we deserve some slack in the system."

"Good enough," I said. "Call me Ted."

The three of us got into a Jeep with Martha driving, Tobruch riding shotgun, and me in the back again, crammed in with my bag. We went back to the massive building by the plaza and Tobruch led me inside as he told me about it. Everyone who worked at the complex was housed here, upward of a hundred or so permanent residents and maybe another hundred temporary workers. It looked abandoned because nobody worked inside it during the day except for the service staff, and they used a back door. It certainly was not a barracks, but it wasn't until we entered the main hall that I realized how much it wasn't a barracks.

"Women on the second floor, men on the first," Tobruch said, pointing at the winding marble stairway as he pulled a key from his pocket and handed it to me. "This is where SS officers stayed, so they spared no expense in building it. There are a few suites for majors, colonels, generals, and visiting politicos, but it was mostly hotel accommodations. You have a private room, no maid service, laundry twice a week, shared bathrooms and showers at each end of the hallways. We have our mess in the building over there, six o'clock in the morning to eight o'clock at night." He pointed out the windows to a building on the north side of the plaza. "They left it all in good working order, so we were lucky."

I still didn't know what he and the others did, but it no longer mattered. I deposited my duffel bag in a room that was the Taj Mahal compared to where I'd been sleeping. I'd have been happy to stay there until they shipped me home, if they'd let me, which made me even more suspicious of what I was going to have to do. Nothing comes for free in the Army.

We walked out of the building to the center of the plaza.

"Welcome to the Dachau Training Center," he motioned in a circle. "This was an abandoned munitions factory in 1933 when Heinrich Himmler, who was an important official in the National Socialist German Workers' Party—that's the Nazis—and also the head of police in Munich, took over the place and built it up to be the national training center for the *Shutzstaffel*, the troops dedicated to the personal protection of Hitler. Under Himmler, they became a lot more. We call them the SS. This complex trained SS troops, SS officers, and the SS Death's Head Division. It was home to the SS medical training and experiments facility as well as the weapons training, and was host to the Dachau Concentration Camp, which held approximately two hundred thousand prisoners over its twelve years of operation and set the standard for inhumane treatment, cruelty, starvation, torture, terror, and mass executions."

I was a little stunned as I climbed back into the Jeep. It was a lot of information to take in all at once. I hoped I wasn't going to be digging graves.

Tobruch continued lecturing as Martha wound through the facilities. "Himmler meant this to be the school where commandants were trained to be managers of concentration camps, so he was personally involved in developing the policies and practices for how prisoners were to be retained, treated, tortured, terminated, and their bodies destroyed so the other camps would be run with the same efficiency."

As we drove around, I saw homes for the camp commanders, large administration buildings, mess halls, restaurants, barracks for the SS troops, training fields, a swimming pool, garages, vehicle repair shops, a bakery, a hospital, two or three infirmaries, a massive herb garden with several greenhouses, and even a facility for raising rabbits. There was a brothel serving both the officers and the troops and the occasional prisoner to make the others jealous.

All empty, except for where I had met Tobruch and Martha. The complex had been abandoned except for a hundred or so troops, who then surrendered to the Seventh Army through an agreement negotiated by the Red Cross. Everyone else ran for the hills as the Allied Army swept through the countryside.

Leaving behind some thirty-two thousand starving and diseased prisoners.

"Let's go see it," Martha said as she drove down a long road paralleled by a tall brick wall and pulled up to an entrance gate.

Tobruch pointed to an iron sign above the gate with *ARBEIT MACHT FREI* in block letters. "It means *Work Sets You Free* and was never true. It should have read *Work Makes You Dead*. It's just one of the pretenses the Nazis used to obscure what was really going on."

We walked under the sign and into a compound set off by ten-foot-high brick walls topped with coiled barbed wire, with similar coils along the bottom. Six towers were spaced along the fences, which I recognized as machine gun emplacements. The odor I had smelled in the plaza area was stronger and more pungent here. It was an ugly smell, dull and offensive, and I couldn't identify it.

To the right of where we had entered was a U-shaped building sitting at the head of a large open barren area that looked like a parade ground, which was in front of a series of thirty-two long, narrow barracks, much like my barracks back at boot camp, but single-storied.

"This camp was opened in 1933 and was originally built to hold five thousand political prisoners," Tobruch said. "Himmler expanded the camp in 1934 to include the 'racially undesirable elements', such as Jews, Gypsies, Serbs, Poles, disabled people, and criminals. Later on, he included Jehovah's Witnesses, homosexuals, and Catholic clergy. It wasn't long before anyone could be arrested and placed here, completely at the whim of the Third Reich. By the time the Allied Army got here a few months ago, they found more than thirty thousand, a third of them sick with typhus, all within this compound."

I wasn't sure I understood. My boot camp complex had four two-story barracks that held maybe sixteen hundred men. Thirty thousand people is a fair-sized city. It would have been impossible to put them in a place this small. The Army bean counters must have missed a decimal place somewhere.

Martha took up the commentary, pointing to various locations as she talked. "A company of the 92nd Signal Battalion were some of the troops who liberated the place on April 29th, about three months ago. They described piles of bodies all along this route. Women, children, old men, babies. They had been starved, stabbed, shot, or bludgeoned to death, and left to rot on the ground. Most were wearing the striped uniforms of prisoners, but many were naked.

"There were groups of children over there," she pointed across the yard, "who had been shot in the back of the head.

"When troops investigated the railroad network leading into the complex, they found boxcars with hundreds of dead bodies. Himmler had tried to get all of the prisoners out of the camp as soon as he knew the Allies were closing in. SS soldiers loaded them into the boxcars but there were too many, so they either shot them or padlocked the doors and let them starve to death. Others had it better—there were gallows back there that still had a dozen men hanging."

Tobruch told me that the odor I'd been smelling was the stench left by rotting flesh.

"Outside the walls in the back are two crematoriums," Tobruch added. "One had a room with a dozen ovens where we found bodies stacked floor to ceiling like cordwood. They were intended to be burned, but they didn't have enough coal. I guess they just ran out of time, and when they finally evacuated, they left behind thousands of prisoners who looked like skeletons, surrounded by mounds of the dead."

I wasn't entirely convinced they weren't making everything up. It just couldn't have been as bad as they were making it out to be.

"After the camp was liberated," Martha continued, "bulldozers were used to scrape out large pits for the dead bodies. The bodies were pushed into the pits, covered, and markers put up to indicate the number buried. In May, the Seventh Army set up their divisional hospitals south of here to treat the diseased and injured while Army kitchens were set up to get the prisoners fed. They had had so little food for so long that their bellies and intestines would have swelled up and killed them if they'd eaten more than a few tablespoons of a regular meal. It took weeks to get people back to eating without becoming sick."

"Dachau was only one of hundreds of concentration camps in Germany and the Nazi-occupied territories," Tobruch added. "We're gathering information now to get counts of how many camps there are, how many prisoners were housed, how many died, and how many survived."

"What do the two of you actually do?" I finally asked.

Tobruch tilted his head as he answered. "Technically, Martha and I and the others are translators. Each of us worked throughout the Allied Armies interviewing German POWs, townspeople, and captured spies, translating signs and captured documents, talking to groups of people, things like that. Our group represents a working knowledge of a dozen or so European languages.

"When the Army started finding camps like this all over the country, we were recruited to be investigators, since a lot of the information about the camps needed to be translated. What happened in the camps was an abomination of mankind, not to mention human decency and dignity. None of these camps should have ever existed for what they were designed to do, but the numbers are already adding up to be far beyond what ordinary people will readily believe. Sometimes, even we can't believe what we've found.

"Our team, and similar teams at other camps, help the American, British, and French intelligence units put all the pieces together—the history, the policies, the timelines, the orders, the treatment, the numbers. We're looking to bring everything into the light: what happened, when, how, why, and especially who was responsible.

"The Allies have, for some time now, been talking about how to handle the atrocities that violated the Geneva Convention. But with what we've learned in the past few months, that was peanuts compared to the genocide actually taking place. Millions of people have been put to death only because of their racial or national heritage.

"But you have to give it to the Germans for being efficient: They had great record keeping, so we're finding policies, historical documents, written speeches, conference proceedings, inter-office memos, diaries, lists of prisoners, and lots of other stuff detailing what they did. That's what we use to build our reports.

"But most of us can't type worth a damn, so you're going to do it for us."

Chapter 36

Tobruch had exaggerated. Many of the translators could type, and the Army had already provided several typists to convert pages of notes written in long hand into formal reports. Those were the typists I had seen around the big office. You'd think with fingers as thick as hot dogs, I wouldn't have made much of a typist, but I was actually pretty good. I admit to being slow and occasionally clumsy, but my tradeoff was the power I had striking the keys when I needed to make stencils. I'd been known for putting a few typewriters in the repair shop.

What Tobruch really meant was that *he* couldn't type. Having a new guy with talent walk in out of the blue was a godsend to him, and my job was to be his shadow. His specialty was interviewing Dachau survivors, so I went with him to take notes and later type them up.

I had arrived close to mid-July, after the final prisoner had left the Dachau camp. By then, many of the remaining concentration and extermination camps had been found and liberated. But there were hundreds of camps, and "liberated" had become a loose term. Large percentages of the prisoners could not or would not physically leave. Disease was rampant, typhus in particular; prisoners had been starved and abused and were physically unable to fend for themselves; injuries and wounds kept people from walking without assistance; and many were dying. At Dachau, a hundred a day were dying before the Army came, and twenty a day afterward.

The prisoners from Dachau were removed from the camp and housed either in large tents, in the SS soldier barracks, or in any of the unused buildings. Having them nearby gave Tobruch a free hand at interviewing them. When he was ready, I took a large notepad and sat with him and his interviewee, while he dictated the information to me.

"Interview" is too strong a word. Since Tobruch was an official investigator, there was specific information he was to obtain, like the interviewees' names, home countries, and home cities, towns, or villages, and whether they had family, and what, if anything, was known about them now. He asked about their previous occupation, their understanding for the reason that they were brought to the camp, how long their prison sentence was, if they knew, and whether there was a trial or any kind of judicial review or appeal process. These things were directly related to the issues of the Geneva Convention or the Versailles Treaty.

It was upsetting to us both to find people who had been at a movie, or in church, or at some other public place when SS soldiers surrounded the place and put everyone under arrest. They herded the people into trucks and delivered them to concentration camps. Those who could do hard labor were put to work, those who couldn't were forced to do menial work, and those who could not contribute were automatically put to death.

Once the treaty information was gathered, Tobruch had a marvelous way of talking to people, making the interviewees relaxed and feeling unthreatened. He never smoked during the interviews, and I had to admire him never being anxious to leave so he could get outside and light up. He never seemed rushed at all. He mainly sat back, and with a little prompting, let the interviewees tell stories about life inside the camp. I recorded the stories as he translated them to me.

Up to that point in the interview, I was a pretty good note-taker, but as the survivors talked about their experiences, I had a harder time writing at the same time I was listening as Tobruch was telling me what they said. Uniformly, everyone spoke of their punishments, their brutal treatment, their daily routine under uninterrupted streams of verbal abuse, beatings, kicks, bruises, cuts, broken bones, refusal of food or water, or even things as simple as not having been allowed to sleep. Everyone had been required to stand for hours in the rain or snow or wind or freezing cold, and been forced to sleep jammed into rows with hundreds of other stinking bodies in spaces where they could not move, covered only by one or two blankets.

Women had repeatedly been forced to disrobe in public and then been slapped and degraded. If pregnant, they were often forced to have abortions. Some women did manual labor, such as carrying sacks of cement on their backs at a work site, moving maybe a hundred sacks a day, and their performance was expected to be the same as the men. Their hair was commonly cut short, as were the men's, and the hair was then used to make industrial felt.

All of this treatment was typical of their everyday existence. The punishment for specific offenses made me sick to my stomach. Floggings were meted out for spilling soup, for being too slow to roll call, for not singing loudly enough as they were marched to work, or even for simply complaining among the others. If that didn't give the bosses enough pleasure, there was being locked in tiny rooms—upright coffins, really—that were too narrow to sit down or squat in and too short for standing straight up—a person would be left for days without sitting, lying down, kneeling, or having a toilet.

Tobruch was a professional. He was compassionate, interested, and sympathetic as the stories were told. Even if the interviewee broke down in sobs, or experienced waves of anger, or shook from remembering the hatred behind each lash of a whip, Tobruch stayed in his role as a neutral fact-finder. Only afterward, outside, would he be silent and intense, his eyes closed, sucking on cigarettes one after another, barely able to calm himself.

We did two or three dozen interviews a week. It was a grind for both of us, but for him especially, as he also had other work to do. I spent my time typing up the interviews from my notes, having them reviewed, and then redoing sections or adding more material. It was tiring, and it was depressing, but the more I heard, the more I was willing to work so we could find the sons of bitches who were responsible.

HE PULLED me from my desk one day. "You asked what we did," he said. "Let me give you a glimpse of the big picture."

We took a Jeep to a large gymnasium I had seen on my first day. Pulling into the parking lot, I saw a more military scene: several Jeeps, three-quarter ton transports, and trucks, all either parked, backing up to loading doors, or driving in and out. GIs were standing around.

Inside the building was a typical basketball gym with a large floor area, high ceilings, and a hardwood floor, but the bleachers had been removed and the floor covered with Army cots, lined up end to end to make long rows. Each cot was jammed with stacks of papers, binders, satchels, boxes, photographs, and whatever. A hundred or more people buzzed around the room shuffling papers, talking, showing photos to others, and pointing at maps, with so much busy-ness it looked like a factory floor. Large maps, photographs, signs, flags, and other visuals covered most of the walls. There was a raised stage on the far end, just like my elementary school gym had, with file cabinets and more formally arranged desks, chairs, and tables.

"We couldn't find enough tables, so we had to use cots," Tobruch said as he and I gingerly walked through the mess. "Each cot holds the materials from one or more concentration camps, either in Germany or in an occupied territory, like Poland. If it's a main camp, like Dachau, with subcamps —Dachau has about thirty—then the complex gets three cots, with the information on the subcamps spread around the main camp. There's usually a map showing where all the subcamps are located."

He looked at me apologetically. "This looks out of control, I know, but we did what we could. What we were attempting to get, and finally have gotten, for the most part, is a centralized information system where we can organize the reports, interviews, source material, and data sheets fed to us by teams at the other camps. We sort through any new stuff that has been brought in and connect it to similar findings in other places. That gives us some confidence in building a true picture of the entire camp operation managed by the Third Reich."

There was a whistle from across the room, and Tobruch looked surprised. "Is it Friday? Is today Friday? I guess I'd forgotten."

People across the room stopped what they were doing, gathered several small recipe-sized cards from their cots or desks, and drifted to the end wall of the gym.

The end wall had been used to create a mosaic of hundreds of three-by-five cards taped to the painted wall-board. Maybe forty feet wide? A few feet high, maybe, so about twenty cards spanned top to bottom. I guessed that maybe two thousand index cards were on display, identical to what the workers were now holding in their hands, all taped up in a rough oval.

There was a single twelve-inch square of space in the very center that was empty.

As the people gathered, Martha Hammer walked in front. I hadn't seen her much in the past two weeks, so this must have been where she was working.

"Well, it's another Friday at 1500 hours," she said as she raised her hand and motioned for people to come forward. "Thank you all for the work you're doing. Thanks especially to the team leaders from the other camps who are here today or who have sent in their boxes of materials. We're doing good work here, people, and the information we're gathering concerns the whole world, so keep your heads clear and your typewriters oiled.

"All right, let's add to the wall. We're looking for items you have found this week that have disturbed you. Torture, terror, policies, ideologies, whatever. Harry will tape them on the wall, being that his arms are longer than mine. After we hear from everybody, we'll take a show of hands for today's winner, and he or she will get a newly arrived case of genuine Coca-Cola given to us by the people in Atlanta, Georgia, who send their best wishes. Let's start with the Polish camps."

I caught on after a few cards. The wall was a mosaic of horrors.

One team member from Poland held up a card. "After the invasion of Poland by Germany, and after tens of thousands of Polish businesses were seized without payment to the owners, the German government posted this sign in public places." The card read:

Entrance forbidden for Poles, Jews, and dogs.

Another member held up his card. "We found a special

edition of *Mein Kampf* in a commandant's office in a camp in Poland." The card read:

```
Mein Kampf lays out Hitler's idea that
Jews and Bolsheviks are racially and ideo-
logically inferior and threatening, whereas
Aryans and the National Socialists are
racially    superior    and    politically
progressive.
```

A man who wore a suit and tie stood up next. "We discovered notes from a secret conference held in January of 1942. The meeting was hosted by Reinhard Heydrich, who was Himmler's deputy at the time." The card read:

```
Approximately eleven million Jews in
Europe will fall under the provisions of the
Final Solution.
```

"This means they were planning to murder them all," the man added.

A woman introduced herself as being new to the group and stated that she had been assigned to investigate a recently discovered camp at Allach. "The Allach camp was a subcamp of the Dachau main group," she said. "It was a camp created to support an aircraft manufacturer in early 1943." Her card read:

```
Allach was created in 1943. Five thousand
prisoners were moved here from other camps
and    eventually    represented    eighteen
different countries, primarily the Soviet
Union and France. The prisoners worked at
the factory producing aircraft engines.
```

A man stood up, held his card high, looked around the group, and asked, "How many have been killed by the Nazis? Millions? Ah, but how many were they willing to kill? We found a document last week where Goering requested a plan be developed addressing the enslavement or elimination of the entire population of not only Eastern Europe, but all of Russia." His card read:

Hermann Goering, in 1941, had a plan developed calling for deporting the entire population of occupied Eastern Europe and the Soviet Union to Siberia, for use as slave labor or to be murdered.

He was followed by a soldier in a US Army uniform with a Technician 5th Class patch on his arm. That's what I used to be. He read from his card with a small quiver in his voice. I wondered if he felt intimidated by the people around him, which I strongly identified with. His card had an excerpt from a document discovered that week. The card read:

But it was also plain that Hitler would have preferred to see Japan attack the Russians rather than draw the United States into the conflict.

It took a half-hour to go through another thirty or so cards, all being added around the edges of the mosaic. I was both horrified and fascinated. I could see the picture Tobruch talked about: the length, breadth, and depth of the Third Reich's program of conquering lands, enslaving the conquered citizens, and then using the conquered territory to raise generations of pure Germans, the Aryan race Hitler so loved.

Finally, at the final call, a woman came forward smiling. "Okay, I've got the winner right here." She held up her card and waved it. "I'll introduce it and then Martha can read it."

"All right," Martha said with a laugh, "but this had better be good."

"It is. My team, which covers the Bergen-Belsen camps, has been going over some of the inter-office memos written during the invasion of Poland. After the country was annexed, the Third Reich destroyed as much of the Poles' cultural heritage as they could. They closed universities, schools, museums, public libraries, and then banned the Polish language. But if they did destroy the culture of the current Polish population, they wouldn't want the next generation to undo what they had done. They needed to keep the succeeding generations dumb and obedient. To do that, they decreed that Polish schools would be limited to teaching only the first four years of elementary school. After that, no education would be allowed.

"My group wondered where the principle of only four years came from. Digging through some of the archives, we found this." She handed the card to Martha, who read it out loud:

A basic issue in the solution of all these problems is the question of schooling and thus the question of sifting and selecting the young. For the non-German population of the East there must be no higher school than the four-grade elementary school. The goals of this school will be: simple arithmetic up to 500 at the most, the writing of one's name, the doctrine that it is a divine law to obey the Germans, and to be honest, industrious, and good. I don't think that reading is necessary.
—Heinrich Himmler

The audience gave snorts and guffaws and most raised their hands in agreement. Martha taped the card in the empty space.

"Thanks, everybody," she said as she gave a final wave. "Bergen-Belsen Team, come get your case of the finest drink in America."

As people walked away, I stayed to read the cards.

Murder, humiliation, theft, beatings, lying, denial of

basic rights, starvation, appalling living conditions, things you wouldn't wish on your worst enemy, all underwritten by a systematic, programmed, pervasive, unquestioned, supposedly divinely ordained ideology that sanctioned the Nazi Party playing God over a hundred million human lives and a couple of million square miles of dirt.

"Now you know what we do here," Tobruch said as he came up behind me. "We're rock-flippers. We go around sniffing and then flip over rocks to see what's underneath. We put it all together to see what the rocks were hiding. We aren't ambulance chasers and nobody's here because of the rewards involved, but we've dedicated ourselves to getting the bastards who did it."

"What's the purpose of the cards?" I asked. "Do you take down the cards, write them all up, and give them to someone?"

"Oh, no. This is just for us. When Martha was appointed the lead for centralizing the information for the intelligence units, she decided to get everybody together on a weekly basis for some social time, expecting that we'd need something to preserve our collective sanity.

"Even those of us who work with this stuff have some level of disbelief at what we've found. We've heard the personal testimonies, seen the death pits, smelled the lingering rot, walked through the barracks, seen the crematoriums, and some of us have even visited train cars full of bodies, and we *still* have a hard time believing the level of disregard for human life the Nazis had.

"Collecting notecards from our members and taping them up in front of everybody allowed us to have a public wailing wall. People stay and talk to each other, asking, telling, sharing, sometimes crying, so others can feel their pain, so we can all feel their pain. Sometimes it takes an hour of listening to each other for people to settle down.

"It's never been a game, even if we do declare a winner

and give away bottles of Coca-Cola. It's all depressing stuff, and we're compassionate people. It hurts our hearts to see what we see. This is a place for us to come together, a harbor to take refuge in, a safe place that keeps us from losing our balance and becoming consumed by sorrow and despair."

Chapter 37

It was the end of August when I sensed we were getting close to the end. Some of the desks in the big room had been empty for a week, there were less people and fewer typewriters clacking across the room, and a few filing cabinets had been disappeared.

"Come with me," Tobruch said. "I have someone special for you to meet."

We left the camp and drove to the countryside. At a small village with a church tower in the center, he pulled into the parking area of the church and we walked inside. Tobruch had brought a coil of rope with him.

Inside, sweeping the floor, was a priest, looking distinguished in his black frock and white collar. Tobruch greeted him in German, warmly embraced him, and introduced me to him. I extended my hand in greeting but then realized he had no hands, only crude hooks at the ends of leather sleeves. When I looked clumsy and apologetic, he gave me a knowing smile and embraced me with his arms.

We sat beside each other in the first pew. It was a small church, but the architecture was of wonderfully carved stone with simply colored windows. An arched ceiling high above us was appropriately uplifting. I was glad it hadn't been bombed.

"Father Hansburger was a prisoner at Dachau for three years, 1940 to 1943," Tobruch said to me. "He is one of only a handful of prisoners who were actually released after a period of imprisonment. When I arrived in May, I learned of Father Hansburger and came to see him. He adopted this church as his parish after his release and serves now as rector and priest. He has also adopted me as a friend.

"He has been a rich source of information for not only the daily atrocities of Dachau, but for understanding the Third Reich's ideologies. He was, among many others, the recipient of every form of torture and sadistic treatment suffered by Dachau prisoners. Father Hansburger is unique, however, in that he was a priest when he was arrested, and the prison guards had a particular disdain for priests. One form of torture you have not heard described in our interviews was common in the early 1940s but was discontinued because it was too brutal, especially after the concentration camps began supplying workers for local industries. I'm going to ask him to demonstrate it for you."

Tobruch spoke to Hansburger and the old man's face grew serious and reserved. He shook his head. He obviously did not want to do what Tobruch was asking. Tobruch spoke in a softer voice, explaining, I assume, the reasons behind his special request. He also motioned toward me several times, so I must have factored in his reasoning.

The kindly man looked at me as if he had a question to ask but finally accepted. The priest led us to the front entryway. Using his hooks, he pulled my arms and hands behind me so my wrists touched and my hands were pointed out. Tobruch tied my wrists together with the rope.

Next, Father Hansburger, being surprisingly dexterous, folded my hands under and in toward my waist, causing me to hunch my shoulders and lean over. Tobruch then pulled the free end of the rope up between my arms, looped it a second time around my hands and cinched it tight. He threw what remained over a stone crossbeam of the church's foyer.

Grabbing the end of the rope, he pulled, raising my bound hands toward my shoulder blades. It was an incredibly awkward position, and I naturally resisted.

Tobruch, with Father Hansburger's help, then pulled hard and I gasped as they briefly lifted me up until my toes barely touched the floor. My hands had come up my back, pulling my arms upward and spreading my shoulders, forcing me to bend almost in half. Another inch and I would have hung completely suspended from the rope. With the screaming my body was already experiencing, I cried out, fearing they would raise me off the ground.

They held me for only a few seconds, but I felt that my wrists were breaking and my arms were pulling out of their sockets. Tobruch gradually lowered me and I collapsed forward until my knees were on the floor and my forehead was fully against the cool stones of the church floor. I fell over onto my side.

The two men had not said a word during the experience. They untied my hands as I laid on the floor, coiled the rope, and left me to consider what had happened while they returned to our pew.

When the pain finally subsided to an acceptably dull level, I rejoined them, still rubbing my wrists and stretching my arms and shoulders. "Why did you do that?"

Tobruch looked at me with a serious expression. "This is why Father Hansburger has no hands. What we demonstrated was called 'poling'. Because of some offense, great or small, he would be tied in that position, but with a longer rope. The end of the rope would have been threaded through a pulley at the top of a pole. A guard would then pull Father Hansburger off the ground several feet and let him hang there for an hour or sometimes longer.

"You have to have a strong heart because of the compression of your chest. You might be able to raise your feet to hang differently for a while, but eventually, your body will pull you down. You will then stretch out until you are hanging almost straight. At that point, the rope around your hands, pulled tight, will likely rip apart all those little bones in your wrists and pull your arms out of their sockets. Many prisoners died before they were let down.

"Father Hansburger suffered poling more than once, and his wrists eventually shattered. He remained in the camp after it happened with only wrapped up, worthless appendages at the ends of his arms."

Tobruch leaned toward me. "And he was still expected to sing as he was forced to work."

I could say nothing, but my eyes probably told him how appalled I was.

"We have had several talks, you and I," Tobruch said, touching my arm, "and we are now going our separate ways. I am going to Nuremburg to help with the trial. At one point, you told me you had learned to hate—to hate the Germans, to hate the Army, to hate your father, to hate your brother, to hate the weaknesses in yourself, to hate the weaknesses in others, to hate the inequality of life. There are many things you should hate in this world, but the hate you've learned serves no purpose. If you take it home with you, it will cripple you as much as Father Hansburger's missing hands cripple him, but it will be much less obvious and far more difficult to remedy.

"If I could give you a gift at our parting, it would be to give you a way to deal with your hate. You know Dachau has hate at its very core. Hate runs through every building, drips from every crevice, and oozes up from every patch of ground. Its history, its role, its very existence is based on irrational hate, a hate that can dominate one's mind if it is all one sees. It feels worse for you because you have been so long without love, honor and mercy that your inner self is running on empty. Where there is emptiness, there are always competing emotions looking to fill up that emptiness, and one of the strongest competitors is hate. You, I believe, have been a prime target for that filling.

"However, it is not too late to unlearn irrational hate. I have learned much from my friend here, and I want to pass on his teachings. It boils down to something simple: Do unto others as you would have them do unto you.

"It is, of course, not easy, but it remains simple. You must convince yourself that what you do unto others is *your choice*, and how they react is *their choice*. It is *your choice* that you must focus on. You now have a taste of the torture of being hung from a pole. That same torture taught some to hate while it taught others to forgive, as it did Father Hansburger. If *he* can suffer all that he has for the sake of his faith, if *he* can hang from the pole and not give up, if *he* can choose to resist irrational hate from becoming the center of his emotions, then *you* can choose to resist hate from becoming the center of yours.

"You have been bothered by not being able to understand war. What I have found is that you really do not understand peace. Peace is so much more than the absence of war, just like love is so much more than the absence of hate. We always speak of desiring peace, but I personally believe that we have hardly an inkling of all that it encompasses. It might take a lifetime to fully appreciate its fullness, and until we do, we must simply *endure*.

"Endurance comes from inner strength, and inner strength comes…well, again, Father Hansburger has come to my aid. It is what he believed then and what he continues to believe now, that God gives our humanness a dimension of himself for our survival. He gives us *grace*. And because he gives us grace, we can obtain the *forgiveness* we need to tolerate ourselves and each other, and to find cleansing from our despicable actions. Through grace we learn to love, through forgiveness we become renewed.

"Again, we must *choose* to accept the grace that allows us to forgive and to be forgiven, no matter how life tests us. If you can choose grace, forgiveness will win out and peace will fill the emptiness inside of you."

Chapter 38

"You're looking kind of lonesome there, soldier." I had been staring at my typewriter and neglected to see Martha making her way across the room to my desk.

I looked up with a guilty smile. "I was wondering what to do next. I've been working on the filing system for almost a month, creating master reference lists of the evidence categories for each camp. Now that it's done, I'm not quite sure what to do."

"Well, this ought to help you out." She handed me a several-page memo from the Seventh Army headquarters with a single paragraph at the top of the first page:

The following are to report 0800 5Oct45 to the Out-Processing Center at Furstenfeldbruck Air Base, Furstenfeldbruck, Bavaria.

The pages listed columns of names, service numbers, and units. My name was underlined on the third page.

Martha looked at me with a kind smile. "You're going home."

· · ·

THERE WAS something I had to do before I could leave.

Tobruch had left the first week of September to support the International Military Tribunal at Nuremberg. He came back twice, once to get a few boxes of information needed by the prosecution, and once to escape the madness and take a break. He was officially a translator for the proceedings, training on a new simultaneous translation system created by IBM specifically for the hearings.

Each time Tobruch came back from Nuremburg, I was eager to listen, but what he wanted to discuss was a bit out of my league.

What part of war is a crime? It can't be the killing, that's been part of war for eons. Is it *murder* versus *killing*? Is the nation that starts a war responsible for what happens? What if the defending nation commits atrocities? Are those also crimes? Are individual soldiers ever guilty, or are they always *obeying orders from higher authorities*? What are *crimes against humanity*?

My mind would be swamped after a few minutes. I had never thought about the basic principles of right and wrong when it was in the framework of war. I had only seen the victims, which made me very much on their side. I wanted every Nazi scumbag to die a miserable death for what they had done.

But it wasn't going to be Hitler. He was dead by his own hand, even though it took a while for everyone to believe it. Himmler was also dead. He tried to go into hiding but was detained at a checkpoint, where he then committed suicide. Reinhard Heydrich, his deputy, had been assassinated. That left Hermann Goering and twenty-one other top Nazi officials to be the first defendants in the trial of the century. There would be other trials, but how they went depended a lot on how this one went.

After the visit from Martha, I was happy to leave it to Tobruch and the lawyers. I wanted to go home. My war, at long last, needed to come to a close. I thought about it, obsessed about it, dreamed about it. I almost wrote you to call Junior and tell him to get me the hell out of here, but I didn't.

When Martha handed me the orders to report to the processing center, I was ready, but I was still wary that nothing might actually happen. I'd been in the Army long enough to know sudden emergencies might suddenly show up and throw schedules out the window. Even so, I had one thing to do before I left, and with the fifth of October was three days away, I needed to hurry.

"The air base is about thirty kilometers from here, so when you're ready, I'll take you over," Martha offered. She was awfully nice. I know she missed Tobruch as much as I did. The teams at the various camps had finished their document searches and interviews and wound their efforts down. Some of the staff had already transitioned back to the States while others were consolidated into teams at the larger camps. The Dachau team had wrapped up its work, while Martha continued putting the information in the right boxes. She was tired, like the rest of us. It was time to be done with it.

"THANK YOU," I said to Martha as Furstenfeldbruck came into view.

"I'm the one who should be thanking you," she said. "You did a ton of work."

"I wanted to do something special for you and Tobruch, so here you go," I said as I reached in the back seat of the Jeep and retrieved a large envelope.

"What is this?" she asked.

"It's the words from the cards in your Mosaic of Horrors. The wall had a little over two thousand cards, so it worked out to be a hundred typed pages or so. Having the group meet every week was something special, and I thought it should be preserved. I didn't have time to make a copy for Tobruch, so maybe you can find some typist who will do it for you. Bribe them with some of the leftover cases of Coca-Cola."

"Well. That's quite a gift," she said.

"I wish I could do more," I said. "Working with you, Tobruch, and the team was special, and it helped me make it through the last few months. I can't say it was fun, but it was significant and meaningful."

"We did good work, didn't we? It was important work, too. I hope people appreciate it. I hope it won't be too long before Tobruch gets back to his congregation."

"Wait a minute. His congregation? You mean he's a minister?"

She looked at me with surprise. "He never told you? He's a priest. In Fredericksburg, Texas. It's a town founded by German immigrants. I hear they make great sausages. His ancestors were from someplace in northern Germany. His grandfather, in fact, was an archbishop before the family moved to America. His mom and dad speak German as well as English, and he was raised speaking both. That's why he's so good at it."

I didn't know what to say. It fit, though. His demeanor working with the victims, his comfort speaking German, his identity with Hansburger.

I'm sure I looked bewildered. "He's not going to expect me to call him Father, is he?"

Martha stopped at a guard gate and I showed them my orders. She drove through and we followed the guard's directions to a nondescript building sitting at the front of a field with endless rows of ten-man wall tents, all in perfect alignment.

Crap. I was going to be in the Army again.

I got out, grabbed my duffel bag from the back seat and

stumbled through some words. "I can't thank you enough. You were a harbor in the storm. You kept me safe and protected, and I appreciate it more than you can ever know."

She smiled and nodded. "You go home, soldier, and live a good life."

Chapter 39

That was it. He was finished.

My dad gave no sign-off, no summary, no expression of thankfulness that he had, after forty-plus years, finally gotten his story told. The TV screen just went blank.

I reached over, pushed the stop button, hit rewind, and sat back in my chair. Nancy was silent, and I hadn't yet found any words that would have been useful.

My dad had started the filming in a clean sports shirt and with an expression of hopeful anticipation. Later, the shirt drooped as his shoulders drooped, and it showed a few wrinkles. He then appeared in a different shirt. Gradually, after another clothing change or two, everything sagged as his energy drained away. Sometimes his expression showed more pain than at other times. Sometimes he sat upright and sometimes he slouched, listing to one side or another. Sometimes his elbows were on the desk and his head was down, focusing on his notes, while the next scene had him upright again, looking better.

One scene after another, one part of the story done, and another started. It was a remarkable demonstration of strength from someone who was dying. Most of the time, he was a consummate speaker, delivering his words distinctly and deliberately. Other times, he grew red and huffy at the shooting of the flak girls, struggled through the escape from the oflag, and became ashen as he described Jake's death in the barn. He never looked at the camera as he recited his conversation with Jake's mound of dirt.

I kept waiting for him, kept hoping for him to finally say he'd made it to a ship and was on his way home, his journey finished at the doorstep of the Gunnarson mansion in the arms of my mother. But once finished with one episode, he'd immediately go on to something else. I wondered how much one soldier could endure. By the time he described his work at Dachau, he was hunched over the desk, speaking more slowly, more concerned with telling of his inner work-ings than outer, more oriented to emotions than the sequence of events. Tobruch had touched him, for sure, and discovering a devout friend was still remarkable to him.

When his orders to go home finally came, his speaking was subdued. He was clearly proud to have reached the end of what he had done in those last months. He sounded satis-fied. At the same time, his voice had a tinge of sadness. Maybe he felt melancholy and wanted reflection and conversation, but knew he had no time. No time at all.

I now understood why he never talked about the war. Even if Task Force Baum had not been classified and he'd been able to speak about it, what part would he have told? What little event would he have picked out for giving his listener a true feeling of what the war was like for him? Which single part of his story would have left him a satisfied storyteller?

You had to hear it all, and Dad probably never found an audience who would have listened that long.

Nancy was still quiet. She said nothing while the tape played, but I had heard her startle and gasp and cry, espe-cially when Dad had stood and put his hands behind his back and then leaned over to show how the rope around his hands had captured him. Jim Powers had come into the shot to grab his hands and pretend to lift him up.

Imagine the pain. Imagine the hurt. Imagine the despair you felt as you hung in the air.

Mom's voice broke our silence. I hadn't heard her come in. I wondered how long she'd been there, how much she could not resist seeing my dad's face again.

"Furstenfeldbruck Air Base turned out to be only one step on the way home," she said quietly. "It took another few weeks of living on cots that were too short, under blankets that were too worn, in a tent that hadn't been cleaned in three years, out in weather alternating between freezing cold and rain or both before he started the trip home.

"The soldiers around him had no interest in the war anymore and certainly didn't want to talk about Third Reich ideologies, the persecution of the Jews, the Poles, the Slavs, the Bolsheviks, or conditions in concentration camps. Other than for maintaining discipline and order, mess hall duties, and keeping the latrine emptied, most of the interactions in the camp went back to being one-upmanship, bragging, and making fun of Dad's big feet.

"Everyone was waiting on the troop ships leaving the harbor at Le Havre, France, and Dad's turn finally came. He was put in a truck convoy, had a layover at a camp in northern France, stayed almost two weeks at an encampment outside of Le Havre, and then walked up the gang plank of a troop ship on October 31, about ninety miles north of where he had landed on Omaha Beach a year and a half before. He sailed directly to New York, stopped at Camp Chaffee in Arkansas to be processed out of the military, and came home to me on November 23."

She took a deep breath and sighed. "That's it. I lived for forty years without knowing anything about his last six months."

Nancy stood and hugged her, and cried on her shoulder, while I did not. I was still wandering in the shadows of the story, my brain still waiting for the next episode.

My mother led us back to the dining room table. "Senior, Lady Gunnarson, my parents, and I all put on our Sunday best and met him at the train station, even though he didn't arrive until four in the morning. Other than looking thin, he acted exactly the way we thought he'd act— excited, full of stories, weary from travel, grateful for having made it back alive, eager to get out of uniform. He wanted to sleep late in a bed he fit, have real eggs and milk, and drive a car with a heater.

"The newspapers were full of stories of men and women coming home, parties being thrown, and I had several friends whose boyfriends, brothers, sisters, or husbands arrived in waves of happiness. From what we know now, I can't imagine any of them were fully right in the head. We didn't have words for PTSD like we do now, but the war had stretched millions of people too thin for too long. That's what we didn't see when he stepped off the train. He was far more messed up on the inside than we ever knew.

"But in the moment, we put the war behind us. Dad and I didn't have any reason not to get married, so we set a New Year's Day wedding date, which nearly gave Lady Gunnarson a heart attack. She had waited years to host weddings for her boys, and now with only one opportunity left, having only a month to plan it almost drove her crazy. That made the next five weeks a total chaos of activity. Of course, Dad had little to do, so he did nothing, which was a mistake.

"We should have involved him in something, given him work to do, or even sent him on a vacation somewhere. Dad had a hard time doing nothing. He became skittish about things and sometimes disoriented, like he didn't understand what was happening. He couldn't sit down for very long, or even read without stopping after a few pages. When he ate, he sat at the table until he ate his last bite and then would automatically stand up, like he wasn't allowed to enjoy it. He talked to himself a lot and paced back and forth, up and down the hallways. I expected him to gain weight and fill out, but he didn't. He kept looking thin, especially in his face, and kept saying he wasn't hungry."

"I bet that put a crimp in your baking," I said.

"Oh, I couldn't boil water before we got married. We'd had a housekeeper since I was in elementary school. I wanted to drive locomotives, not operate an oven. It was after we were married and had moved to Boston for Dad to go to school that I learned anything about cooking. Dad never failed to be home for supper. We always ate together in the evening, even if it was pancakes or toast or tuna fish. He showed me how to make a cowboy stew from his horse-packing days at the ranch. After a few nights of that, I started reading cookbooks, and that's when we made the kitchen the center of our home."

My mother stopped talking and looked down at the table, struggling to control her emotions.

"Mom?"

She jerked up, her eyes wet. "He was committed to making the kitchen a welcoming and safe place. He used to refer to the kitchen as the family harbor, a place anyone could sail into for protection from the storms. He and I were the harbormasters, always there, always available, always ready to listen. It was a choice he made that he never backed away from."

She nodded and bowed her head as if agreeing with a ghost.

I hate to cry. Always have. Being fascinated by processes and events, I became a history major so I could be an observer of life. I liked to stand outside the circle, watch, understand, digest, theorize about events and people, and then write it up in a paper. To look but to not become involved.

My father had revealed himself over the past few hours —his wants, his needs, his weaknesses, his frustrations, his courage, his curiosity, his hates, his fears, and his incredible resiliency. He also showed, from before our family existed, how he wanted to raise his children. Whether it came naturally to him or whether he'd learned it from two priests who taught him to choose grace and peace as his inner core, the results were the same.

I have always been surprised by tenderness, compassion, and active love. No theories, no strategies, no plots, just people wrapping their arms around the ones they love, guarding them, doing whatever they needed to do to protect them. That's what my dad did for himself, my mother, my sister, and me. From the beginning, he chose to cherish his family and it was a choice he made every day.

I cried, my hands held over my face.

I missed my daddy.

Chapter 40

"I have a couple of questions," Nancy finally said after we all held each other and shed our family tears. "What happened to Jake's body?"

Mom took her seat next to the trunk, looking better from her break in the sunroom.

"Once they'd been told he had died, Senior decided Jake should be buried in Europe in a cemetery in France or Belgium since there were no American cemeteries in Germany. Sometime later, Senior got a letter detailing the location of Jake's grave. He opened it, glanced at the information, and then burned it in the ashtray he used for his cigars. He only told his wife after the smoke cleared.

"That's the only time I saw Lady Gunnarson have a fit. She screamed and cried and tore into him like a banshee. He was stolid for a while, but then pushed her out of his office and shut the door. She grabbed her purse and her hat, walked out of the house, and didn't come back for two weeks. Senior remained aloof over it all and never asked where she had gone, even after she returned.

"To this day, I'm not sure why he burned the letter. It

could have been part of his grieving for his son, or an overt rejection of Jake's decision to enlist, or his regret at not bringing Jake home. I don't know. By that time, I was too excited by the war being over and too busy imagining your dad coming home, even though it wouldn't be for three more months. The location of Jake's grave became a skeleton in the family closet."

"I read about the Hammelburg raid in college," I said, rotating my neck to find the kinks. "It was the worst defeat of Patton's career and of the Third Army. When he was confronted with the fact he'd squandered a task force only to rescue his son-in-law, he absolutely denied it. He said the task force was a diversionary tactic while he moved the Army north. Since he had classified the existence of Task Force Baum, people couldn't talk about it, and in particular, the press couldn't write about it."

"But he was a *hero!*" my sister yelled, jumping up and banging her hand against the table. "He risked his life to save his brother!"

I absolutely agreed with her, even if his efforts had failed. The Hammelburg raid was a great miscarriage of power. General George S. Patton should have admitted his responsibility for what he'd done, but he did not. He should have recognized the sacrifice of those three hundred men, but he did not. He should certainly have recognized the bravery and tenacity of Captain Baum, but he did not. Captain Baum did survive and was later given a medal by Patton, but Baum didn't say a word when it was presented.

Mom settled into a chair and took a deep breath. She was looking worn out again. "You have any more questions?" she asked. "If so, I hope they're easy."

Nancy sat back in her chair. "I have to ask something, but you don't have to talk about it if you don't want to. When Dad got Jake's belongings, the GRU guys gave Dad

Jake's shirt with a V-mail letter in the pocket. Was the letter from you?"

Nancy never missed a trick. I had picked up on Dad's being given a letter but had forgotten about it.

My mother stood up, took a moment to consider her words, and then laid her hands on the small trunk. "I love you kids to death, but I hope I don't have to be this honest for the rest of my life. When your dad mentioned the letter, I knew it had to be one of mine. Jake wouldn't have kept a letter from Lady Gunnarson, for sure. It had to be months old because I had stopped writing to him back in the summer. I doubt Dad knew I had been writing to Jake, but he would have recognized my handwriting from the address.

"After the videotape, as we sat and talked, he reminded me he'd been given the letter. He told me he hadn't read it, hadn't even taken it out of the envelope, and had not looked at the address. He considered it Jake's business and not his, and he threw the letter into the fire outside the Hammelburg hospital."

"Do you think he told you the truth?" Nancy asked.

My mother, her head bowed toward the trunk, rubbed her forehead and looked up. "No. I think he did not tell me what he really did when they gave him the letter. He told me what he wanted me to believe. But that's okay. Sometimes people who love each other choose to not tell the truth because the truth would not serve the purposes of love. I think he read the address and recognized my handwriting; he may have even read it. But when he brought it up, what he was telling me was that whatever the letter did say, or might have said, made no difference to him, then or now. He wanted me, for the time he had remaining, to accept what he'd told me as the truth, so neither of us would ever have to think about it again. That's what I did.

"I never told him about my affair with Jake and he never

confronted me about the hour at the airfield. Each of us chose to let who we were prove our love, not what we did or didn't do. We had both lived through a war, had dramatic things happen to us, and had changed deep inside, but the war was over.

"Well, okay," Mom said as she sat back down. "It's been a long day, so let's finish this up. I want to tell you what happened after he came home.

"His bedroom in the Gunnarson mansion was down the hall from my suite, and I didn't hesitate to jump into bed with him. I was tired of waiting and wanted to start my campaign of making our marriage the most important thing in my mind and heart. I always made it back to my room before morning, so I was properly discrete. If Lady Gunnarson suspected anything, she decided not to look."

"I don't remember you not looking," Nancy said with raised eyes. "If I had been casual about sex, I'm pretty sure you would have handed me my head on a platter."

My mother smiled. "I apologize for nothing. If you had been twenty-two and had a fiancé come back after being gone for three years, I would never have said a thing.

"The wedding and everything was on track, but then Dad started having nightmares. He'd wake up in a sweat and be breathing hard. He'd seen terrible things and was being haunted by them, even to the point of smelling blood and hearing screams. We made it through December, got married on January 1, went to Chicago for our honeymoon, and then moved into the north wing of the mansion. Lady Gunnarson had remodeled the second floor to be a suite of rooms, including a big bedroom, two dressing rooms with closets, a large bathroom, a reception room, and even a study for your dad.

"It was February before I finally understood Dad was more seriously ill than what we'd thought. His nightmares continued, and he began having panic attacks. He'd jerk up out of his sleep and would have to get up and walk around before his mind would settle down. He would say he'd been awakened by the sounds of artillery, sometimes even feeling the floor shake.

"As the nightmares and attacks got worse, he became seriously depressed. I was afraid he'd make it back to the go-kill-everybody state of mind and run away. Lady Gunnarson was ready to plop him in a sanitarium, but I wouldn't let her. I felt I owed him whatever it would take to get him healed."

"What was Senior doing all this time?" I asked.

Mom shook her head, pursed her lips, and her eyes took on a bitterness. "I wish I had known how your dad was strung up by that priest. I would have done it to Senior and left him for the crows to eat. Basically, he didn't believe in depression. He told me it was a bunch of hooey. He believed hard work solved everything so, beginning in March, he required your dad show up every day, go with him to the downtown office, and write business reports for the sawmills.

"I finally couldn't stand it anymore and moved the two of us to my mom and dad's house. Lady Gunnarson hit the roof, and Senior would have fired me if I'd been on his payroll, but I wouldn't back down. Lady Gunnarson finally put the blame on her husband and not on me, and she began visiting every week, which made your dad happy. He had missed his mother as much as he had missed me. She enjoyed visiting and was surprisingly affectionate towards us both.

"I thought Dad needed to verbalize his experiences instead of keeping them inside, so I set a schedule for each day. We would have a nice breakfast every morning, then would sit and talk. I had him start from the moment he left for the army, describing everything that happened. I never rushed him. Sometimes he'd creep along with his descriptions of the day-to-day activities, and other times we'd talk about a week at a time. I always kept him in check and wouldn't let him summarize or jump ahead.

"Every day, we had lunch downtown. If it was a nice day, we'd get something and go to the park. We'd walk, or go rowing on the lake, or go to an amusement park, even if we didn't ride anything. He always wanted ice cream. And cake. He always wanted cake.

"We'd come back home and we'd talk again. I even read him the letters he had written to me. I wanted him to remember, and I wanted him to talk about it. He'd gone three years without talking to anybody, except for Jake and Father Tobruch. We'd eat supper with my mom and dad, then go to the movies, or take a walk around the property, or go to a concert. The evenings were for taking a break from the past, for living in the present.

"For all the minutes spent talking, it was still surprisingly hard for him. He felt he was betraying the trust of his buddies, that the stories should have been told only to those who'd been there. He had been a member of an exclusive brotherhood and outsiders had no claim to its experiences.

"I kept working on him, keeping him in factual details, asking him the names of things or places or people or numbers of troops or distances and things like that. I even had him draw out maps of where he had been. He learned to remember without feeling the terror.

"He gradually improved. His panic attacks became less frequent, his nightmares moderated, and he started gaining weight, like a new husband ought to. We talked up to where he had left Bastogne but before he had written the kill-them-all letter. That's where we quit. With what he talked about in the videotape, I'm glad we didn't go further. His last six months of the war were a whole level of emotion above the other memories, and I don't know if he could have survived it.

"By summer, Dad was strong enough to make the decision to go to Harvard in the fall. He had talked a lot with my dad about accounting and business management, so he declared them as his major. Senior had a deep disrespect for accountants, and Dad's choosing to be one was a slap in the face. He took back his promise of money for Dad's tuition and living expenses and just wrote him out of the books.

"Dad didn't even confront him about it. He said if Senior wanted to help, fine. If not, that would be fine, too. We'd make it somehow. He didn't even let my dad help. That's when I knew he was becoming his old self again.

"Your dad and I only had what I had saved from his Army pay and what I could earn working. Even back then, tuition for Harvard was not pocket change, but we were determined to make a go of it. He applied, got accepted, and then was surprised by being given a full-ride scholarship.

"He had never applied for a scholarship. We thought he'd gotten lucky or something, but then found that it was Junior. Junior had funded the scholarship by making a sizable donation to the college. He'd worked for Senior for a decade or so, made his own investments on the side, and had a sizable fortune of his own. Nothing was ever said, but I think Junior turned out to be a good brother to your dad."

"Now we know how you ended up in Boston," Nancy said.

"I wish Dad could have seen more of the overall picture," I said. "There's no doubt it was a war of attrition and we won because Germany and Japan could not come close to matching the industrial strength and resolve of America. But blaming officers for sending men to their deaths is a dark view of war. There were thousands of officers killed, just like the enlisted men. War is complicated, but it's not selective. Everybody suffers.

"Lots of men died from mistakes. Lots died when the weather went bad. Lots died merely by chance. You can see in his letters that Dad somehow felt like it shouldn't be that way and that he felt bad not being able to do anything about it. If you throw in his desire to be a hero," I said, "he put himself in a no-win situation. War is brutal: It grinds everyone down eventually, and the real heroes never come home."

Chapter 41

Mom put the videotape back into the trunk and added Dad's written story about the ranch. "I'm going to bed," she said. "When you're done looking at the rest of the letters, put them back in here. Oh, here's another Gunnarson family mystery you can solve."

She took another large envelope from the trunk, removed an eight-by-ten photograph, and laid it down on the table between us. Two men sat on what looked like a concrete bench on a patio while a woman sat between them. Behind them was a tall, trimmed hedge.

"That's Lady Gunnarson." Nancy said, pointing to the center figure. "Isn't this Junior?" she asked, pointing to the left figure. "Oh, wait, is this Dad? It is! He's so thin!"

Mom smiled. "Yup. Those are the two remaining Gunnarson sons and their mother. This envelope, with the photograph inside, was found in her desk in New York after she passed away. Her name is on the back of the photograph, but the envelope has my name written on it, in her handwriting. I assume she meant to give it to me, but I don't know why she didn't.

"I'd never seen it before, don't know when or where it

was taken, or why. I showed it to Dad and he couldn't recall ever sitting for a picture with the two of them. He said he had no idea about it, so I put it away with the letters."

"You see that Dad has his Army uniform on, right?" I asked.

"That's why I put it in the trunk. I figured it had to be related to the war. When I pointed it out to Dad, he was even more puzzled, but he assumed his mother had asked him to put his uniform on when he got back and had someone take the picture in the backyard. I didn't ask him any more about it and chalked it up to memory loss."

I looked closer at the image of my dad. There was something wrong with his uniform.

"Okay, time to quit," Mom said. "You've worn me out. Besides, we can't talk anymore because I'm out of sugar." She gave us a big smile. "When you're done, put everything back in the trunk." She turned around to go upstairs.

"Mom," I said.

She turned back to me.

"You saved my dad. Thank you. You're my hero."

She smiled. "We were a matched set, weren't we?" She slowly walked up the stairs to her bedroom. My sister and I sat in silence for a moment, but then Nancy moved to the chair next to me and leaned her head in like a conspirator.

"Okay, so we now know that both Mom and Dad could keep secrets for their whole lives. Do you think Dad told Mom everything Jake said? Do you think Jake fessed up?"

I thought for a few moments. "Okay, I hear your questions and I raise you several more. I don't think Jake would have admitted to having sex with Mom, and I doubt he would have admitted to writing letters to her. But Dad had to know that Jake considered himself quite a stud, that he would have no trouble seducing women, and that Jake would never have spent an hour giving Mom a tour. If Dad suspected they had had an affair, he would never have considered rape to be a part of it, just seduction, which meant mom was complicit."

"Rape is still rape," Nancy said in her lawyer voice. "Don't ever think it isn't. And don't think a woman ever forgets, no matter how debatable Mom makes it sound."

"Well, I'm sure Dad never thought Jake would rape anybody, much less Mom. But he had an imagination, he had months to think about it, and he was thousands of miles away. I believe he had only remotely imagined Jake's seducing Mom until Jake lied to him. Jake couldn't remember meeting his fiancé? Not true. Jake had been home only a day or two? Not true. Jake hadn't spent any time with Margie? Not true. The plane ride was on Monday? Not true. He wasn't in town on that Wednesday? Not true.

"Jake told one lie after another, so Dad knew something had happened. Even if he didn't know exactly what, the two of them had to be somewhere for an hour while Paul Avery was looking for them."

"And, on Mom's part," Nancy added, "she never mentioned Jake coming home. That's way too important for her to not have mentioned it. I think Jake having the letter confirmed what he had feared all those months."

I nodded in agreement. We both leaned against the backs of our chairs.

"And now we've got one more thing to think about," she continued, holding up the photograph. "This is getting ridiculous. A photograph appears after our grandmother is dead, it has Mom's name on the envelope, and nobody knows where it was taken or why or when? What's up with this family? Are we dysfunctional or what?"

I took the photograph from her and stared at it. I still thought there was something wrong with Dad's uniform.

Ah. Okay. "Here, look," I said. "What uniform is Dad wearing?"

Nancy took the photograph, studied it, and replied, "It's a dull green shirt with a dull black tie, a dull green pair of pants and really ugly boots with those things…weren't they called leggings?"

"Yes, they were called leggings. It was a common piece of clothing worn by World War II troops. The clothes are dull because it's a wool uniform, at least the shirt and pants."

"Okay, so what?"

"Dad is wearing the uniform of a soldier who hadn't come back from the war yet. If you were, for example, in somebody's backyard on a bench in America, you would have worn your dress shoes and your Class A uniform."

Nancy looked at me. "I'm lost. What are you getting at? He's wearing the wrong uniform?"

"No, he's wearing the right uniform, if he's still in the military and in Europe at the end of World War II."

Nancy stared at me. "You think the photograph was taken in Europe? That's not right. Lady Gunnarson was never in Europe, and I doubt Junior was, either."

"Remember Mom saying that when Senior burned the letter with the location of Jake's grave, Lady Gunnarson went ballistic and disappeared for two weeks?"

Nancy's eyebrows shot up and her mouth dropped. "You're kidding!"

I had to smile. "I bet she walked out of that house, found a phone, called Junior, told him what Senior had done, and within days Junior had found out where Jake was buried and they were on the way to Europe to locate the grave. Junior also had enough pull to get Dad a pass, and he met them over there. I bet this photo was taken at the cemetery where Jake is buried."

"You can't prove any of this. Oh, wait a minute. Dad couldn't admit to knowing about the photograph because all that stuff was classified: the task force, how Jake died, where he was buried, all of it."

She shook her head and leaned forward to put her elbows on the table. "A Gunnarson family soap opera. So, where does that leave us?"

I leaned back in my chair, stared at the remaining mounds of goodies on the table, and took a deep breath. "I think we don't *know* anything for sure, but everything points to the fact that our parents are truly remarkable people. Our mother keeps secret a rape that led to infidelity, knowing the information could ruin her marriage, and our dad, even if he guesses about the infidelity, makes a choice to love his wife in spite of it.

"Mom had it right: Sometimes the truth doesn't serve the purposes of love. When Dad decided to film his story, he knew he was going to tell her things she would think about for the rest of her life. Why tell her anything that might embarrass her or make her feel guilty? If he had known or even guessed about her and Jake, what good would it have done to tell her after all these years?"

"And on her part," Nancy continued, "who would a confession have served? If she had told the truth, even forty years after the incident, they would both have been worsened by it. Why not continue with what had worked for them all these years? In fact, Dad could have left out that Jake's letter even existed. But why not use the opportunity to set both their minds at ease?"

"Why not," I said, "let her know he had chosen to forgive her for anything real or imagined, at the beginning of their marriage, and her confessing would not have made a difference? We're talking about a man who had learned how powerful grace and forgiveness were, and a woman who knew how to accept both of them."

Mom came down the stairs in her nightgown and robe, and we both watched silently as she walked into the dining room. "I thought you might like to see these. I found them in your dad's things when I had the safe open."

She laid two silver objects on the table and placed an aviator's hat next to them. They were Jake's captain's bars, his Air Force pin, and his hat.

"I remember playing with this hat when I was a little kid!" I exclaimed as I picked it up. "I never knew it was for real."

"I have one more question, Mom," Nancy said.

I looked at her with questioning eyes. Did she really want to ask a question?

"What's with the locket? You've never worn a locket before, and that is one really nice-looking piece of jewelry. It must be something special."

Mom smiled, undid the clasp, and sniffled as she set it on the table. "Oh, your dad! After we finished talking about the videotape, he told me to go buy the prettiest locket I could find, with all the diamonds they could fit on it. It took me all the next day to find one, but when I came back and showed it to him, he opened it and put a little slip of paper inside. He told me not to read it until after he was gone. With everything that's been going on, I haven't had a chance to look at it.

"I'm going to bed," she said, wiping her cheeks. "You kids have cured my restlessness. Leave the locket on the table and I'll put it back on in the morning."

She left, and the room felt a whole lot emptier.

Nancy's eyebrows were raised as she looked at me, grabbed the locket, opened it, and removed the piece of paper. She unfolded it, read it, and handed it to me. I had been waiting impatiently, trying to guess what was written on it.

I wasn't even close.

Plot J, Row 9, Grave 46

Margraten

It's a beautiful place. Jake would have liked it.

We stood together, my mom, me and Nancy, in the back portion of the Netherlands American Cemetery, outside of Margraten. The cross was white granite and the inscription, though stained by weather, was still deep and clear.

JACOB F GUNNARSON
CAPT 322ND FIGHTER SQD US ARMY AIR FORCE
MINNESOTA APR 1 1945

"You guessed about the photograph?" I asked my mother.

She had been silent most of the day. It had been forty-plus years since she'd been this close to Jake, and I suspected she was putting all the memories into perspective.

"I was never sure," she said quietly, "but I didn't give Louisa enough credit. If she had wanted to know where Jake was buried, and I know she did, Junior could have found it with no problem. When she did find out, she wouldn't have made the location known to the rest of the family because she was afraid of making Senior even madder than he was.

"I'm happy she did something extraordinary, that she came here and she even brought her sons. She would have asked Junior to travel with her, and I'm sure it was her idea for Dad to meet them so they could all stand at the grave. It would have been late summer or early fall in 1945. I'm sure Dad wanted to come. He would have liked to know that Jake was finally settled, and I'm sure he desperately wanted to see his mother."

She smiled up at me. "Boys are like that."

I knelt, unscrewed the top of the small plastic jar, and

shook out a small cloud of gray dust at the bottom of the cross. There were probably rules against it, but I hadn't asked.

It wasn't all of Dad, just a portion—the rest was back in Minneapolis. Mom thought he would appreciate the gesture but wanted him to be substantially intact when her ashes were placed beside his.

"It was an enormous thing in history, our Second World War," I said as I stood up. "Maybe that's one reason why the people who lived through it never talked about it. They had spent so long at it, had used so much of their lives doing it, had been part of something so outlandishly huge and complex, that they found what Dad had found—telling pieces would never do it justice. They all needed a long time to tell what there was to be told, but no one ever sat down long enough to listen."

Mom took the large bouquet of flowers she had been holding and divided it into three bunches. She handed one bunch to me, the other to Nancy, and we stood together in front of the cross.

"Your dad and I had secrets," she said quietly but deliberately. "Perhaps we shouldn't have, but we had secrets and we kept them for all of our marriage. He had the war, and I had Jake. He taught me that grace and forgiveness were sometimes a better choice than honesty.

"Dad left me the location of Jake's grave because he knew I would want to come here. He also knew you two would come with me. We would all be together: him, me, our son, our daughter, and Jake. Without violating our secrets, he meant for us to find closure in the context of the family he so dearly loved, and to affirm it was okay to be who we were."

"Remember what Tobruch told Dad?" I said, struggling to hold back my tears. "It was when they were at Father Hansburger's church. He said that peace is so much more than the absence of war, just like love is so much more than the absence of hate. Dad knew that by choosing to make peace and love a priority in his life, he would make them a priority in our lives. It leaves us with a mission, and it should be the mission of everyone. As Dad's generation was consumed with war, our generation should be consumed with peace. Where he saw hate oozing out of the ground, we should sow love in its place."

Mom bowed her head, tears sliding down her cheeks, and stood silently. She then leaned down and placed her flowers against the granite cross. Nancy and I reached down and placed ours.

It was time to go home.